Henri Joly, Mildred Partridge, George Tyrrell

Saint Ignatius of Loyola

Henri Joly, Mildred Partridge, George Tyrrell

Saint Ignatius of Loyola

ISBN/EAN: 9783741192937

Manufactured in Europe, USA, Canada, Australia, Japa

Cover: Foto ©Andreas Hilbeck / pixelio.de

Manufactured and distributed by brebook publishing software
(www.brebook.com)

Henri Joly, Mildred Partridge, George Tyrrell

Saint Ignatius of Loyola

The Saints

SAINT IGNATIUS OF LOYOLA

SAINT
IGNATIUS OF LOYOLA

BY
HENRI JOLY
AUTHOR OF "THE PSYCHOLOGY OF THE SAINTS"

TRANSLATED BY
MILDRED PARTRIDGE

WITH A PREFACE BY
GEORGE TYRRELL, S.J.

LONDON
DUCKWORTH & CO., 3, HENRIETTA STREET, W.C.
NEW YORK, CINCINNATI & CHICAGO: DUBLIN:
BENZIGER BROS.   M. H. GILL & SON
1906

First Impression, 1899
Second Impression, 1906

AUTHOR'S PREFACE

IT has been thought desirable that the lives forming
this collection should not make any parade of
learning. Nevertheless, it is well that the reader
should be informed as to the guarantees of accuracy
which he has a right to expect in them. This, then,
is the manner in which this new life of St Ignatius
has been composed.

Among the men who heard, questioned, consulted
St Ignatius, or held close intercourse with him,
there are three who made a careful compilation
of their notes and recollections; they are Gonzalez
(*Acta antiquissima*), Ribadeneira (*Vita altera*), and
Polanco (*Vita Ignatii—Chronicon Societatis Jesu*).
The writings of the first two are incorporated in
the large volume of the Bollandists, but Polanco's
work was not published till 1894, at Madrid. It is
quite equal to the others in precision of detail, in
clearness of distinction, in felicity of expression, for
Latin had laid bare all its secrets to these men.
Therefore, I broke up the life of my Saint into a
certain number of fragments, and I compared the
testimony of these three contemporaries concerning
each of them. It is needless to say that I have
added the critical observations of the Bollandists,
and I have striven to vivify the whole, as far as
possible, by the writings of St Ignatius himself, the

Exercises, the Constitutions, and especially the Letters. When I have had recourse to other sources I have been careful to acknowledge them.

This book has been written with perfect freedom. If it is not found to contain many concessions to inveterate suspicion and bias it is because nothing is more calculated to destroy a host of prejudices than prolonged intercourse with a man above the common. There are some legends which belittle human nature, just as there are others which hide it from view under improbable marvels. It is an understood thing that the aim of this Series is to refute those contradictions of exact truth which have been propagated by both classes.

I should be most ungracious and most forgetful of my duty, if I did not here take the opportunity of thanking the numerous members of the Society, who, from Paris to Brussels, have supplied me with valuable sources of information. Owing to them, I have been able to read many documents, if not all unpublished, at least very scarce. With as much pleasure as profit I consulted at Saint Acheul the curious library bearing upon the *Spiritual Exercises* collected by Father Watrigant—books by fore-runners in the same path, books by commentators, books by friends, books by enemies, translations into every language (including Arabic). Neither must I forget those many Protestant editions published in England and America by clergymen, with very slight "expurgations," to the end that other religious com-munities might avail themselves of the work of the celebrated Jesuit. I trust that I have not profited very ill by these aids and resources.

EDITOR'S PREFACE

AS a biography is not merely a catalogue of facts and circumstances determining an individual life, but an attempt to make a personality evident in all its characteristic distinctness, we have no reason to complain that the life of St Ignatius has been written once more. There is room for endless approximation towards perfection in biography without any danger of so attaining it as to leave place for no further endeavour. It were comparatively easy to take the man as he was, the child of his age and country, formed by the society around him, educated in its beliefs and its ignorances, its enthusiasms and its animosities; to record his words and actions, to trace the diverging streams of his influence from his own to after times; and thus to know him as mingling with and embedded in the history of a given place and period; but far more difficult is the subsequent task of getting at his own precise and separate self, of discerning in his life what was due to that passive receptivity which has the most to do with a man's making, from the residue which is to be credited to his own originating activity. It is the latter which reveals that individuality whereby each man is distinct from all others, and is so far a theme of special interest.

As a typical sixteenth-century Spaniard, aristocrat, soldier, student, ecclesiastic, Ignatius may offer a valuable study to the historian, but the biographer's interest is in what is individual, not in what is typical. Was he a mystic only because mysticism was in the air all round him, and was the " methodism " which appears in the *Exercises* the truer manifestation of his personal bias ; or contrariwise, was the latter merely a prudent concession to growing or prevailing fashions ? Are we to judge him by the violent anti-semitic prejudices, which to some extent he shared with the society which formed him, or by the recorded instances when he went counter to that tide of bitterness ? When does he think and speak and act simply in obedience to the law of imitation, as others round him thought, spoke, and acted ; and when, because he has reflected and judged independently ? In a word, the biographer's task is to discriminate what is original from what is derived, and thereby to reveal to us the unique essential spirit which is distinctive of the character he desires to portray.

I do not think M. Joly has underrated the difficulty of his task, and though there will always be something to attain in the way of clearness and precision, yet his psychological handling of the subject has done more to make St Ignatius stand out as a human reality than has hitherto been done by any mere narrative of the Saint's life and times. For those who have leisure and ability for the investigation, it is doubtless in what remains to us of his writings that " he being dead yet speaketh." There, as we read and ponder, underneath the manifold letter, the unity of spirit betrays itself and takes shape in our minds as something altogether simple and distinct, like a flavour or a fragrance, scarcely to be analysed or even compared to anything else. Those who have known him in the "Acta quaedam" of his own dictation; in his letters; in the *Exercises*; in some of those rules that came straight from the heart of the man; who have unlearnt and blotted from their minds the harsh-featured Ignatius that unskilful biographers have popularised, will be independent perhaps of M. Joly's labours—except so far as we all owe gratitude to the artist who gives clear utterance to what we ourselves had felt and failed to express. But for many, this biographical essay, slight though it be, will do much to create a true first impression, or to correct a false one elsewhere derived.

Saints suffer more than others from uncritical biographers, who usually approach their subject *genibus flexis* predetermined to see sanctity in everything, and to load with pregnant meaning each of that multitude of literally "insignificant" actions which make up the bulk of even the most reflex life, and are in no sense original or characteristic. Further, the biographer is certain to look for, and therefore very easily to find, his own particular ideal of sanctity in this unsorted mass of material before him. A harsh, unloving nature will be governed in the selection and ordering of these materials by the desire of approving from the example and authority of Ignatius its own views

and conceptions. For such a one, there is enough
and to spare in the account of the earlier stages of his
spiritual transformation, ere the softening influence
of grace had done its full work, out of which to construct a somewhat angular and repellant portrait—
and yet surely an untruthful one, if we are to judge
the Saints, like other men, not by what they are at
any given moment, but by what they are shaping
towards, what they have fixed their heart on becoming. This end, this goal, answers to and reveals
the true character of the man, helped, it may be,
and elevated, yet not changed by grace. The progress of that development by which the radical
personality asserts itself, and the governing ideal
is more clearly conceived and gradually realised, is
blocked and impeded in a thousand ways, sometimes
fatally, always with much loss. But to confound
the consequent deviations and wanderings with the
straight course, as conceived and willed, is false
criticism. As the marble takes shape under the
sculptor's chisel, masses of rejected matter fall
away, freely at first, then more sparsely; but it is
from what remains, not from what is cast away, that
we are to judge his work, and so with the soul that
shapes itself laboriously under the guidance of divine
grace.

To determine the aim of a man's endeavour is
the true key to his character; yet it is a key by
no means easy to find. M. Joly, consciously or
unconsciously, has proceeded by this method, and
we think the result is a nearer approximation to
the true Ignatius than hitherto attained.

For many reasons, intrinsic and extrinsic, he is perhaps one of the least knowable and least known of the saints in any intimate sense of the word; for he has been "a sign of contradiction" as few other saints have been, and has suffered much doctoring from the hands of friends and foes; and along with this, he has it in common with all men of transcendent power to be slowly comprehended in the lapse of time, to be perhaps better appreciated in the age he divined and prepared for, than in the age he lived in. This being so, it need not surprise us if we lay down the book with a sense of unrest, as though there were something still wanting to the unity of our conception of this strange man. Had we instead a satisfied sense of comprehension, it would only indicate that some violence had been used to produce an appearance of completeness beyond what can really be attained consistently with truth. For the less cannot compass the greater, nor perhaps can any man ever more than partially understand another.   G. T.

Easter, 1899.

CONTENTS

CHAPTER I

CONTENTS

CHAPTER FIRST

THE CONVERTED AND PENITENT KNIGHT
PAMPELUNA AND LOYOLA—MONTSERRAT AND MANRESA

IS it a fact that St Ignatius was born in 1491 on Christmas night as the tradition of many asserted? or did his birth really take place in 1495, as the Bollandists of the present day, in conjunction with Polanco, are inclined to think? The question is not of sufficient importance, nor are the *data* in our possession sufficiently certain to detain us long. Suffice it to say that he was born in the reign of Ferdinand and Isabella, the last monarchs of old Spain, and that he died two years before Charles V., that is to say when the monarchy may truly be described as at the zenith of power and conquest.

That his family was noble is a well-established fact. It belonged to the number of those whose head was invited by the king himself to the ceremony of taking the oath of fealty. Bertrand of Loyola, his father, had, by his marriage with Dona Marina Saenz, thirteen children, eight boys and five girls. Ignatius (in Spanish Inigo) was the youngest, if not of the thirteen (the registers are not clear on this point) at least, without any doubt, of the sons. Like all his brothers and sisters, he was born at the Castle of Loyola, at a short distance

A 5

from the town of Azpeitia, in Guipuscoa, in the
country of the Basques, quite close to the French
frontier. He was baptised in the church of St
Sebastian at Azpeitia, where his brother, Dom
Martin, in his will, which has been preserved to
our day, begged at a later date to be buried.

His stock of knowledge was limited to reading
and writing (a good deal for a Spaniard in those
days) when John Velasquez, high-treasurer to their
Catholic Majesties, begged Bertrand of Loyola
to entrust him with the education of one of his
sons. The father's choice fell upon Ignatius, as
even then showing signs of being the most gifted
of the family, though we learn that all his brothers
were also valiant knights. He set forth for Arevolo
in the diocese of Avila, where the feudal castle of
Dom Velasquez stood; but he afterwards accompanied his patron to the court of Spain, where, as
we know, he remained for some time. In 1517
Velasquez fell into disgrace, and at about the same
date young Ignatius left the court in order to join
the army, which he entered under the protection
of his relation Dom Manriquez, duke of Najera,
one of the greatest nobles in Spain.

In 1521, when the war began between Francis I.
and Charles V., he had reached the rank of captain,
and was defending the stronghold of Pampeluna
against André de Foix, who was besieging it. The
town capitulated without consulting him, whereupon
he retired into the citadel with a handful of men,
and began a struggle of hopeless resistance. The
disparity of numbers forced him, despite himself, to

enter into negotiations, but not being able to bring himself to accept the terms offered, he broke them off almost immediately. At last, on May 21st, 1521, he received, in a *sortie*, a wound which broke his right leg, and threw him into the hands of the besiegers. His two-fold career of courtier and soldier was ended.

What had it been like? What memories did it leave with him?

Not one, amid all the Jesuits who have written the history of their founder, has tried to conceal the fact that his hero's life had been far from edifying. Maffei does not hesitate to speak of his " blind wanderings and vices " (*cæcos errores et vitia*).

These words, coming from a Latin theologian, are possibly a slight exaggeration of the truth. Bartoli, with more delicacy, and we would fain believe with more accuracy, says that he practised with regard to woman a gallantry induced rather by the vanity incidental to his age than by a vicious disposition. We see by documents unpublished till 1894, when the Society began to issue them, that Polanco steers a middle course between the two, though his language is rather more akin to Bartoli than to Maffei. "Up to the age of twenty-six," he says, " the life that he had led was by no means spiritual; like most young men whose affections are centred in the court and the army, he lived a somewhat unrestrained life, divided between the love of women, games,[1] and disputes about points of honour."

[1] Polanco says plainly " games " (*ludis*). The other biographers have made a great point of observing that the young knight had not cared about " play " properly so called.

Heaven knows that the youth of that day allowed themselves a good deal of licence in these respects.

There can be no doubt that Ignatius' gallantry was of a noble kind, mingled with the uses of chivalry and with elaborately poetical language. He himself related how, shortly after receiving his wound, the thought of his lady constantly occupied his mind. For three or four successive hours he pictured to himself how he would soon go to see her, how he would salute her, what conversations full of ingenious conceits he would hold with her, what military accomplishments he would display in her presence.

This lady was, according to the confidences of her devotee, "neither a countess nor a duchess, but something greater," which causes Father Genelli to surmise that she must have been either Germaine de Foix, the young widow of Ferdinand the Catholic, or the princess Catherine, daughter to Queen Joan. Thus the brilliant young knight had already formed the habit of aiming very high, but at the same time, even thus early in life, he pressed into the service of his ambition remarkable constancy, skill and gentleness, amusing himself, so to say, by the adaptation of, I will not say small, but ingenious means for the furtherance of his great end. We may add that, according to the very detailed testimony of his confidants, he was then exceedingly particular about his personal appearance, taking more care of his hair, hands and nails "than was reasonable."

He had received more than an ordinary share of natural gifts; besides an ardent courage, which manifested itself equally in braving danger, in rejecting yielding and compromise, in surmounting difficulties and in enduring pain, he showed wisdom beyond his years in his knowledge of men, in his skill in dealing with them and in gaining their friendship. In his endeavours to win their goodwill he was aided, not only by the prestige of his valour, but by a greatness of soul, in which were even then discernible, so his relations tell us, "the unmistakable tokens of a religious mind . . . great respect for holy things, a horror of blasphemy . . . scrupulous care about deviating from truth . . . contempt of avarice, and even indifference to worldly advantage, . . . readiness to be reconciled with his enemies." Sometimes he gave up to his comrades his share of the booty obtained on the battlefield, sometimes he himself distributed among the enemies who had wounded him the different parts of his armour.

In the gallant, romantic, believing Spain of those days, every knight had, as well as his lady, a patron saint to whom he was devoted. It is worthy of note that the future champion of the Papacy felt a peculiar devotion to St Peter, in whose honour he had even written verses in the Castilian language, just as he had composed sonnets for the lady of his thoughts.

Thus his ignorance was that of a nobleman, whose mind had nevertheless been cultivated after the fashion of his day. Let us again follow him into his room in the castle of Loyola, whither the French, full of admiration for his courage, had caused him to be carried in an almost dying state. They made a point of themselves providing him with medical attendance, and with everything which appeared

necessary for the treatment of his wound.   We know
how he bore unmurmuringly the diverse tortures of
a series of unskilful operations.   "He gave," we read,
"no sign of suffering, save the tight clenching of his
hands."   "Being vigorous and well made, very much
preoccupied about a graceful and elegant carriage,
and fully determined to pursue the profession of
arms," he caused the bone of his knee to be sawn
through, in order to get rid of a malformation resulting from the first operation.   It was partially removed,
but left him through life a slight lameness.   When
at the point of death, the day before the feast of St
Peter and St Paul, he had invoked his favourite saint,
and during the feverish night which followed he
seemed to behold the apostle before his eyes.   From
that moment he considered himself cured.

Nevertheless worldly thoughts had not yet left
him.   Knowing that he would have to be a prisoner
to his bed for many long months, he asked for
"Amadis of Gaul," a book whose success throughout Europe was to be ensured twenty years later
by the French translation, which was the favourite
reading of Francis the First.   What did our knight,
who was not as yet a true penitent, seek in this
romance?   Apparently what is actually found in
it, an exaggerated picture of the manners of
knighthood, seeking adventure, battle, and love,
which was destined to be parodied by Cervantes,
"a phantasmagoria of heroism, of heroes cloven
through and slain, of knights overcome in twos
and threes, men-at-arms in eights and tens, soldiers
in thousands on the battlefield, one single hero, such

as Amadis, Galaor or some other, being apparently
capable of accomplishing all these feats; children
lost and found again, husbands and wives and lovers
parted, attachments of indescribable passion and
depth, witchcraft, oracles, fabulous geography." [1]

But it was the will of Providence that those who
were nursing the sick man should not have a romance
at hand. They brought him two books, which he
had not asked for, and which he accepted, says Ribadeneira, in order that he might not remain entirely without occupation, the " Flower of the Saints," a popular
book, of which Ribadeneira himself was later to bring
out a famous edition, and the Spanish translation
of the " Life of Christ " by Ludolph the Carthusian.

The old biographers of St Ignatius passed lightly
over his reading of these volumes, and yet it must
have exercised deep influence over the thoughts of
the young man. In order to discover what he found
in the " Flower of the Saints," we have only to take
an edition of Ribadeneira, and read with especial
attention the lives of those who flourished before
the sixteenth century, and they would be found sub-
stantially identical with the Castilian edition of
that date. Scarcely recovered, as he was, from the
two-fold fever of the fight and of his illness, con-
strained, by the helplessness of his body and the
tediousness of his convalescence, to serious reflection,
limited in his comparisons by the small number of
his books, he must of necessity have eagerly devoured
these chronicles of the many and marvellous deeds
of prowess, wrought by another order of chivalry, in

---

[1] Lanson, "History of French Literature."

the service of the greatest of kings. Thus it is easy
to call up before our eyes the pageant which gradually
set his imagination aflame ; the daily triumph of
charity—the power obtained by means of mortifications, rendered sweet by that very charity—humility
overcoming brute force—obscure anchorites trans-
forming countries and men's hearts—popes bowing
before the sanctity of a monk or of a virgin,
and in their turn humbling before them the dukes,
kings and emperors whose rebellion always ends in
conversion or humiliation—voluntary poverty compensated by the conquest of souls in this world,
and the guerdon of Heaven in the future—miracles
rewarding the faith of some and the disinterested-
ness of others—sin seen everywhere in the shape of
an attack of the enemy—an incessant struggle with
the devil, who is vanquished by penance and prayer
—a perpetual contrast between the blind, passionate
and bloodthirsty sensuality of sinners, and the
prudent gentleness of the children of God—Jesus
sometimes coming back to earth, showing Himself
there in apparitions, enduring His Passion afresh
through the crimes of His enemies, but pouring
forth before men's eyes the saving effects of that
Passion in the virtues and miracles of His elect—
the renewal of the wonders of the life of Our Saviour
in the prodigies accompanying the birth, life and
death of the saints—the whole creation, inanimate
objects and the very animals pressed into the service
of these heroes who finally bore away by " violence "
the Heaven which they so ardently desired to gain
for themselves and for others. — Such was the

spectacle constantly offered to the contemplation of the knight by the perusal of these lives.

No one can deny that with these accounts are mingled fables, incredible to the most Christian historian of our day, that apocryphal miracles are found there in far too large numbers, and that too many accidents or sicknesses, arising from a natural cause, were attributed to the intervention of Satan. Scholars and learned men have laid great stress on this "fabulous" side of the subject, and have made it the text of their severe denunciations of the "coarseness" of the Middle Ages. They have pointed out that the literal sense is often substituted for the figurative; that moral virtues and intellectual inspirations are often transformed into apparitions, into voices, into a sudden metamorphosis of natural elements; that, consequently, material greatness, instead of being the symbol of moral greatness, easily came to usurp its place; and that thus the visible world, encroaching little by little upon the domain of the invisible, materialised all conception of it; that in short we are confronted with a kind of mysticism, which is not merely uninspired by spirituality, but is frequently, they affirm, its very contrary. There is truth in all these observations; and whenever we review and criticise popular notions left entirely to themselves, we should make a great mistake in overlooking the fact. But at the same time we must remember that the saints themselves, whose character and mission were thus misrepresented by credulous minds, did not share these childish errors. Nay, they struggled energetically against them, as did the prophets against the carnal spirit of the Jews, their humility and their delicate feeling for spiritual things alike protesting against the species of transfiguration which the populace, even in their lifetime, strove to impose upon them. We do not mean to say that St Ignatius, when reading the "Flos Sanctorum" for the first time, had progressed to such a degree, but it is possible that the pious legends contained in the book were necessary in an age when criticism was unknown, to introduce the future saint into the supernatural world by the substitution of the histories of martyrs and confessors for the fictions of "Amadis." Nevertheless, if we glance at Ribadeneira's edition, it does not appear to us that the over-imaginative part of these histories is detrimental to the authentic and deeply Christian portion. For example, why not believe that Ignatius laid to heart these words said of St Bernard, whom later in life he quoted more than any other Father of the Church: "He himself was the first and greatest of all his miracles"?

This great miracle of self-conquest, which, in order to be successful, must begin with self-knowledge, was to be accomplished by St Ignatius in his turn, and the Bollandists, following in the track of his earliest biographers, are at pains to explain how it was that during his lifetime he wrought no other; they consider that this, coupled with the founding of the Society, was sufficient for his own sanctity, for the glory of God. But at present we are a long way distant from that heroic period of his life. Providentially for himself, he was at this time intent not only on the "Flower of the Saints," but on the pages of Ludolph the Carthusian which he read and meditated deeply.[1]

It is not very surprising that the authorship of the "Imitation of Jesus Christ" should sometimes have been attributed to this Saxon monk, for, in his "Life of Christ," the idea and the word "Imitation" recur in many different ways, and, when this beautiful book is studied as it deserves to be, the author will not be regarded as unworthy of such an honour. Undoubtedly it would be very difficult to deprive France of the merit of having written the "Imitation," a book equally remarkable for its depth, the closeness of its reasoning and its perfect clearness, even when soaring to the heights of the most touching and tender mysticism; but whether it is that the anonymous writer has gathered up and set forth, in a fashion peculiarly his own, an idea already scattered amidst all religious orders, or whether he was its originator, it is certain that in the fourteenth century we meet with it everywhere, and, as I have just said, Ludolph the Saxon is full of it. In common with every chapter of the book the introduction closes with a prayer, and we make no excuse for quoting this first prayer in all its eloquent simplicity: "Lord Jesus, grant that I, a weak and miserable sinner, may always have before the eyes of my heart Thy life and virtues, and may imitate them to the best of my power."

[1] He read it in the Castilian translation, recently brought out, by the Observatine Franciscan, D. Antonio Montesino. Neither the date of Ludolph's birth nor death are known with certainty. His biographers say : "He flourished in the year 1330."

When he turned from the "Flower of the Saints" to the "Life of Christ" Ignatius had no longer before him a crowd of different exploits performed in every country and under circumstances differing widely from one another. Nevertheless the severe unity of Our Saviour's life was presented in these pages in a guise well fitted to captivate the imagination of a man still so young.

There are many points of comparison, it seems to me, between Ludolph and those German painters, whose progress was abruptly checked by the Lutheran Reformation. They are at once learned and simple, religious and familiar; they intermingle scenes taken from everyday life with moving descriptions of the most solemn mysteries. Their colouring is, I own, not invariably harmonious or delicate, but it is warm and vivid, and proof against the ravages of time. In the pictures of the Saxon Carthusian, the Spanish nobleman came here and there on a few scattered legends, like the accessories which give a picture an appearance of reality and sometimes of tranquillity. He saw that the apocryphal gospels were made to contribute all kinds of details with regard to the life of Our Lord, or of the Holy Family. Thus the good monk displays minute care in his description of the person of Christ, omitting neither His dress, nor the colour of His eyes, nor His complexion, nor His hair, with its parting (*discrimen*) down the middle, after the fashion of the Nazarenes. In other passages depicting human sins or weaknesses, he has touches taken from the life in the ordinary ceremonies of public worship and its incidents. Thus he compares people who are offended by truth with those who in church, during the *Asperges*, put their hands before their face for fear of being wetted by the holy water. But these episodes, which stamp the book with its personal character, its local colour and its date, nowise impair the effect of teaching full of the memories of the four Gospels, of the doctrine of the Fathers, and of the pathetic tones of St Bernard—who indeed is met with everywhere in the thirteenth and fourteenth centuries.

What effect did these studies produce on the mind of our convalescent? They awakened in him an emulation quite as eager as that aroused in another direction by the warlike chronicles of the Castilian knights. "Well," he would say to himself, "supposing I too were to do what St Dominic and St Francis have done." "And he turned over in his mind many projects," adds Gonzalès, "and constantly set before himself great and difficult things, and whilst reflecting upon them he believed that he felt within himself the power of accomplishing them, solely from the following motive: 'St Dominic did this, then I will do it; St Francis did it, I will do it too.'"—Have we not often seen many a great vocation decided thus, in war, politics and art?

We are far from saying that even at this time his recollections of the world and of the camp did not fill his head at times with dreams of very different exploits, of quite contrary roads to glory. "Sometimes," says Polanco, "he felt within himself a powerful inspiration, leading him to give himself entirely to God, and to imitate everything that he had just read; sometimes vain imaginings urged him towards the greatness and the glories of the world. For, since his soul was great, he always aimed at great things in either of the two paths which he was pursuing. Never did he read of any kind of penance practised by the saints without feeling confident that he too could practise it. In those days, like a conscript going through the severe training of the spiritual army, holiness specially presented itself to him in the form of rigorous penance, accepted for the love of God. But, as during his former life he had had very little practice in spiritual things, he still allowed himself to be excited quite as much by worldly as by virtuous thoughts."

But here took place the decisive event which was to settle his conversion; he was to take new shape in the innermost depths of thought and liberty, and then to attain immovable consistency and strength with great rapidity.

Persons who are possessed of much imagination cannot fail at first to experience many temptations; for the imagination revives within them the original sensations of which it is but the inward reproduction; moreover, it increases and diversifies in a thousand fashions these revivified sensations. Therefore men often yield to these deceptive suggestions of the imagination, even though they repent afterwards with the bitterness which accompanies every awakening from a state of intoxication. But when

this vividness of mental picturing is united with a
reflective tendency, a man soon learns to check one
conception by means of another, and guards against
fresh stumbling and falling on his own part, for he
looks the suggestions with which he has already
made acquaintance straight in the face, and to a
certain extent exhausts them by foreseeing all their
consequences and tasting in anticipation all their
fruits, whether refreshing or poisonous. This is
exactly what happened to the soldier of Pampeluna;
he made, unaided, a psychological discovery which
he was to consider from every point of view, which
was perhaps the leading factor in his thoughts, his
doctrine, his piety, his teaching, his foundations, in
short, throughout his whole life.

In proportion as these contradictory ideas of
temporal glory or of sanctity succeeded each other,
or were mutually supplanted in his mind, he carefully noted how the two arose, and how they ended.
He observed that the last-named were not merely
good thoughts (because they were in conformity
with the law of religion) but that they fortified his
soul, consoled it, and, so to say, filled it with solid
food; whilst the first, though apparently agreeable
during the time of his indulging in them, left his
soul, on their departure, empty and unsatisfied.
By this sign he was in future able to distinguish
what came to him from the "good spirit," from
God or one of His angels, and what came from
the "bad spirit." By this means, according to
the testimony of those who gathered together his
own recollections, he definitely established the theory

of the discernment of spirits which was to be brought to perfection in his *Spiritual Exercises*. It was undoubtedly on his sick bed at Loyola, when reflecting on the contradictory feelings which alternately filled his suffering and tormented soul, that he conceived the first idea of them.[1]

Needless to say, the theory was not new; it is most clearly set forth in one of the dialogues of St Catherine of Siena. Jesus Christ says to the saint: "If you ask me how you are to recognise what comes from the devil and what comes from Me, I answer that this is the sign for your guidance:—If the idea comes from the devil, the soul receives all at once a feeling of lively joy; but the longer the state lasts, the more the joy diminishes, and it leaves you in weariness, confusion and darkness.—But if the soul is visited by Me, the Eternal Truth, it is, at the outset, seized with a holy fear and subsequently receives gladness, sweet prudence, and the desire of virtue."

Had St Ignatius read St Catherine of Siena when he was reflecting, as we have just seen, on the aspirations of his own mind? We may safely reply in the negative. It is quite certain that he perceived and drew this distinction of himself. The touch of kinship, in these two souls, differing in so many respects, is worth observing, less for the honour of the knight in the first stages of his conversion than for the honour of this profound truth,

[1] " Electionum rationem particulatim asseruit elicuisse se ex illa spirituum varietate quam sensit tum cum in Loyola aeger ex tibia decumberet " (*Gonzales*).

presenting, as it does, one of the most important aspects of the psychology of the saints.

It would have been strange if the sensitive imagination had not been affected by all this deep and close reflection. Whither did it lead him, nourished as it was by the dreams of convalescence, and by the reviving fire of youth? We know as a fact that he had a fresh and more distinct vision: the Blessed Virgin, holding in her arms the Child Jesus, appeared to him brilliant with light (*clarissima*). It was during the night, but he felt wide awake (*noctu, vigilans tamen*), says Polanco. Was it merely the result of intense thought concentrated on one of the mysteries most familiar to believing souls? Was it a movement of human love, raised to a higher plane, desirous of contemplating in spirit the grace of woman, yet seeking it purified and ennobled? Was it a hallucination? Was it the gift of a supernatural action substituted for nature or mingled with it? In his old age Ignatius himself questioned himself on the subject and hesitated; he did not dare to say whether this phenomenon had come from God or no (*divinitus contigisse*). But those in his confidence learnt from his own lips that after that day both his body and his mind had been spared impure temptations. We feel no surprise at the whole framework of his good resolutions gaining in strength from that date. His brother and those of his household who were nursing him, alike observed the change just wrought in him.

As soon as he was able to be about, and was confirmed in his purposes of amendment, one side of his nature and disposition were endued afresh with innocent liberty; he set about occupying himself. He wished to work at the perfection of his soul with that patient love of careful detail, and even with that attention to adornment, which we find later on in the literature, art, and schools of the Society. As he steadily found more and more pleasure in pious reading, he conceived the idea of making extracts of what appeared to him most important in the life of Christ and of the saints. Ribadeneira has already related the fact, but St Ignatius, in his confidences to Father Gonzalès, gives in addition interesting details. " When he was beginning to get up," he says, " he began to write with extreme care a book of three hundred quarto pages. The words of Jesus Christ were painted in vermilion (and doubtless he used gold for certain points and for the miracles, as Ribadeneira says), those of the Blessed Virgin in blue, the remainder in various colours, according to the inspiration of his piety. The paper was very fine, the lines carefully ruled, the handwriting excellent, for he possessed the art of forming letters exquisitely.[1]   But we

---

[1] We may with reason believe, that as time went on many a page which St Ignatius had copied and left among his papers was attributed to him. He is by no means the only person to whom such a thing has happened. For instance, most people accredit St Ignatius with the authorship of the beautiful prayer which opens the *Exercises* :—

> Soul of Christ, sanctify me,
> Body of Christ, save me,
> Blood of Christ, inebriate me.

Now the Jesuits tell us that it had been widely known for two

know from the same source that this work was alternated with the contemplation of the sky, and particularly of the starry sky. It seems to me that this fact instinctively turns our thoughts to Kant, who, in the same way, considered the study of the interior law and the gaze fixed on the starry firmament as the two great attractions of the intellectual life; he too set between these two great delights certain regular habits of rather minute detail, either simply in order to relax the tension of the mind, or in order to exempt himself once for all from reflecting on things not worth the trouble.

.   .   .   .   .   .

But neither pleasant employments nor lofty contemplation could satisfy this young Spaniard, who treated himself with such harshness, and to whom the term *"exalté"* might not unfitly be applied. God had given him the grace of conversion, and had cured him of his sickness; the time had come for doing penance and shunning the occasions of falling into sin. One of his first ideas was to enter the Carthusians at once. He even desired, by way of consummating his sacrifice at one blow, to present himself at the monastery without revealing his name. But nothing appeared in his own eyes sufficient to satisfy what two of his disciples have described as his generous indignation, and even his hatred against his own person. He bade one of his servants get for him the Carthusian rule, he read it, and was, we are

centuries among the faithful in Spain, and that it was inscribed in barbarous orthography over one of the most beautiful gates of the Alcazar of Seville.

told, satisfied with it, but he desired first to go to
Jerusalem and impose on himself of his own free
will severer penances than those invented by the
Carthusians.

Everyone knows that the idea of the Crusades had
lasted in Spain longer than anywhere else. The
spirit of chivalrous piety, excited and kept alive by
seven centuries of struggle against the Moors, had
been preserved in that country in all its vigour, says
a recent historian of the Papacy,[1] " even at a time
when amidst other notions of Europe it had long
given place to more material notions, or degenerated
into fierce rivalries." It was not long since a Pope
of Spanish origin, Alfonso Borgia, having become
Pope Calixtus III., had awakened the ardour of
Europe (1455) in order to save Hungary from the
invasion of the Turks. He would have liked to do
more; for he aspired to the reconquest of the Holy
City. He had inaugurated his pontificate by a kind
of solemn oath, which ended with these words: " If
I forget thee, O Jerusalem, let my right hand be
forgotten! May my tongue cleave to my jaws, if I
do not remember thee, if I make not Jerusalem the
beginning of my song."

Well, in 1521, this echo was not quite silent in the
country of Calixtus III., and the young Ignatius, like
the Pope, desired that Jerusalem should be the
beginning of his spiritual joy. It was not now a
question of war or conquest; but was not a journey
to Jerusalem for the sake of sharing in the Passion
of Our Saviour and in the sorrowful humiliations of

[1] Pastor, "History of the Popes," French edition, II. 321.

His Sepulchre, held captive by the infidels, a sort of crusade in the eyes of pious people? Such was the gate through which our convert wished to enter upon the way of salvation.

He therefore made ready to start. I have said that the change in his habits had been observed by his family, who suspected him of cherishing designs of a monastic life, or of a solitary existence full of mortifications. So, when he made known his approaching departure, his brother, Martin Loyola, who occupied in the family the place of the father, now dead, took him aside and spoke to him with a curious mixture of respect and authority. He reminded him of the expectations aroused in their part of the country by his talents, courage and prudence, and of the confident hopes cherished by his kinsfolk of his increasing the family glory. " I am," said he, " your elder in years, but your reputation has outstripped mine; do not do anything unworthy of our ancestors "; by which he doubtless meant to warn his brother, not against dishonourable actions, but against a life in which the penitent might forget his earthly nobility and his warlike honour.

Ignatius answered gently but vaguely, that he would neither forget nor compromise the honour of his family. He used as a pretext for departure a visit which he owed to the duke of Najera, and, accompanied by two servants, started for Montserrat. I shall not lose time in relating at length the episodes with which everyone is familiar—the dispute with the Moor and the vigil of arms.

Who has not read the account of that meeting

between the Catholic knight and the imperfectly-converted infidel, both on horseback, both armed, both engaged in a violent argument concerning the virginity of Mary? The Moor was quite willing to admit that she had, when a virgin, brought forth Christ, but maintained that she had afterwards lived like other wives. Ignatius, angry at seeing the glory of his Lady unacknowledged, asked himself whether it were not his duty to avenge her. On the other hand he was reluctant to shed blood. He got out of the difficulty by letting the reins fall on the neck of his mule, and saying to himself that if it followed the same road as the blasphemer, he would follow the man and kill him, certain that God would have thus given him a sufficiently clear indication of His Will. The saint's biographers have not failed to point out that according to all likelihood the mule would have followed the level high-road taken by the Moor, and that on the contrary it set off by itself down a mountainous path, and they conclude from this circumstance that invisible intervention hindered Ignatius from unlawfully seeking to take human life. We may, without much subtlety, be allowed to think that the former soldier showed, by leaving the decision of such a case to his steed, that he had anticipated the bloody solution, and been disposed beforehand to accept it.

However this may be, the conclusion of the adventure ought to have shown him that arms were henceforth useless to him. But the spirit of chivalry, which still dwelt in his imagination, suggested to him another expedient in which the old and the new spirit were again intermingled, before parting company for ever, we may venture to say. He was about to enter on a life of renunciation and penance, and, being a beginner, stood in need of preparation and armour. He therefore entered the chapel of Our Lady at Montserrat—it was on the 24th of March, the vigil of the Annunciation, 1522— and spent a whole night in keeping his spiritual "vigil in arms." Those who have most carefully collected his own statements affirm positively, on his authority, that he drew his inspirations from the old customs of chivalry, nay, that he was acting from recollection of the accounts of "Amadis" and other writings of the same kind. But his armour was no longer the same. He had hung up in the chapel his baldric, dagger and sword. His spiritual armour consisted of the clothes of a poor man, for which he had exchanged his own, a kind of gown of coarse cloth, shoes of esparto-grass, a rope girdle, a gourd, and a sort of wallet, destined to carry, together with his bread, the book which he had taken away from Loyola—probably the volume composed by himself of all sorts of extracts from pious works.

What was Montserrat like then? A member of the Society of Jesus has given us a charming descrip- of it. A statue of the Blessed Virgin, which worked miracles, was discovered there. "Gradually first a church and then a Benedictine monastery were built near the statue, and, scattered about in the most desolate spots, hermitages to the number of thirteen arose. A delicate and indefinable poetical perfume was mingled with the pious and austere life

of the hermits. The descendants of St Antony
and St Paul had tamed the mountain birds; the
young fledgelings often came in springtime to be fed
and petted by the solitaries. Green coppices, kept
constantly fresh by the pure and limpid water of the
mountain torrents, seemed to soften the severity and
wildness of the bare rocks and dark precipices."
As time went on the "pilgrimage assumed pro-
portions that Lourdes alone was destined to exceed
in that district, and it had exercised considerable
influence over the destiny of Catalonia and over the
morals of the inhabitants. In the beginning of the
sixteenth century, the monastery of Montserrat
numbered a hundred and forty Benedictine monks.
There were confessors in Spanish, French, Italian,
German and Flemish. In spite of the extreme
difficulty of communication, the sanctuary was
visited every year by about a hundred and fifty
thousand pilgrims, rich and poor, of all nations,
among whom were to be found kings and princes.
One priest in a single year had to hear nearly six
thousand French or Flemish confessions; and
within the same space of time, hospitality had been
given to seven thousand seven hundred priests and
religious; Charles the Fifth went as often as nine
times to Montserrat."

But everyone knows that however different are a
man's surroundings, he will feel, think, and act
according to his dominant idea, always provided
that he has one. It is certain that Ignatius did
not .suffer his attention to be much distracted,
either by the charms of nature, or by the excite-

ment of the numerous pilgrimages. He spent only a short time at Montserrat, just as much as was necessary to enable him to read to the French Benedictine, Dom Chanones, his general confession, which he had written down. Moreover, he had begun those austerities, those frequent disciplines, which were added to the mortification of coarse clothing and scanty food. These practices had rather strengthened than modified the, as yet, entirely exterior nature of his asceticism. He set about spiritual things, says Polanco, in a military spirit (*militari adhuc spiritu*); he regarded them from the point of view of a knight, not of an apostle. " He thought less," says Gonzalès, "of really doing penance than of showing himself devoted and generous to God. He could not hear the mention of any austerity practised by any saint without desiring to inflict a similar one on himself. But he knew nothing then of the interior reasons for penance, nothing of charity, humility, or prudence. He only saw one thing, that he must do great actions, since the saints had done them for the love of God."

In these dispositions he promptly left the great monastery and the picturesque solitudes of Montserrat in order to go to Barcelona, whence he intended to embark for Jerusalem, but he was first to remain at Manresa close to Montserrat for almost a year. These ten months had so important an effect upon his whole life that we must pause with him.

He had left his mule at the monastery, and, being

desirous of henceforth appearing as a "pilgrim," he started, his right leg still lame, staff in hand, in the dress with which we are already familiar. It was then that the beggar to whom he had given his own clothes was stopped by an alguazil, who suspected him of having stolen garments clearly belonging to a nobleman. He protested his innocence, and gave information which enabled the authorities to start in pursuit of Ignatius and ask him for an explanation. The pilgrim only answered what was absolutely necessary for the exculpation of the beggar, and seeing that his first act of charity had nearly cost a poor man his liberty, he could not help lamenting within himself over the difficulties of doing right. He even shed a few tears, the first, according to Polanco, that had fallen from his eyes since he left his father's house.

It was at this date that took place his meeting with Agnes Pascual, the first of those pious women destined to foresee his sanctity and help him to attain it. The account given by John Pascual, son to Agnes, has been quoted in all the biographies, and deservedly so, for it gives us an authentic portrait of the saint. "One day, when she (his mother, then a widow for the second time) was returning, in company with two young men and three women, from a pilgrimage to Our Lady of Montserrat, she was accosted by a poor man, dressed from head to foot in a coarse serge pilgrim's gown. He was of middle height with fair and bright colouring,[1] and an expression of such modesty that it seemed as though he

[1] According to Ribadeneira, his light hair fell on his shoulders.

scarcely dared to raise his eyes. He walked as
though overcome with fatigue, limping with the right
leg. He came up to my mother, near the chapel of the
Apostles, and asked her if there were by chance a
hospital in the neighbourhood where he could take
up his abode. At the sight of his gentle and noble
countenance (*honoratum et bonum*), of the expression stamped on his brow, whence the hair was
already slightly worn away, she felt moved by feelings of devotion and piety." She proposed that he
should mount her donkey, he refused persistently.
Having reached Manresa, the charitable lady sent
him part of the supper prepared for herself.

We now see Ignatius installed in the hospital
of St Lucy, nursing the sick, living on alms, in-
flicting upon himself the most severe mortifications,
spending seven consecutive hours on his knees in
prayer, sleeping little, scarcely eating at all, striving
like almost all the saints at this period of their lives,
to do and suffer everything most repugnant to nature,
making a parade of dirt, allowing his hair, beard and
nails to grow long and unkempt, seeking the company
of the poor and sick, and meeting with nothing but
mockery from anyone. Every day he read the
Passion of Christ, but rather in the same manner
that he would have read the account of a battle, in
order to excite his courage. His health was
weakened, and the inevitable result, which later on
he strove to avert from all his disciples, followed;
—troubles of various kinds fell upon his soul.

At first they were only comparatively unimportant
temptations, which he overcame without much diffi-

culty. Thus one day he involuntarily asked himself whether he should be able to endure this kind of life and carry it on, for instance, to the age of sixty or seventy. But he instantly made this answer to himself: "Why do you talk of seventy? Are you even sure of living two years?"

But after the temptations which assail strong natures came the scruples which more commonly fall to the share of overheated imaginations. He was constantly asking himself whether his confessions had been full, and having the eyes of his soul constantly turned upon himself by these unhealthy doubts, he was amazed at the dryness and weariness which had suddenly replaced his passionate transports of piety, and he conceived a disgust for life. Before long this disgust assumed the form of a temptation far more serious than the others. He had exchanged the shelter of the hospital for that of a Dominican monastery. There, when praying one day near a yawning chasm, he was seized with a moral and physical giddiness, urging him to put an end to his sufferings by flinging himself into the abyss.

It is true that in this terrible peril he checked himself by exclaiming, "No, Lord, I will never offend Thee." But he had recourse to a remedy, which was perhaps worse than the disease; he wished, so to say, to do violence to God after the example of certain saints, who, as he had read, had fasted until they had obtained the grace which they were imploring. He resolved to abstain from eating and drinking until peace was restored to his soul. He thus went two, three, and even seven whole days without taking anything, and without pretermitting any of his occupations or penances. And yet his strength remained unimpaired, and he felt no symptom of weakness. This dangerous experiment was brought to an end by the advice of his confessor, who threatened, if he persisted in it, to refuse him absolution; he was also advised to be more simple about his confessions. Two or three days later, despite a violent return of the evil, the penitent found himself cured. His past life was forgotten. He felt, says Gonzalès, like a man awakening from a long dream, and, as it were, entering upon a new existence. One result of this trial, in which he had nearly been overwhelmed, was a peculiar skill, which he retained through life, in driving away scruples from the souls of others.

After this final calming of the storm his whole being was, as it were, raised up by a buoyancy independent of any factitious shackles. He had arrived at one of those crises, when thoughtful minds, and still more great souls, casting away everything that is artificial and conventional, everything lending itself to illusion or self-deception, see, more clearly than they will ever do again, danger on the one hand, safety and duty on the other. The complications, the agitations, the false hopes of life will usually silence the truth-speaking voice, or close the ears to its warnings, but on that day at least it had made itself plainly heard, and the listeners will call it to mind sometimes, either to reproach themselves for having disregarded it, or to congratulate themselves on having recognised and obeyed it.

Something of this kind was going on in the case of Ignatius, but there was undoubtedly a more powerful factor at work, for it was then that he had those celebrated visions in which we are told that he received more light than in all the other visions and all the other meditations of his life.

I say advisedly *those* visions, for if we read Polanco and Gonzalès carefully, we see that he had several, in which he believed that the contemplation was vouchsafed to him either of Our Lord's Humanity, or of Our Lady, or of the Holy Trinity, or of other mysteries, upon which he then proceeded to meditate, doubtless with more imagination than serious consideration, and especially with but little science.

It has been possible to locate exactly the spot where he received those favours, which left in his mind deeply-cherished memories. It was almost a thousand paces from the town of Manresa, on a path hollowed in the rock, which overhung the little stream, the Cardone, and looked down upon the picturesque hills of the neighbourhood; the place had received the name of St Paul's balcony.[1] Did he in truth there behold real objective visions, which might be described as hallucinations? In two or three instances the expressions used in the accounts seem a little doubtful. This much we

---

[1] On account of a church and priory of that name which are at the end of the road. The priory is still in existence. The present road is lower, having been reclaimed from the river-bed.

may safely affirm, that his imagination and his reason were always in perfect harmony and that the latter had the upper hand. A visible form exterior to himself, made manifest to him that which his mind received inwardly, but there is no doubt that the essential part of these visions (to use the words of St Teresa at a later date) was an intellectual vision. The testimony of his secretary is explicit. "Then," he says, "the eyes of his mind were opened and illuminated, not that he beheld a shape or image which affected the senses, but that he had then a marvellous comprehension of things referring either to the mysteries of faith or to science,[1] and he beheld them so clearly that it seemed to him as though the realities themselves were before him lighted up with new brilliancy. After having remained for some time with his mind fixed on this interior sight, he knelt down before a cross that was near at hand, and thanked God for so great a benefit."

Some biographers of the saint have appeared to think that, from that day forth, he was fortified by a supernatural agency, with all the knowledge and all the strength required for carrying out his life-long work. This appears to us a curious simplification of the hard task always set to a saintly hero. Let us hear what St Ignatius himself says in a passage of the *Exercises* which may most fitly be quoted here:

[1] Ribadeneira says "scientiarum cognitionem," Gonzalès "litterarum peritiam." Natural science being at that period only composed of deductive reasoning and of speculative philosophy the two writers are in substantial agreement.

"When the soul has received consolation from God, there always comes upon her *a second time*, to which she ought to pay great attention, for though she may be still all on fire and filled with the consciousness of divine favour, nevertheless, through her own reasoning, as a result of her habits, and in consequence of her conceptions and judgments, she forms, when under the dominion of either a good or a bad spirit, resolutions and decisions which do not come from God."—It is to this "second time" that we are now about to devote our attention.

On his return to his solitude, he was still under the confused impression of these great ideas, and his mind was anxiously fixed on retaining the understanding of them.   He who scarcely knew more than how to read and write began to compose an *opusculum* of eighty pages on the Holy Trinity.   The book has not been preserved.

Such a tension of mind could not continue without weakening a nervous system that was already overwrought.   Not that much importance need be attached to the recurrent phenomenon of a luminous image from which the form of a serpent suddenly emerged before his eyes, for he soon succeeded in putting this vision to flight, and it does not seem that the "attacks of Satan" ever exercised much influence over the course of his thoughts.   But some time after the great interior scene just related, he had what his first biographers call a rapture (*raptus*).   He remained for a whole week in a state of lethargy, his body being insensible and like a corpse, a slight flutter of the heart the only sign that life was not extinct. When he returned to himself he uttered the simple exclamation: "Oh! Jesus," but held conversation with no one as to what had taken place within him during that period.

The physical trials were not over. Three times did this Spanish neophyte resume his excessive austerities, three times he fell seriously ill; he was already afflicted with that disease of the stomach which was to trouble him all his life. As he was well known in Manresa, and all his actions were watched with a certain curiosity intermingled in the minds of some with admiration, of others with contempt, he divided the town, so to say, into two camps. Some pious women, of the number of those who had observed him most closely, went to nurse him at the hospital; then the magistrates of the city became interested in him and had him moved to the house of a citizen, who was delighted to receive him, despite the sarcasms of those who were annoyed by these manifestations and turned them into ridicule.

As for him, he became a prey to fresh temptations, but this time they were of the kind well known to contemplative souls, and even to those who examine themselves frequently and attentively. He believed himself to be virtuous, and then he reproached himself with this excess of confidence and accused himself of not corresponding sufficiently with divine grace. These scruples were laid to rest like the others. The effect of this kind of

contact with death, of this foretaste which he had
had of it, was a state of mind unusual in ordinary
men : he was from that time unable to think of
death without experiencing a thrill of joy, and
being filled with an ecstasy which moved him to
tears.   We need hardly say that this state was
not the gloomy weariness of life, which had weighed
him down for a short time; it was love of the life
of free and unfettered expansion in the breast of
perfect goodness.   The feeling continued to be so
vivid and persistent that he was compelled to turn
his mind away from the thought, "for fear of finding too much consolation in it."

Between a year and a half and two years had gone
by, ten months of which were spent at Manresa,
since his wound had suddenly stopped his worldly
life in mid-career.   This space of time had been
filled with many attempts, we may likewise say with
many spiritual excesses.   Let us suppose for a
moment that his life had ended there, and that
nevertheless his reputation, attributable as much to
his austerity and piety as to his noble birth, had survived, many critics or self-styled historians of matters
religious would have made him the text of their dis-
sertations on the diseases of mystics or the neurosis
of the saints.   But, thanks be to God, the pilgrim
of Montserrat, who was still in the stage of painful
apprenticeship to sanctity, was to learn its real
marks in the sweat of his brow.   He had already
begun to turn from this purely external exhibition of
imprudent heroism towards the life of the soul.
There he had crossed the road of scruples and fear

in order to make his first steps in that of confidence
and love. Then he had extracted from the feeling
of interior consolation the idea that he might make
use of his own experience for the good of other
souls; he said to himself that by inspiring his neighbour with piety he should doubtless see the increase
of his own. But in that case he must alter his
manner of life: indeed the illnesses through which
he had been made him feel the necessity of that.
Therefore, before the end of his stay at Manresa, he
had modified his dress and his diet. He had cut
his nails and hair, assumed more ordinary clothes,
resumed the custom of covering his head, lessened
his vigils, abstinence and different austerities. He
disdained no opportunity of acquiring instruction and
of imparting to others the little that he had learnt.
He gradually accepted the company of people living
in the world, and ceased to refuse to eat at the
table of those who invited him. To confess the truth,
it appears from the testimony of Polanco that when
he tried to prepare what he was going to say, he did
not succeed particularly well. But when, on the
contrary, he spoke on the spur of the moment,
taking the words of some other guests as his text,
he was eloquent. Only, his disciple adds, his hosts
perceived that on these occasions he took no part in
the meal, and being desirous of making him eat like
other people, ceased to put questions to him.

The visions with which he had been favoured,
whatever their exact nature, had left in his soul deep
faith and peace. Thenceforth he could no more be
contented with that kind of light than he could stop

short at mortification pure and simple. It was not
even enough to continue to put down in writing
what was revealed to him by the reading of pious
books, the advice of his confessors and his own
meditations, for he realised that in order to influence
other people, and to work with profit for the good
of their souls, he needed real knowledge, both of
human nature and society. It has been frequently
stated that it was only on his return from Jerusalem
that he had resolved to acquire learning. Polanco
quotes this opinion, but in order to refute it
positively. Although he was unable to begin a
methodical course of study till after his return from
Palestine, it is certain that his resolution was taken
at the end of his stay at Manresa, when he was
about to depart for Barcelona. So anxious was he
to avoid delay in at least beginning the execution of
his project, that he began to learn grammar.

Nevertheless all this gives but a very imperfect
idea of the vigour with which he was laying the
foundations of his new life. In the midst of all
these episodes, important and closely connected
though they might be, he was carrying on in a
grotto of Manresa, in the "Santa Cueva," a work
destined to produce far greater results—namely,
the first compilation of the *Exercises.*

CHAPTER SECOND

WHAT is the book of the *Exercises*? A series of meditations, prayers, resolutions and pious actions, divided into several weeks, and arranged on a strict plan. This is the definition of them given by the author himself: "As walking, marching and running are bodily exercises, so the different methods of preparing and disposing the soul to get rid of all its ill-regulated affections, and after having got rid of them, to seek and to find the Will of God in the ordering of its life, with the object of securing its salvation, are called spiritual exercises."

It was shortly after his conversion—but subsequently to his great vision, Polanco thinks—when he was no more than a faithful believer ardently seeking the way of salvation, that he sketched the plan of his work, in a grotto at Manresa.

The book, or rather the quires of manuscript that he wrote there, was evidently not the book in our possession. For twenty-five years[1] he continually retouched it, till eight years before his death, in

---

[1] So say the Bollandists. Father Roothan thinks that the *Exercises*, as we know them, were laid down as early as 1541. It seems to me that the date must be rather later. Father Watrigant reckons three stages in this long work : (1) the first compilation at Manresa in pure Spanish ; (2) a second, increased

1548, he, with the approbation of the Holy See, had it printed, and therefore must have considered it finished.

But it is probable that these additions and annotations, the result of scrupulous attention to minute details, did not, to any appreciable extent, modify the broad outlines. As often happens in the history of art, the sketch must have been no less interesting, nor less full of ideas than the fully-completed work. Moreover the instant success obtained by Ignatius when he gave his *Exercises* and " had them made " around him is sufficient to prove the fact.[1]

Two parts must be clearly distinguished in this work. There are first of all the principles designed to direct from above the entire life, then the means or methods, which in the actual course of the *Exercises* are to penetrate the whole being of the man who is practising or receiving them.

and corrected, after Ignatius had learnt Latin at Alcala; (3) additions suggested at Paris, partly by his greatly increased knowledge of philosophy and theology, and partly by the use of the *Exercises* as given to people of more advanced spirituality. But I think that to these should be added the annotations and additions, the idea of which was given to him by directing the infant Society. The rules concerning orthodoxy and benefices are evidently the work of a man who had priests under him. It is therefore my opinion that the latest date that can be decidedly maintained is 1548.

[1] He began to impart these spiritual exercises, which he had himself received as instruction from God, to a great number of persons at Manresa. Those, before whom he set them thus, remained under the action of the Lord by these admirable lessons, by the spiritual consolation which they received from them, and by their increase in all virtues (Polanco).

I am convinced that among these fundamental principles that one which is likely to have first attracted the mind of St Ignatius, is that Jesus is a king, a leader of an army, or, as the first Spanish text had it, "a captain-general," whose knight the convert looked upon himself as being. It is with this noble chieftain that we are to set about the business of conquering the kingdom *par excellence*; it can only be accomplished by Him and with Him, but, in order to share the glory which He so liberally offers us, we must first share His labours.

We must do so, since God is our leader and our end; the first meditation convinces us of this, and an examination of conscience, the indispensable preliminary to every pious action, shows us how far we are from realising the inspiration of this idea. But God is also the most liberal and gracious of kings, and it would be an act not only of disobedience, but of ingratitude, to disregard His appeal.

In a German periodical deservedly held in high esteem, "Stimmen aus Maria Laach," Father Kreiten, a Jesuit of our own day, has most ingeniously linked this idea to the chivalric recollections with which, as we have seen, the soul of Ignatius was filled. The appeal of a king or hero to the knights and nobles of his kingdom is of constant occurrence in the history of Charlemagne and his peers; . . . it is found both in the ancient poems and in the later romances. Here, amongst others, is an instance taken from one of the best-known romances of chivalry, William of Orange.

William has rendered to his king, Louis, signal services, accompanied by marvellous adventures, but nevertheless he has received no reward, whilst gifts and fiefs have been bestowed on courtiers and knights. The hero, roused to indignation by others, feels doubly hurt by this forgetfulness, and goes to court in order to make a complaint to the king. But, on the way, the thought strikes him that it is not worthy of a true knight to claim a right from the king in this fashion.[1] However insignificant Louis may be, William is his vassal and as such has pledged himself to the Emperor Charles to defend his son against all enemies. Therefore, when Louis declares that he has no fief to give William, the latter demands as such Spain, that is to say, the southern provinces of France occupied by the Saracens. At this request the king smiles, thinking that a country still in the power of the enemy is a curious fief. Nevertheless he yields to William's desire, and consents to make him donation of Spain, with a glove, the sign of the imperial supremacy over every country. Accordingly, in presence of the assembled court and before the counts, barons, nobles and knights, William receives the symbolic glove, then he springs upon a table, and says in a loud voice to those who surround him :

" Listen, noble knights of France. By the Lord Almighty I I can boast of possessing a fief larger than that of thirty of my peers, but as yet it is unconquered. Therefore I address myself to poor knights, who have only a limping horse and ragged

[1] This idea is likewise to be found in St Teresa.

garments, and I say to them that if up to now they have gained nothing by their service, I will give them money, lands and Spanish horses, castles and fortresses, if, together with me, they will brave the fortunes of war, in order to help me to effect the conquest of the country and to re-establish in it the true religion. I make the same offer to poor squires, proposing moreover to arm them as knights."

In answer to these words all exclaimed: " By the Lord Almighty! Sir William, haste thee, haste thee, he who cannot follow thee on horseback will bear thee company on foot." From all parts there crowded to him knights and squires with any arms which they could lay hold of, and before long thirty thousand men were ready to march; they swore fealty to Count William, and swore never to abandon him, even though they should be cut to pieces.

In this episode, says Father Kreiten, we find a living picture of true chivalry, that is to say, a natural expression of the generous ideas and sentiments which animated the most noble minds for centuries, gave rise to the Crusades, and drew the noble Genoese to the discovery of a new world.

" These sentiments must needs have been peculiarly intense when, at the beginning of the sixteenth century, the Turks advanced in countless hordes, and threatened to overrun the whole of Western Europe. . . . Belgrade was taken in 1521; in 1522 it was the turn of another bulwark of Christianity, namely Rhodes, which fell before them with the flower of chivalry. Is it surprising that these exact sentiments should appear in the *Exercises*, when, in the meditation on the reign of Jesus Christ, he made an appeal similar to that related in the history of Count William of Orange?   Therefore, if the close analogy existing between the scenes related in the romances of chivalry and this meditation cannot be ignored, we must also again take into consideration the manner in which St Ignatius utilised his human ideas. . . . Just as the conclusion of the *Foundation* re-echoes in the second week, so the first meditation of the second gathers up from the outset everything that appears under the image of 'the appeal of a temporal king.'   It is not an ordinary prince or nobleman, summoning his peers, who are not strictly obliged to follow him, as in the case of William of Orange; it is Jesus Christ, a King chosen by God, to whom all Christian princes and subjects owe respect and obedience.   This prince might simply order them to follow him; that is the idea of the first week; but now the King presents as the object of His desires what He might claim as a right.   That is why St Ignatius calls Him a gentle and generous King; and from these two facts, the obedience owed by the subjects, and the liberal nature of the appeal which is addressed to them, he deduces the unworthiness and infamy of those knights who will not follow their prince . . . and do what is necessary in order to gain the victory, the fruits of which He has promised to share with them."

All these analogies of Father Kreiten are remarkable equally for their ingenuity and their probability, and for this reason we have reproduced them here.[1] Nevertheless we must not exaggerate them, for, however vivid the recollections of chivalry might still be in the soul of the author of the *Exercises*, we shall see that, as time went on, they were more and more, not stifled, but absorbed in all the ideas, all the reflections, nay, even all the turns of speech which he borrowed from the monastic surroundings wherein he took such great delight.

There are then (to follow the course of the ideas of St Ignatius) men who would like to gain the victory and live happily without fighting. In other words they wish to save their souls, but cannot make up their minds resolutely to crush the obstacle to be met with in affections, which are, if not absolutely unlawful, at least ill-regulated, since they clash with the sacrifices necessary for the desired result. They do indeed want the end, but as for the means, they will have none of them, they drive away the idea or put it off till the hour of death. Others understand the necessity of sacrifice, but a large number of them expect and desire that it shall be slow of coming and as incomplete as possible, whilst a few, a very few, begin and carry it through with right good will. What we have to do is to advance steadily and gently, according to our strength, from one step to another.

During our progress we may, if we choose, be encouraged by comparing the two states of consolation or desolation, of which we are conscious within

[1] For this communication, as well as for many others equally valuable, I am indebted to the kindness of Father Watrigant.

ourselves, each in its turn; they are governed by those two spirits, the discerning of which should always be our great care. The one, in what is called by men pleasure, destroys the strength of the soul, whereas the other, even in what appears like sorrow, restores and builds it up. It falls to the lot of no human being to be constantly under the influence of the second of these two spirits; but it is within the power of everyone to choose the period when he feels its influence for the forming of decisive resolutions, so that when the hour of desolation, rendering him incapable of arriving at them, comes, he may experience, if he holds faithfully to them, the benefit of that spirit of consolation which inspired him with them.

But, besides these partial resolutions, which follow each other in succession through the life of all men, there is one designed to dominate them all, namely, that which refers to the choice of a state of life. If the man entering upon a course of the *Exercises* has not yet settled this, the moment has arrived for him to make his choice, by the light of these principles. If he has entered upon marriage or any definite way of life he has nevertheless to fix upon the method by which he will make use of it, and to render that method more perfect from day to day.

Such were in fact the three great principles which Ignatius was then turning over and over again in his mind. He had just inaugurated the spiritual warfare with a greatness of soul and a courage which were at first slightly rash, but which strove to become prudent and moderate. He had caught his first glimpse of the distinction of the two spirits on his sick-bed, and every day of temptations and scruples had afforded him fresh opportunities of studying the subject thoroughly. Lastly, was not his great anxiety the choice of his way of life ? There is no doubt that at a later period he found it necessary to set himself free from all personal anxiety, to make his maxims of universal application to the needs of all souls, in every possible position, with a view to the needs of the Church, and, above all, that he, year by year, brought to perfection the art of *giving* to others the *Exercises* which he had at first practised in order to strengthen himself in the spiritual life. But we have already, I think, laid the roots of the tree sufficiently bare, they reach far down into the already deep soil of his personal reflections, troubles and consolations.

Having glanced at the principles which he intends to *exercise himself* in impressing deeply on his soul, we come to consider what are the practical means which appear to him best fitted to make them strike deep root in his life and cause them to produce abundant fruit.

To begin with, there is of course the great Catholic method in which the solitary of Manresa had no innovations to make, more frequent prayers, examinations of conscience, confessions, communions, regular and detailed meditation on the life of Our Lord—all these resources must have been utilised by the author of the *Exercises*. Although he regulates wisely and carefully the use of them all, though he assigns exactly to each, both in the day and the night, its fixed hours, it is not in that direction that we must look for original talent.

The case is different when we turn to the *technique* of his process, and meet for the first time with the distribution of parts between him who gives the *Exercises* and him who receives them. The first should strive, not to subjugate the other, but to serve him gently. Then for him who is receiving the *Exercises* [1] we find the advice to make use in his own meditations of the help of his imagination, to *construct* mentally the *place* of the sacred scene, whose mystery he is studying and contemplating, to represent to himself with numerous imaginary details, the persons, their words, their actions, the material circumstances of the surroundings in which he places them. " I will look first at the men on the earth, so different in dress and appearance—some white, others black,—some at peace, others engaged in war,—some weeping, others laughing, some healthy, others ill, some just born, others dying." But it is not sufficient to provide oneself with the help of the visual imagination. All the senses in their turn should be employed in strengthening this contemplation by addressing itself to the different aspects of the truth, which are of a nature to interest each one of them. We must in imagination touch, hear, smell and taste everything which refers to the mission of Christ, to our last end, in short, to everything on which we are obliged to meditate. " I will listen to the words,

[1] Or who is able to give them to himself without the aid of another, for this case is, I believe, provided for in the practices of the Society.

first of men talking to each other, how they condemn and blaspheme—secondly, of the persons who say: ' Let us bring about the salvation of the human race,' thirdly, of the angel and of Our Lady. I will meditate on these speeches, so as to draw profit from them."

Lastly, if any particular position or attitude of the body seems to have resulted in, or at least contributed to, a good disposition of the soul, it should be continued, according to the special advantage which is experienced from it, so that thus the whole body may share in the spiritual exercise and may do its part in the preservation of all its fruit.

. . . . . .

We now begin to enquire what portion of this treatise on the interior and spiritual life is more or less borrowed from other sources, and what is strictly personal.

Did Ignatius of Loyola invent the *Exercises*? No, neither as to name or substance. The *Exercises*, that is to say the acts, guided by reflection, the practical studies and the graduated attempts belong to the very essence of every industry, science and art, of every religion, but especially of the Catholic religion. We may, in proof of this assertion, go back to St Paul, who wrote to Timothy: "Avoid foolish and old wives' fables, and *exercise thyself* unto godliness ... for godliness is profitable to all things " (1 Tim. iv. 7 and 8).

Nevertheless, it does not seem that the notion of systematising these exercises was entertained as long as the princes of the Church were busy, either with great theological struggles and the extermination of heresies, or the conversion of barbarians, and the cultivation of waste districts, or in social struggles. Though the word *exercises* may be met with in St Jerome, it is scarcely to be found in St Augustine, St Ambrose, St Anselm, St Bruno, St Benedict. This last-named does indeed, in his rule, speak of the "instruments of the spiritual life," but these instruments are simply the fulfilling of all the commandments of the Decalogue, of all the commandments of the Church, and of all the precepts of Jesus Christ. The distinction between the different exercises and the detailed theory of them begins with St Bernard.

"One day," he says, "when I was occupied in manual labour, and had begun to consider the exercises of the spiritual man, I saw, in my thoughts, four steps to be ascended, reading, meditation, prayer and contemplation. They are the ladder of the cloister, which leads from earth to Heaven." [1]

The great abbot of Clairvaux devotes a whole treatise to the explanation of this division; he often sums it up in his letters, in one, amongst others, in which he reminds his correspondents that the "spiritual exercises" are not made for the corporal, but the corporal for the spiritual, just in the same way, he adds, "as man is not made for woman, but woman for man," [2] and he commands that the different hours of the day shall be carefully portioned

---

[1] Ladder for monks (*Scala Claustralium*) or treatise on the method of prayer (*tractatio de modo orandi*).

[2] Letter to the brethren of the mount of God (*ad fratres de monte Dei*).

out between both, according to the rules of the Order.

After that date there was probably no religious who did not know the *Exercises* explicitly and put them into practice. In the next century, St Bonaventura wrote for a nun of the Order of St Clare a meditation on the life of Jesus Christ,[1] over which we must pause a little, for we know (Father Watrigant having recalled it to our memory) that a Catalonian translation of it had been brought out at Montserrat at the beginning of the sixteenth century. This book, the authorship of which is generally attributed to David of Augsburg (we are not now concerned with the examination of the question), gives us in anticipation a portion of the *Exercises* of St Ignatius. "The course of this meditation is divided amongst the seven days of the week. On Monday you will go as far as the Flight into Egypt. . . . Having left Our Lord in that country, you will return there on Tuesday. Thence on Wednesday you will go on to the ministry of Martha and Mary, and so on." But all these pious visits, all these conversations, are contained in a whole, of which St Bonaventura gives us the broad outlines, in his own winning language. All the doctrine and all the practical wisdom which he sets forth are borrowed from St Bernard, who is quoted on almost every page. He tells us that St Bernard inspired him in dividing the exercises both of the active and the contemplative life.

[1] Translated into French by M. de Riancey (*Paris: Poussielgue*).

In the active life he distinguishes two parts: the
first in which a person is striving, for his own special
advantage, to reform himself, to amend his faults,
and to train himself in virtue; the second, in which
he turns his exercises to the profit of his neighbour,
whilst still labouring at his own merit.   "Between
these two parts of the active life stands the contemplative life, so that its method may be duly regulated;
we must first exercise ourselves, give ourselves up
to prayer, to the study of sacred literature and other
good works and pious practices; secondly, rest in
contemplation by seeking solitude of the heart and
occupying ourselves with God alone; thirdly, once
thoroughly imbued by means of the two first
exercises with virtue and true wisdom, devote
ourselves to the salvation of others."

In the fourteenth century, the cloister cherished
the benefit of these lessons, every day more valuable.
For instance, in St Gertrude we constantly find the
distinction between these three kinds of exercises
mentioned as a well-known, habitual and familiar
truth: exterior exercises, training the soul in humility,
charity and patience,—the exercises of piety, such
as those belonging to the choir, the Way of the
Cross and the like . . . and, lastly, the *interior and
spiritual* exercises.

Therefore, when we reach the days of St Ignatius,
these interior practices had been very often described
and explained in books that could be carried about
and were put within the reach, first of religious, but
also of the faithful living in the world. I am not
now speaking of the " Imitation of Jesus Christ " or

of " Inward Consolation," which is the secular French edition of it. According to Ribadeneira it was later,[1] at Barcelona, when he began to learn Latin, that the saint read thoroughly the " Imitation of Jesus Christ, by Thomas à Kempis," says his biographer, and at the same time that work of Erasmus, entitled, the " Christian Knight." The mistrust, and even antipathy with which the latter inspired him was equalled by the delight caused him by the former; he became so saturated with it, says Ribadeneira, that his life was an exact reproduction of it. Gonzalès also writes with equal energy: " To see, hear and watch him was to see the book of the ' Imitation of Jesus Christ ' put into practice." It is not surprising that in the complete edition of the *Exercises* the " Imitation " should be often recommended, together with the Gospel and the " Lives of the Saints "; we see that the author couples it, and it only, with the two kinds of reading which had settled his own conversion. But whether Ignatius before his stay at Barcelona, in his solitude at Manresa, became acquainted with any Spanish translation of the " Golden Book," as Polanco calls it, remains an open question. The probabilities are that he had not studied it with the deep attention which he devoted to the few volumes of his choice, but that the spirit of it had been communicated to him through one of those monasteries, which may

---

[1] Also according to Polanco, who says that Ignatius took great pleasure in making others read it. We may notice that whereas Ribadeneira attributes the authorship of the " Imitation " to Thomas à Kempis, Polanco attributes it to Gerson.

be almost described as international (like the universities), or in simpler language, Catholic, in visiting which he took so much delight.

Before the year 1522, spent at Manresa, and marked by the composition of the *Exercises*, with what monks had he made acquaintance, and with whom had he held intercourse? With the Dominicans, since at Manresa a Dominican monastery afforded him shelter, when he left the hospital of St Lucy—with the Cistercians, likewise at Manresa, for after his pilgrimage to Jerusalem he was delighted at again meeting there a holy and learned Cistercian, whose instructions he desired to attend; it was after hearing of his death that Ignatius decided to go to the university of Barcelona—Carthusians, for, according to Gonzalès, he had also felt a desire, on his return from Jerusalem, to enter the Chartreuse at Seville—also, as we shall see, Benedictines. Now each of these Orders must have had, besides its special rules, reserved for its own religious, certain methods of direction adapted to the varying needs of its penitents. It would have been strange if such a penitent, seeking for his true way of life, eager for light, still more eager for pious practices, making himself acquainted with the rules of the most austere communities, had got nothing from the Fathers whose sermons he frequented, and who heard his confessions.[1]

Among the Orders then in repute there is one

[1] He was not satisfied with one, and the researches of the different historians of the Society have discovered several, Dominicans, Benedictines, and Cistercians.

which deserves that we should pause a little over the keen discussions which it has provoked among the biographers of St Ignatius, we mean the Benedictines. The Benedictines then possessed more than one house in Spain. They had one at Oña, where it was long believed that one of the community, D. John de Castanisa, had composed the first issue of the " Spiritual Combat," of which another edition was to be brought out at Venice in 1589, enlarged by a commentary which has become incorporated with the original text.[1] They had another house at Montserrat, where Ignatius had met the French Benedictine Chanones, who left the world at the age of thirty-one, a monk greatly and universally esteemed, to whom, for the space of three days, he had been occupied in making his general confession. It was there also that another Benedictine, Dom Garcia de Cisneros, had published, twenty-two years earlier, that is to say, in 1500, a book entitled "*Spiritual Exercises*."

This last book had been published in the vulgar tongue, so as to be, said the author, within the reach of simple and devout souls. It is clearly acknowledged now that Ignatius might have read those exercises. Not only he *might* but he *must* have done so; for Dom Garcia de Cisneros, nearly related to the great Cardinal Ximenès de Cisneros, was far from being an ordinary monk. He was the life and

---

[1] We may note in passing that what is nowadays known as an author's self-love was then unknown, either with regard to himself or others. A good book belonged to the Church, and anything equally good added to it neither involved nor compromised any rights of literary proprietorship.

soul of the monastery at Montserrat, where he had not only made a library, but also a printing-press. He had founded the school, and, as we should say, the choir-school of the "Pages of Our Lady," a body of educated choir-boys who were recruited from the ranks of the nobility. Finally his reputation was solidly established outside the cloister, since he had been one of the two negotiators to whom was entrusted the task of making peace with Charles VIII.

Why then should we not give credence to this passage of the French Benedictine Dom Thevard, who in 1655 faithfully repeated the traditions collected by Dom Yepès and carefully preserved in the Order? It runs as follows in the preface to the translation[1]: " It has been thought that these same exercises might perhaps produce some good effect on the souls of those who will read and practise them in the same spirit as several persons in days gone by, who from them have gained light as to sanctity, which has led them to the highest perfection, for instance, among others, the blessed Ignatius of Loyola, who being sent by an inspiration of the Holy Ghost to this holy place (Montserrat) there met a good, religious and great servant of God named John Chanones, who, after having in the course of three consecutive days heard his general confession, taught the way to Heaven to this devout pilgrim, who held the *Spiritual Exercises* of the Abbé

---

[1] Paris, 1655. It is in the National Library. The work of Cisneros had had a great success and had been translated into several languages. A Latin edition has been recently brought out by Mantz, at Ratisbon.

de Cisneros in such high esteem that at the beginning of his conversion he not only incited those with whom he held intercourse to practise them, but likewise imitated them in a book which he afterwards composed for his own religious, to which he also gave the name of *Spiritual Exercises*."

If we now turn to the Benedictine volume, what do we find in its pages that may have remained in the mind of St Ignatius, and from which he may have drawn profit? First of all the title,—no small matter, for the words composing it belonged to that class which contains within itself many ideas. In it was involved what is expressed by the older of the two books in the following terms: "The necessity of subjecting oneself to certain fixed and strictly regulated exercises arranged in order, so that the devout religious man will be able to practise them throughout the whole week." In this regular series we come upon the division, old enough, it is true, and yet one that a recruit in religious life must needs learn somewhere, of the purgative, illuminative and unitive way. This division, which is most explicitly set forth in the first of the two authors, is only hinted at in the second, but it is actively present, as all the authorised commentaries of the Society have acknowledged.

Certainly the Spanish Benedictine's book lacked depth, and therefore there were ample grounds for making another, but it was drawn out in every part with the greatest clearness, and the apparent dryness of its sharply-defined divisions may possibly not have repulsed a man who was thoroughly penetrated with its spirit: sixteen considerations to induce the soul to carry out the spiritual exercises well, ten reasons for condemning the want of fervour and diligence of some religious; the unitive love, passing through five degrees; the Passion of Our Lord divided into six portions; all the days of the week having, as in St Bonaventura, a text for meditation,—Monday sin,—Tuesday death,—Wednesday hell,—Thursday purgatory,—Friday the Passion,—Saturday the Blessed Virgin,—Sunday the glory of Paradise, — none of that could have seemed unworthy of the attention of a man who was in his turn to multiply preparatory prayers and preludes, points of meditation, colloquies, and the like.

Lastly, was that man unworthy of feeding with inspiration the soul, at once strong and gentle, of the servant of Jesus, who, without being weighed down by all this apparatus of divisions and subdivisions, wrote: "The way to find out whether one is purified, is to examine oneself seriously as to whether in the soul these three qualities are to be discovered: fervour, which drives away all cowardice; love of mortification, which conquers movements of sensuality; and cheerfulness, which gets rid of all bitterness and malice"? If I had not read these lines in the first of the two treatises, I should be ready to believe that they are in the second, they express so happily the dispositions and, as it were, the spiritual genius of our saint.

I must now crave leave to retrace our steps, or, in other words, take up again Ludolph the Carthusian's "Life of Christ," many pages of which had been copied by Ignatius, after he had read it in his sick-room. The Saxon monk had already perceived, in meditation on the Life of Our Saviour, what he described in distinct terms as the "spiritual exercise" *par excellence.* "Nowhere," says he to the faithful soul, "wilt thou find wherewith to defend thyself against the empty and transitory flatteries of the world, against tribulations and adversities, against the temptations of the enemy, and against vices, as in the life of Our Lord Jesus, who was of such great and never-failing perfection. Frequent and careful meditation on this life will bring thy soul to confident love and to familiarity with Jesus. If the world has been sweet to thee, know that Christ is still sweeter: if the world has been bitter, know that for thy sake Christ endured all bitterness. Arise then and walk, be not idle on the way, for fear of losing thy place in thy true country."

But there is one idea, or if the expression is considered preferable, one method, the honour of which is attributed by the whole Christian and literary world to St Ignatius, and which, after having been glanced at by St Bonaventura,[1] is plainly recommended by Ludolph the Carthusian; namely, the use of the imagination, that which the *Spiritual Exercises* describe by the now famous name of the "*Composition of place.*"

Let us open the *Exercises* written at Manresa

---

[1] St Bonaventura says: "Meditate on the action of Our Lord making the event present to you, as though it were taking place under your eyes, and according as it offers itself *simply* to your mind." This "simply" was not enough for St Ignatius.

afresh, and read once more the numerous passages
in which for instance it is said : " the composition
of place will consist in looking at the road—from
Bethany to Jerusalem—from Jerusalem to tne
valley of Josaphat—is it wide or narrow ? smooth
or stony ?   In the same way with the supper-
room, is it large or small ?—arranged in such and
such a way and the like ? "   Then going back to
the Carthusian whom he had studied, let us ask
ourselves if he must not have copied, in his book
of extracts, pages like the following :—

" Be present at the Nativity and the Circumcision,
like a good foster-father, with Joseph.   Go with the
magi to Bethlehem, and adore with them the little
King.   Help the parents to carry the Child, and to
present Him in the Temple.   With the Apostles
accompany the Good Shepherd working His glorious
miracles.   Render Him service at His death, together
with His Blessed Mother and St John ; suffer and
lament with them.   Touch with pious curiosity each
Wound of the Saviour Who has just died for you.
With St Mary Magdalene seek Him risen, till you
are worthy to find Him.   Admire Him, ascending
into Heaven, as though you were in the midst of
His disciples on the Mount of Olives.   Sit in
conclave with the Apostles," and so forth.   And
after all these enumerations, this is the general
theory, " Read the account of the events as if these
events were actually taking place.   Place before
your eyes the past facts, as though they were
present, and thus you will feel much more relish
and sweetness.   For that reason I have often noted

the places (*annotavi loca*) in which such and such things took place; there is great importance in knowing *the situation of the place* (*multum valet si scit loci situm*)." [1]

I think that these comparisons leave no room for doubt, and that they show how quickly St Ignatius had profited by a tradition of which Ludolph the Carthusian, who was as full of St Bernard as was St Bonaventura, had given him a picturesque and often pathetic résumé, very frequently marked by loving familiarity. St Ignatius has carefully studied this tradition with his own peculiar perseverance, guided by a psychology, naturally deep, though not very extensive, nor very learned, even in mysticism: he draws a distinction, I admit, between meditation

---

[1] I have thought well to maintain these comparisons, which I set forth for the first time in the "*Quinzaine*" of the 15th of September 1896. Shortly afterwards Father Watrigant published in "*Études*" (and in 1897 as a separate work) a book which, as I have since learnt, he had been preparing for a long time; he goes far beyond me in the collection of "borrowings" which he believes to have been made by St Ignatius from a number of his forerunners.

The main thing that I gather from his pamphlet is that the extensive borrowing from Ludolph is, by his skilful comparisons, proved beyond all doubt. He is likewise of opinion that many passages in the *Spiritual Exercises* are taken from the *Brothers of Common Life*, from Gerard of Zutphen (and he might also have added from Gerson). Each of these hypotheses, taken separately, is ingenious and probable, but if they are put together in succession, we say to ourselves that, considering his small amount of knowledge and the short time at his disposal when at Manresa, Ignatius could not have accumulated so many quotations. Nevertheless the fact remains that he must have gathered up from his surroundings, from sermons, conversations and exhortations, many ideas which formed part of Christian asceticism.

and contemplation, but often using the two words together, or putting one indifferently in the place of the other, and above all practising and recommending active and reflective meditation, although comprising in it a certain kind of contemplation, reduced to an easy exercise of the imagination and the senses.[1] He desired particularly that this mingled operation should be supported by an upward soaring of the soul and guided by a very practical spirit, which did not disdain preliminaries.

He has specially adapted this spiritual method to the needs of certain classes of society, which the other Orders had not so clearly in view. Some, as the Cistercians or Carthusians, had worked especially for the life of the cloister. Others, like the Dominicans, watched over the preservation of the faith in general, and preached to the whole assembly of the faithful, whom they met in the churches or in the public squares. The Franciscans had specially taken upon themselves the task of succouring the misfortunes of the populace. The Benedictines, as we have just seen, had begun to address themselves to men who were not ignorant, but not necessarily cloistered. The founder of the Society of Jesus drew up his *Exercises* for himself first, next for those whom he wished to attach to himself with a view of making them ardent, faithful, believing and docile

[1] A learned Capuchin, as well known by his works about mysticism as by his social labours, told me with an evident shade of regret that the Jesuits have contributed to the diminution of the part played by contemplation in the Christian life, to the advantage of meditation pure and simple. Many will question if this be an evil.

companions of his apostolate, and lastly for men who were pious or desired to become so in the middle or upper classes of society. As we shall see in the course of this narrative, there the novelty is to be found, and there the strength of his work abides.[1]

---

[1] We shall have to return to the *Exercises*, when we endeavour to discover what may have been added later to the compilation made at Manresa.

CHAPTER THIRD

PILGRIM AND STUDENT—JERUSALEM, BARCELONA, ALCALA, SALAMANCA

THE "pilgrim" (to use the name of which he him-self was so fond) arrived at Barcelona far less inexperienced in religious matters than he had been on his departure from Loyola. He only spent twenty days there. Nevertheless, despite the shortness of his stay, he was able to assure himself that he had made progress in more than one direction. The temptations were gradually departing, and the dis-cernment of spirits was growing more and more easy to him. He was desirous of meeting men capable of leading him, by their instruction, further on in the road of Christian perfection, but not there, any more than at Manresa, says Gonzalès, did he find what he sought.

On the other hand, he came across there too, without looking for them, pious women who attached themselves to him. As he was begging his bread from door to door, it chanced that a lady of high rank guessed him to be a nobleman, by his distin-guished appearance and the whiteness of his hands.[1]

---

[1] It is doubtful whether this was the woman who said to him : "So you wish to go to Rome. Many have done so, and have come back none the better."

The sight of him reminded her of a son of hers, who had left her in order to indulge in various kinds of adventures, and she at once began to abuse Ignatius with a sort of frenzy.   But his answers were so humble and yet so dignified that she begged his pardon for her anger, and conceived so great an esteem for him that on his return from Jerusalem she took pleasure in seeking his advice.

He inspired still greater affection in the mind of Elizabeth Roser, whose name will often recur in the course of this narrative.   It is true that she one day saw his head encircled by a halo as he knelt upon the altar-steps in church, and therefore she brought him joyfully into her husband's house, as a guarantee of happiness to herself and her household.   Lastly, let us not forget that woman whose name has remained unknown, but whose reputation for sanctity and wisdom is said to have been so great that Ferdinand the First, king of Castille and Arragon, consulted her on matters of conscience.   Ignatius had already spoken to her at Manresa, where she had addressed to him those words which he always bore in mind: "Oh! if only Our Lord might appear to you!"   With his memory filled with legends, and his imagination still hungering after sensible marvels, he had taken the words literally.

But he only stayed at Barcelona, because he was obliged to wait a little for his departure to Italy. He received from many quarters offers of help for the voyage; money and travelling companions were pressed upon his acceptance.   As he had made a vow to live upon alms, from day to day, and as his devotion was still of the kind that would be nowadays described as very formalistic, he had scruples about refraining from begging, even on the ship. However, at the orders of the captain and by the advice of his confessor, he made up his mind to lay in a store of biscuits, but he would not keep anything else and threw into the harbour the few coins which he had left.   He started thus, unacquainted with either Latin or Italian, and unable to count upon the help of any human being.   Later, he warned his disciples against imitating this noble imprudence; for he always desired that they should have with them a small reserve fund in case the charity of others should not suffice them.

He had chosen the smallest of the two boats which were on the point of sailing, although the other had on board a bishop, related to Elizabeth Roser. History has not failed to remark that this ship, which the humility of the pilgrim caused him to reject, foundered at sea.   As for Ignatius, he arrived first at Gäeta, then entered Rome on Palm Sunday, 1523.

The city was suffering from the ravages of the plague, and the poor traveller entered it much exhausted, and therefore in great danger of catching the prevailing epidemic.   He did not remain there long, but was able to receive the blessing of the Pope, then Adrian II.   Those whom he informed of the ultimate goal of his journey tried to deter him from it by speaking of the war with Soliman, who had just captured the island of Rhodes, and whose fleet covered the waters of the Levant.   Nevertheless he received for his journey seven or eight gold crowns, which he accepted with regret, almost with remorse, and which he speedily, in his turn, distributed among the poor. Then, after innumerable difficulties, repulsed everywhere as a plague-stricken person, on account of his thinness and pallor, abandoned on the high-roads by companions, who found difficulty in walking no faster than he did, he at last arrived at Venice. A vision of Christ, during a night spent in the open air, had strengthened and comforted him.

He arrived there, as we may easily believe, without resources of any kind, and was obliged to sleep at first in the arcades of the Procurators' Office in the Piazza San Marco. There he was discovered by the Senator Marco Antonio Trevisano, a man whose custom it was to shelter the poor and to care for them in his own house. But Ignatius declined to profit for any length of time by this magnificent hospitality, he preferred that of a Biscay merchant, who, moreover, procured for him from the Doge a free passage on a ship just sailing for the island of Cyprus.

He embarked at Venice on July 12th, 1523, in a worse plight still than at Barcelona, for a doctor had declared that he would certainly die at sea. After a passage full of adventures and perils, "perils of waters," perils from the coarse sailors, who strove to make him suffer for the admonitions with which he had wearied them, he reached Jerusalem on September 14th. Entering the town in procession under the guidance of Franciscan friars, he and his companions were seized with a kind of involuntary and nervous mirth, a reaction from the deep emotion experienced by their faith on first touching the sacred soil.

Was the project which had possessed him so long, which had enabled him to endure impassively so many different trials, about to be realised? And first of all are we quite sure as to what that project was? His persistency in going alone, without preparation, without companions, without resources, sufficiently proves to us that he was only guided by interior purposes, and had nothing in view but the sanctification of his soul. It is certain that he intended to remain at Jerusalem, and that he cherished within himself a vague scheme of which he hardly dared to speak to anyone; namely, the establishment there of a society, which should take every means of converting the Mussulmans. Even if it were unsuccessful, it would at least be a blessed thing to suffer for Our Saviour in the place where He had undergone His Passion. He said a word or two about it to a Franciscan Father-guardian, to whom he had a letter of recommendation, but who gave him scant encouragement, and bade him wait for the return of the Provincial. The reception accorded to Ignatius by this letter was what might have been expected. The monk, well aware of the dangers to which ill-timed zeal would expose all the Christians in Palestine, bade the imprudent visionary leave the Holy Land as speedily as possible, even threatening, if he resisted, to use a right of excommunication which he held from the Sovereign

Pontiff. There was nothing for it but to obey. Nevertheless, the pious pilgrim was able to climb the Mount of Olives, and to kiss the print left upon the stone by the Feet of Our Lord on the day of His Ascension. He even succeeded in going there twice; for, after his first visit, he reproached himself with not having noted with sufficient care the separate places of the right and of the left Foot. We see that the author of the *Exercises* made a great point of practising with scrupulous care his method of " composition of place." In order to accomplish his double visit successfully, with the permission or toleration of the guards, he had, in default of money, sacrificed the only two articles which remained to him, the knife with which he mended his pen and a small pair of scissors. Resigned to the leadings of Providence, consoled by the image of Christ, which tradition says he saw go before him in the air, and bearing with him the remembrances of six blessed weeks, he prepared to beg for the means of return from the charity of his neighbours. The captains of two well-built ships repulsed him with great mockery (for they said that if he were a saint, as he was popularly reported to be, it was quite easy for him to walk upon the sea) and he was reduced to embarking in a third vessel, very small and leaky. For the third time he brought good luck to the ship which bore him; he arrived with it in the middle of January 1524, the two others were lost at sea.

The return-journey to Spain was also long and painful. Between Venice and Genoa he had to go in turn through the Imperialist and the French armies. The first-named treated him very roughly, for one of their officers, who had at first taken him for a spy, came to the conclusion that he was nothing but a poor lunatic incapable of giving rational answers, and allowed the soldiers to drive him away with blows and kicks. A little later the French also stopped and examined him, but they showed him kindness, and suffered him to go on his way. At Genoa he at last found a Spanish captain who recognised him, and took him to Barcelona, which he reached at the end of February or the beginning of March 1524.

     ·   ·   ·   ·   ·

Jerusalem would have none of him. He must needs make up his mind as to his vocation in life. Should he enter an Order, and, if so, which? He was inclined to make choice of one where the dis- cipline was relaxed and needed reformation, since he would thus be provided with opportunities of suffering and merit. He desired to obtain advice from a Cistercian, whom he had known at Manresa, but this religious was dead. Ignatius returned to Barcelona, and, having decided to retain his liberty for the time being, began to look about for the means of entering upon a regular and complete course of study. Two persons enabled him to carry out his desire; a professor named Ardebalo, who gave him free instruction, and a woman already known to us, Agnes Pascual, who supplied his necessities.

It was no easy matter for a man who had recently led the life of a nobleman, and had never studied except in order to learn to read and write, to set about the task of acquiring a knowledge of Latin. He never, it is true, arrived at being a great scholar; his terse and picturesque style was always rather incorrect. Moreover, his habit of contemplation and his predilection for supernatural imagery formed an obstacle difficult of surmounting, and the harder he strove to give his mind to his grammar, the more strongly he felt himself drawn towards the purely intuitive action, whose sweetness he had experienced. He considered the matter, and said to himself that the enemy was doubtless laying snares to stop his purpose by leading him away from the work necessary for it. Therefore, he one day asked his confessor to accompany him into a church, and there besought him to cure him of his negligence, by treating him, if necessary, like a little school-boy; in return he bound himself, by what may truly be described as a vow, to redouble his attention. In order to ensure success, he again modified his way of life a little, though he evidently did not entirely leave off working for the good of souls, and giving the *Spiritual Exercises*. He even drew down upon himself a great deal of abuse and personal violence, which nearly cost him his life, by strengthening in piety ladies of the highest rank, such as Dona Stefana de Requesens, Dona Elisabeth de Badajoz, Dona Guyomar Gralla, and Dona Elisabeth Josa, and by assisting in the reform of a convent of Dominican nuns, with more success than was to the taste of the fashionable young men of Barcelona. But he shortened his time for prayer, as he had modified his austerities, and soon made such progress that he was able to extend his range of studies.

It was at this period that he had occasion to compare two very different books, the "Imitation of Jesus Christ" and the "Christian Knight" by Erasmus. He conceived for this last book, and for the class of literature to which it belonged, an aversion in which time only confirmed him; not that he was insensible to the author's grace of style (for it is said that he made extracts from it in order to familiarise himself more with the niceties of the Latin tongue), nor that he found heterodox propositions in it, but the colour in which the author presented his ideas and the things of which he treated seemed to Ignatius calculated to quench little by little the fervour of piety in the souls of his readers.

As for the "Imitation" it delighted him, and was henceforth one of his favourite books, but the study of it did not prevent his desiring to add to his interior life schemes for a more active and a more apostolic existence. Up to this date his demonstrative piety, his mystical demeanour and the marvellous accounts (doubtless exaggerated) by which simple souls expressed the admiration they felt for him, had specially appealed to the imagination of the Spanish women; henceforth he thought it necessary to associate with himself male companions, and found that the plan offered possibilities of success. He met with three, whose temporary union constituted his first attempt at collecting a following, and making any serious propagation of his views. They were Calisto, who had made the spiritual exercises under his direction, and who later on made a fortune in the Indies; Artiaga, who also went to the Indies, but who died there as a bishop; and finally Diego de Cazérès, a young nobleman in the service of the viceroy of Catalonia.

This first little band, which was destined to break up in a few years, accompanied Ignatius when he went to the University of Alcala. Ardebalo had asserted that he knew enough Latin to follow a course of higher studies, but the pupil insisted on passing the regular examination. A distinguished theologian confirmed Ardebalo's opinion, and the student, reassured, set out with his friends for his new place of residence.

.   .   .   .   .

The University of Alcala had been lately founded by Cardinal Ximenes with special reference to the instruction of young converts from Mahometanism. It was impossible for Ignatius to take up his abode in such surroundings without being speedily brought into conflict with the narrowness, hardness, and paltriness which then marked the Church in his own country. Temporal events touched the depths of his soul so slightly, the political changes which Spain and Europe underwent before his very eyes exercised so little influence over the course of his thoughts, that it is not necessary, I believe, for us to occupy ourselves much with them in order to understand the rest of his life. But it is scarcely necessary to say that we cannot be as indifferent as he was to the religious crisis of his century.

At the moment when Ignatius was entering upon the spiritual life, two great calamities, which we may reasonably feel surprised at finding in conjunction, were rife in Spain. They were on the one hand the laxity of morals which prevailed in all ranks of the clergy from the lowest to the highest ; on the other, in one word, the Inquisition. I have said *the* Inquisition, but it is important to remember that there was more than one, for the overlooking of this fact causes too much credit to be given to those common accusations which lay to the charge of Catholicism all the cruelties and follies of the last Inquisition.

The first had been the Episcopal Inquisition, that is simply the charge given to the bishops to seek out whatever might warp the faith of their dioceses by distorting tradition. The second was the Dominican Inquisition, that is to say, the creation of a special tribunal, taking cognisance of a particular heresy. The Order of St Dominic had been chosen, as everyone knows, to denounce the heresies, social as well as religious, of the Albigenses. A brief of Innocent IV., in 1248, extended the jurisdiction of the sons of St Dominic over the whole of Spain. There is nothing to be said here, concerning this institution, which affects the life of Ignatius. The case is quite different with regard to the third or political Inquisition, established in 1478; it was this last which was in force in the time of our hero.

It was political, by reason of the method of its

composition, and still more by the ends which it
sought. In the different statutes which were suc-
cessively given to it (more particularly in 1484) we
meet everywhere with mention of "their Highnesses,
the most serene sovereigns," nowhere with that of
the religious authorities, nor of the commands of
the Church, strictly speaking.[1] The Papal See
always considered it as an encroachment on the
part of the civil power, and strove to limit its
operations as much as possible. But royalty, on
its side, made use of this tribunal in order to re-
strict, for its own advantage, the privileges of the
clergy as well as of the nobility. Afterwards it was
especially used as an instrument against the two
divisions of the population which caused such un-
easiness to the royal power, namely, the Moors and
the Jews.

Here policy and religion were closely intermingled,
and it is easily understood that the Inquisition might
sometimes make itself popular with those who beheld
in the infidels enemies quite as dangerous to the
integrity of Spain as to the unity of the Catholic
Faith.

In order to escape death, Jews and Mussulmans
had been compelled to choose between baptism and
exile. Many had accepted baptism, but had secretly
kept their religion, and had even made proselytes,
some of whom were recruited from the ranks of the
clergy. In 1498, Peter Arando, bishop of Calaharra,
was deposed by the Holy See as convicted of connec-
tion with Judaism by the testimony of a hundred and

[1] Héfélé. Cardinal Ximenes. (Paris, 1862.)

one witnesses. As a recent historian of Ferdinand and Isabella has said, " Judaism was the great heresy of Spain in the sixteenth century." [1]   Those who did not make compacts with the Jews manifested against them and their doctrines a passion whose ardour was warmed by the fire of national senti-ment no less than by that of the faith.   " The popu-lace found a solution of their own to the Jewish question under the form of periodical massacres. The Inquisition bestowed upon this hatred judicial form and the prestige of a double authority.   Never-theless it would be unjust to say that the Inquisition only aimed at the Jews, though the " General His-tory " just quoted asserts in a somewhat astonishing sentence: " It was against this apostate race that the Inquisition was established."   It was also estab-lished, as everyone knows, against the Moors, and was unavoidable, in order to satisfy popular senti-ment.   In 1526, when St Ignatius arrived at Alcala, there was still a kind of crusade against the uncon-verted Moors of Valencia and Arragon.   "Valencia, which numbered more Moors than Christians, beheld its fields laid waste and depopulated by this furious orthodoxy."

That was not all, for the doctrines of the Albigenses, which were themselves the outcome of Gnosticism and Manicheism, had left behind them in the pen-insula a perfect train of anarchist sects.   Among the number was that known as the " Illuminated " (alumbrados).   We shall soon see that they were

[1] " General History," under the direction of Messrs Lavisse & Rambaud.

not yet free from pursuit.[1] Lastly, the Inquisition did not refrain from seeking out every view and opinion which seemed to it heretical. For instance, Protestantism has never caused Spain to incur danger comparable with that with which she was threatened by the Mussulmans. Nevertheless, to make acquaintance with it was with the Spanish people to hate it, and to take against it, even in our days, terrible precautions. The remark has been made that it " was from his subjects in the peninsula that Charles V. got his open and sincere intolerance, his impetuous hatred of heresy." The interests of his vast Empire imposed concessions and compromises on him in Germany. But where he could act with a high hand, as in the Low Countries and Spain, he showed himself in his natural character, eager in the pursuit of heretics and infidels.[2]

[1] A book recently brought out asserts that the "Illuminated" did not appear in Spain till 1575. It is a mistake. The year 1575 is the date, not of the appearance, but of the momentary disappearance of the sect. Peter Martyr of Anghiera spoke of it in 1509.

[2] The Spaniards saw in all heresies the consequences of the same revolt against the unity of their belief. An illustrious member of the family of St Francis Xavier, who was a second father to the saint himself, Don Martin d'Azpilcueta, known under the name of Don Navarro, wrote in 1511 : "It is a subject of rejoicing to me that I am a Navarrese and a Basque. Up to the present day no Navarrese has been found to abandon the faith preached by St Saturninus, the disciple of St Peter; not one, despite alluring offers made to them when in prison or under torture, deserted the Catholic Church to embrace the heresies of the Jews, Turks or Lutherans." (Extract from Father Cros' "History of St F. Xavier," vol. i., p. 71.)

If they identified themselves with this passion the Spanish Inquisitors ought at least to have moderated it by a spirit rather more in conformity with that of the Gospel; but as they were frequently plunged into this office through political ambition, and with no preparation for it beyond a pile of scholastic formulas, they displayed in its discharge the scrupulous, narrow, cruel folly of the official, who is resolved at all costs to find out transgressions where no one else perceives them. The whole system of denunciation, of " questions," of indefinite imprisonment was certainly terrible for the accused, but his being cast into this network entirely depended on the good pleasure of the " qualificators." " Now," says a historian,[1] " it was through the folly of unreasonable and excessive ' qualifications' that the Inquisition was most compromised, as, for instance, when it kept in prison until his death a professor of rhetoric, the father of twelve children, for having said, in explaining Pliny to his pupils, that Jesus had been circumcised by His Mother, and not by St Simeon, and for having refused to believe that eleven thousand virgins, all on board the same ship had been massacred; the words " XIM. Virgines," " meaning," said he, " eleven martyrs and virgins, and not eleven thousand virgins."

Whilst relentlessly pursuing such offences, the Inquisition allowed a swarm of abuses, which were the disgrace of the Spanish Church. Intercourse with Mussulmans and Jews had caused laxity of morals in every rank of society; and every kind of

[1] Forneron, " History of Philip II."

disorder, with its inevitable results, was openly allowed. Thus Don Martin of Loyola, brother to Ignatius, mixes up in his lengthy will pious recommendations with the frank declaration, unaccompanied by any sign of repentance or any excuse, of the measures which he has taken in favour of two illegitimate children. But at least he was only a layman; it was far worse that the idea was not even received of the necessity of giving up any sort of licentiousness because one was going to enter Holy Orders or live in a monastery. Moreover, as the profession of cleric carried with it exemption from taxes, men flocked into the ecclesiastical career, which was thus burthened with entirely unworthy individuals. Historians affirm that in the time of Philip II. there were in Spain 312,000 priests, 200,000 clerics in minor orders, and 400,000 religious. A quarter of the adult population belonged either to the secular or regular clergy. In the diocese of Calaharra alone, the native country of St Dominic, there were 17,000 clerics, the greater number of them unoccupied and " so deserving of punishment that the office of alcalde in the episcopal prison was worth 1500 ducats." Promotion to ecclesiastical offices, involving the most serious responsibilities, was far from being a sign that it had been deserved by learning or morals. The scandal was not unknown of a bishopric passing from father to son, and being claimed by the latter as a right. The very questions with which the national councils struggled (the synod of Aranda in 1473, the Council of Seville in 1512) serve to give us an idea of the extent of the evil, by the nature of the astounding prohibitions which they felt themselves obliged to issue. How often do we see saints like St Ignatius, and again after him St Teresa, perceive with terror, in the course of their confession, that they have before them an unworthy priest, and that it is their task to attempt the conversion of him who was listening to them. Nevertheless, Ferdinand and Isabella had, with the aid of Ximenes, at last brought about some steady improvement. It is true that Isabella, in particular, took the trouble to seek out, in the retirement of the cloister, in order to raise them to the episcopal dignity, the religious who were there striving to expiate by secret penance the open crimes of others, and that in order to conquer the scruples of these humble souls she was obliged to call to her aid the orders of the Pope.

This is doubtless the explanation of the unparalleled contrast (the word is not at all too strong) between pagan licence and fearful austerity then presented by the Church in Spain. In the days preceding St Ignatius the great ecclesiastical figures of his country are deservedly conspicuous for the severe, and to a certain extent tragic, dignity with which they pass through this world of debauchery. For instance, we have Cardinal Juan de Carvajal, commonly called the "incorruptible and the indefatigable," the enemy of the Hussites, who contributed to the success of the battle waged with the Turks under the walls of Belgrade in 1456; a man born in the diplomatic office, yet destitute of pride and ambition, as much famed for his spirit of strict obedience to duty and for the mortifications which he vainly strove to conceal as for the nobility and seriousness of his disposition. Again there is the man, who has been styled the greatest theologian of his day, who was at the Council of Basle, the resolute defender of the rights of the Holy See, and who, when made a Cardinal, observed none the less exactly all the rules of his Order;—when I say that his name was Torquemada, his portrait will be complete. The advent of Ignatius was required to moderate the pitiless ardour of such zeal, and to effect the assigning of wide space and friendly welcome to the optimism and gentle charity of St Teresa by the side of St John of the Cross and St Peter of Alcantara.

.   .   .   .   .

Let us now return to our poor student. He arrived at Alcala in 1526, with his three companions, who had been joined by a young Frenchman, named John, a page of the vice-king of Navarre. They had all three adopted a fashion of dress which, besides being very poverty-stricken, attracted notice by its uniformity. This was a mistake. Ignatius was the most observed; he was arrested three times.

On the first occasion surprise had been excited by the fact that women went to see him at the hospital, and held converse with him concerning spiritual things; in truth they sought him out there with as much eagerness as at Manresa and Barcelona. In the prison where he was confined he was visited by three women, one of whom was Eleanor Mascarenas, maid of honour to the Empress, and governess to

Philip II.: we shall see later, when Ignatius is at Rome, that she will write to consult him, for she never ceased to regard him as a saint. Meantime it was supposed that this popular student and his companions belonged to the number of those who aspired to do away with the work of the clergy, by raising the soul directly to God. In other words they were taken for members of the sect of the "alumbrados." Then, as it was easy to see that he had many dealings with the clergy, this charge was abandoned and another invented. He himself, in a subsequent letter (March 15th, 1545) to John III., king of Portugal, explains this persecution in the following terms:

"If your Highness desires to know why I have been the object of so many enquiries and so much examination I can assure you that it is not because any errors of the schismatics, the Lutherans, or the 'Illuminated' have been discovered in me, for I have never had any relations with them, but because it was considered strange, particularly in Spain, that, never having studied, I should take the liberty of speaking at length and discoursing about spiritual things."

In truth it was this last complaint which was most energetically preferred against him. He had been released once, not without having carried on the following short dialogue with his interlocutor: "Well, has this complicated examination made you discover anything bad in us?" "No! not at all; had anything been found out you would have been driven away, nay, even burnt." To which Ignatius replied;

" But, if you were to fall into error, would you be burnt too ? "   " Undoubtedly," said the other, and he departed.

But Ignatius was soon apprehended a second time; it was not to be borne that he should speak of religious matters before having finished his studies. His friend Calisto, then ill at Segovia, hastened to join him and share his imprisonment. Lastly, proceedings were taken against him a third time because he was accused of having advised two widow ladies, mother and daughter, to make an im- prudent pilgrimage (the fact being that he had tried to dissuade them from it). These women were of the number that sought his advice and strove to make it their guide, but nevertheless exaggerated it in several particulars. It must even be admitted that the ecclesiastical authorities were not wholly without excuse, if it is true that when the pious and enthusiastic student spoke of God to these audiences of women several amongst them fainted.[1]

However that may be, this last accusation speedily fell to the ground. But the opportunity was seized to demand from the prisoner some explanations of his devotions belonging to Saturday, a day which he had simply consecrated to the Blessed Virgin. His interlocutors thought that they had laid an ingenious trap for him by putting questions to him concerning the Sabbath and asking his opinions thereon.   Genelli is of opinion that the witches'

[1] See Serrano y Sanz "San Ignacio de Loyola en Alcala de Henares," Madrid, 1895, in which will be found the authentic *procès-verbal* of the researches made in 1526-7 at Alcala concerning St Ignatius.   F 5

Sabbath was in their minds, not the Jewish; but what we have seen of the way in which fifteenth and sixteenth century Spaniards viewed the "Jewish peril" would make us incline towards the second hypothesis, even if we had not, after Genelli, the express witness of Polanco. Certainly the question was childish, but the Inquisition was not likely to trouble itself about that, and it was of the kind which had so large a share in filling the prisons of those days.

What was the result of all these persecutions and of these forty-two days' imprisonment ? Very little, if the merit gained by the saint, through his patience and humility, is left out of the reckoning. He and his companions were set at liberty with the injunction not to attract attention by their dress for the future, to which the student, always bold and free in his speech, answered, that if they wished to see him wear a different kind of garment, they had only to give it to him. The hint was taken. The authorities added that, without having found anything exactly blameworthy in his actions, or his writings, they should prefer his holding his peace. "We should like to see you avoid all novelties." "I should never have supposed," Ignatius answered simply, "that it was a novelty among Christians to speak of Jesus Christ." Nevertheless, he was enjoined to refrain from all public meetings and all speeches until he had finished his four years of philosophy, under pain of being excommunicated and banished from the kingdom.

This sentence against him obtained only in the diocese of Avila, which he therefore hastened to leave. In the past year he had certainly gained

experience; he had acquired a knowledge of some
kinds of men, but had profited little by his studies,
properly so called. He had carried them on un-
methodically, attending " at the same period all the
lectures in the University " ; moreover, the assiduity
of the pious people who answered his appeals ended
by taking up a great deal of his time. [1]

He left Alcala for the University of Salamanca,
where he hoped to prosper better. There fresh but
similar tribulations awaited him, and resulted in
twenty-two days of imprisonment. What was his
offence? He had allowed himself to speak of mortal
sin and venial sin without waiting for the completion
of his studies. Therefore the Inquisitor wished to
make sure that he had not got to deal with one of
the " illuminated," who relied on immediate and
direct relations with the Divinity. He set before him
the following problem, which recalls some of those
captious questions in which the judges of Joan of
Arc sought to ensnare her, and whence she extricated
herself so prudently. " You speak of virtues and
vices ! These things are learnt by study or by
the revelation of the Holy Ghost. Now, you are
ignorant men. What revelations have you had ? "
To which the student answered with much good
sense : " But tell me whether what I have said is
true or false ; let me know whether you approve
of it, or disapprove of it." This question of his
remained unanswered, and as he persisted in saying
no more, he and his companions were put in irons,

[1] He bore this in mind, and in his Constitutions laid down the
rule that the last years of studies should be freed from all dealing
with others.

all being fastened to the same chain. It is true that they were soon to give a striking example of their spirit of obedience. One night all the prisoners made their escape, but they alone remained, though they could have got off just as well as the rest. They were released after due formalities, but not without having been warned more than once that they must refrain from speaking about mortal sin and the distinction between it and venial until their four years were really and authentically finished. "Does this sentence please you?" asked the Inquisitor. "No," replied Ignatius. "And why?" "I do not understand your forbidding me to treat this question when you found nothing wrong concerning it in my writings." And he declared that he would rather leave Salamanca, as he had left Alcala.

His mind was made up. He considered the studies he had pursued in Spain absolutely inadequate, and he determined to go to the University of Paris in order to resume them completely.

First of all, however, he had to return to Barcelona, and he accomplished the journey, with a donkey loaded with his books. His friends there tried to dissuade him from his project, speaking of the severity of the winter, of the obstacles sure to be put in his way by the war, which was raging more violently than ever, and reminding him of all kinds of current stories with regard to the cruelties of the enemy. Nothing moved him. Finally Elizabeth Roser offered him help, both in money and in letters of credit for Paris. He accepted it, and starting at the beginning of January 1528, arrived safe and sound in the capital of France in the beginning of February.

CHAPTER FOURTH

BARTOLI, one of the first historians of the Society of Jesus, desiring to explain all the links connecting it with the principal countries in the world, wrote as follows: "Spain gave it a father in St Ignatius, France a mother in the University of Paris."

The testimony of Ignatius himself goes to confirm this judgment. He had already spent four years in Paris, when he wrote on the 15th of June 1532, to his elder brother Don Garcia, whose son, being destined for Holy Orders, was to come and study in his turn in the famous University. Ignatius admits that the anxieties of living, the masters' fees, and the requirements of study demand more sacrifices there than elsewhere; but he adds: "In my opinion, if you consider the expenses, they will be less in this University, where one gains more profit in four years than in some others that I know in six, and if I were to say still more I do not think that I should be departing from the truth."

Doubtless the University of Paris did not then enjoy quite that high position which the two preceding centuries had given it all through Christendom. It had reached its zenith, when at the closing of the

Council of Constance (1418) it had, through the
instrumentality of d'Ailly and Gerson, prepared the
way for the end of the Great Schism.   Since then
its prerogatives had diminished in proportion as the
power of the king extended, and as the unity of the
monarchy became consolidated.   Moreover, the time
was drawing near when, being attacked simultaneously by the spirit of the Reformation and that of
the Renaissance, it was to lose the leadership of the
intellectual movement.   Nevertheless, at the particular time when the Spanish student, so ill-satisfied
with Alcala and Salamanca, came to attend its lectures, the Sorbonne was still a kind of theological
international parliament, which nations and kings
consulted on great political and religious questions.
Ignatius had not yet left France, when Henry VIII.
demanded a consultation at the University of Paris
(as also at the Universities of Angers, Bourges and
Toulouse), on the annulling of his marriage with
Katharine of Aragon.   Francis I., who then favoured
the King of England,[1] and who was very much
inclined to impose his good pleasure on the great
bodies in the State, neglected no means of obtaining
from the Sorbonne a declaration agreeable to the
wishes of Henry VIII.   " He got it at last, or
rather," says Dareste, " he wormed it out of the
members, by having the questions put in a mislead-
ing manner, and the other Universities gave in their
approbation."

[1] It is a well-known fact that the object of the conference at
Boulogne in 1532 was an alliance between Francis I. and Henry
VIII. against Clement VII. and Charles V.

Still, for all that, the University of Paris continued to form against heresy and schism a rampart
behind which the kings of France were fond of taking
refuge. In Spain Ignatius had only caught a far-off
glimpse of the struggles of the Church against the
Lutheran revolt: he was to be a near spectator of
them in Paris. As early as 1521, the University
had condemned a great many propositions taken from
Luther's book, the "Captivity of Babylon." In
1527, the condemnation of the "Colloquies" of
Erasmus was pronounced, and Ignatius, on his
arrival, saw himself justified in the suspicions which
he had formed on first reading the brilliant writer.[1]
In 1529 the Protestant, Louis Berquin, was burnt
on the Place de Grève by the king's orders. A few
years later, the very year in which Ignatius was to
return to Spain and then to Rome, a band of reformers were entering into negotiations with Francis
I. about a journey to be taken by Melancthon to
Paris, and conferences to be given there by him.
The king then addressed himself to his University,
which laid down the fundamental propositions which
it was necessary to prescribe beforehand as the

---

[1] Erasmus was not openly heretical, and it is probable that the
Reformation did not please the sceptical humanist any better than
the purely Catholic tradition. His strictures on the celibacy of
monks and on the morals of the clergy were seasoned with a good
many doubtful details which increased the sale of his books. One
Paris printer struck off as many as twenty-four thousand copies of
the "Colloquies." He often defended Luther, but prudently strove
to at least appear orthodox. "He died," says Pallavicini, "with
the reputation of a bad Catholic indeed, but nevertheless not a
Lutheran" (Council of Trent, I. 23.).

basis of every discussion, and the meeting was put off. These propositions were drawn up with equal precision and elegance, and Father Watrigant is of opinion that the author of the *Spiritual Exercises* must have long and accurately preserved them in his memory to his own profit.[1]

Those who have been accustomed to regard Francis I. as a personage connected only with battles and pleasures would be perhaps rather surprised to read in du Boullay the enumeration of the religious festivals in which the knight-king constantly took part; mingling with the procession, holding in his hand a large taper, "the socket of which was wrapped in crimson velvet." In 1527 his return from Madrid had been celebrated first by a solemn entry into his capital, then by a procession, the object of which was to restore to their ordinary place the relics which had been publicly exposed during the whole length of his captivity. When we turn over the history of the University of Paris in the years corresponding to Ignatius' term of study,[2] we come every moment upon "Te Deums," solemn processions in which the king figures—not only for Corpus Christi, but for different religious events, such as expiatory ceremonies, now in consequence of some profanation of images, now in reparation for the insulting placards against the Sacrament

[1] These propositions are reproduced in Father Watrigant's opus-culum; "*Formation of the Exercises*," p. 7 1. I shall add to the authorities quoted in it a manuscript volume (a collection of documents referring to the history of the University of Paris), belonging to the library of Saint Sulpice.

[2] Du Boullay, vol. vi.

STUDENT AND APOSTLE   89

of the Holy Eucharist, which were stuck up in
Paris, inspired and some say dictated by Calvin. This
was likewise the period, du Boullay tells us, of the
development in Paris of the devotion to St Joseph,
for which St Teresa was soon to labour in Spain.

The students of the University and their professors took an important part in all these festivals,
which awarded a place of honour to literature. In
1530 our hero was able to witness Queen Eleanor's
entrance into Paris. "She presented herself on a
stage erected in front of Saint Ladre, and was
seated upon a chair covered with azure velvet,
scattered over with golden fleurs-de-lys, in order to
receive and hear the harangues of the Church,
the University, of the Châtelet, of the heads of
the Courts of Justice, of the Treasury, and of
the Tribunal of the Parliament of Paris. . . .
Next came the University, and quite two or
three thousand scholars must have marched in
order; then next walked the Bachelors of Arts,
of Medicine, of Law, and of Theology, wearing
their black capes. Next followed the Masters of
Arts and the Bursars of the 'Nations,' with their
caps. Next the Proctors of the said nations,
dressed in red capes, before whom were the four
little bedels of the aforesaid four nations with their
silver maces; and behind them walked the Doctors
of Medicine with their red capes, and in front of
them the two bedels of their faculty," and so on.

This was on the 16th of March, but in spite of
the part that it had played in this grand parade
the University had not yet paid its quota. Five

days later its members went to greet the Queen at the Louvre, and a "very eminent professor addressed her in a harangue" agreeably enriched with quotations taken partly from the sacred writings, partly from profane history, and from the annals of nations (partim sacris litteris, partim profanis historiis et annalibus non illepide locupletata).

To a hard-working student, already penetrated with the spirit of sanctity, there was a reverse to the medal. Under the pretext of reform, in the general sense of the word, the spirit of emancipation and of intellectual licence strove to make way. On the 15th of July 1524, the Faculty of Theology censured the following proposition which had been found, I believe, in one of its theses:[1] "What had we to do with so many constitutions, decrees, and traditions? We had done quite well without them, our law has become more severe than that of the Jews, and nevertheless Jesus Christ desired that Christians should live in freedom and liberty."[2]

If this spirit of theoretical emancipation was repressed with comparative ease within the precincts of the University, it was a different matter when it came to the practical conduct of life. Following the example of the king (which had better have been put aside in this respect) the

[1] Extract from the manuscript volume already mentioned belonging to the Library of St Sulpice.

[2] Work already quoted by Father Cros, p. 263. This book abounds in autograph documents curiously engraved.

University combined a considerable amount of licentiousness with the display of its devout zeal. To begin with there were a good many varieties among the twelve or fifteen thousand students whom it numbered. Besides the *Caméristes*, rich youths, lodging in rooms under the control of their tutors, besides the poor *Martinets*, or free day-scholars, some of whom were exhibitioners, and some earning their living as servitors and attending the lectures as best they could, there were, as Father Clair reminds us, the *Saloches*, "amateur students, too often lazy and noisy, tramping from lecture to lecture without presenting themselves for examination."

Blessed Peter Le Favre, who had been in Paris before Ignatius, informs us, though with great reserve, in his "Memorial," of the trouble he experienced at the sight of the faults of his neighbour, and of the scruples (amongst many others) which he had when confronted with "innumerable imperfections," until then unknown to him, and "this trial," he adds, "lasted until my departure from Paris." The good Le Favre had come from a pious village in Savoy. As for Ignatius, he had already seen so much of the sort in Spain, that this kind of scruple was probably spared him. Later, Francis Xavier, when chatting familiarly beyond seas with a chaplain of St Tomé, said even more about it than his friend. He told how a great number of his companions were given up to debauchery, "*and our master with them*," he added. . . . Many and many a time they left the college at night (despite the enactments which the authorities were obliged to make in order to hinder the students from wandering about at night), and they took me with them; the master was with us; but I was filled with such a terror of contracting the diseases, with which I saw the scholars and master attacked, that I never dared to behave as they did. This fear sustained me for a year or two, till the master died of these shameful complaints, and there was sent to us a chaste and virtuous master (Don Juan Peña), whose good example I followed."

If masters and pupils were thus in collusion for the satisfaction of the grossest pleasures, it is not surprising that both were equally responsible for other abuses, and that there were so many trials, "for great intrigues, monopolies and scandals, brawls, and acts of violence," which marked the election of the Rectors. In 1533 the counsellors appointed by the King for the reform of the University set forth in their report that they had seen "the statutes of the governing body," and found that there was "not a single article of the same observed." They added, that in the said Faculty "great extortion was practised, and unnecessary banquets were given in the evenings," whence it resulted that the authorities were compelled to make decrees for the cataloguing of examination-expenses and the regulating the number of guests whom every newly-received licentiate has the right to entertain.

Such were the surroundings amid which Ignatius and his famous companions were to live. As in so many other, nay, I may venture to say, in all other surroundings, everyone might find almost what he wanted, what he was seeking for, or at any rate that to which the bent of his mind inclined him. Everyone, it is incontestable, met with what might help him in a power of resistance proportionate to his strength, and what would allow him to build up his spiritual edifice according to his own design. As I have said, St Ignatius arrived in Paris in the beginning of February 1528. The University had scarcely seen the end of the long altercations which had disturbed it on the occasion of the election of the Principal of the College of Montaigu. It does not appear that he experienced any of the consequences, or that he took any part in these disturbances, beyond giving good advice to one student or the other.

His extraction destined him to form part of "the nation" of France. It is well known that there were in the " Rue de Fouarre " four old public schools, among which the students were divided, according to their nationality. " Four nations " were reckoned as follows :—nation of France—nation of Picardy—nation of Normandy—nation of Germany. In time, and owing to the increase of students, who flocked in from every quarter, this division, which had been supposed to be sufficient, had certainly become rather extraordinary. As all, from whatever country they might come, had alike to speak Latin at the University, there had seemed no objection to sending the English students to the German nation, and to augmenting the French nation by students from Spain, Navarre, Savoy, Italy, Egypt,

and Syria. Be that as it may, it is interesting to
note that by this classification the future founder
of the Society of Jesus was destined to find himself
at once in a specially intimate fashion in the company of Navarrese like Francis Xavier, Savoyards like
Peter Le Favre, and finally Spaniards such as those
whom we shall soon see gathered round him.

.   .   .   .

He had arrived in the February of 1528, and was
not to depart till the March of 1535. Therefore his
stay did not extend over eight years, but it certainly
covered more than seven of real and anxious study.
How did he divide and spend them?[1]

At Salamanca he had studied everything in a
promiscuous fashion, and had not been satisfied.
"As," according to Polanco, "nothing imperfect
pleased him," he resolved to begin everything again
on a fresh plan, as though his former studies were
no longer worth taking into consideration. He
devoted himself exclusively to Latin and grammar
for a year and a half, nearly two years, according
to Ribadeneira. At the end of 1529 he began his
studies in philosophy, and it was then that he left
the college of Montaigu to enter Sainte-Barbe.
Let us glance at the following explicit passage in
the Memorial of Peter Le Favre. "In that same
year Ignatius Loyola came to the college of Sainte-
Barbe in order to take up his residence there,

---

[1] Polanco, indeed, says " octo fere annos." The reckoning up
of the different courses of study is in the main easy, despite the
confusion in calculating, caused at the outset by the Paris University's method of reckoning, which extended a year to the Easter
of the following year.

and to share the room which we occupied, intend-
ing to begin with us the course of arts or philosophy
on the next Feast of St Remigius. This chair was
to be occupied by Master Francis Xavier. Blessed
through all eternity be Divine Providence who thus
arranged things for my welfare and salvation! For
having been charged by Master Xavier with giving
lessons in philosophy to the holy man just mentioned, I had the happiness of enjoying, first his
conversation on ordinary topics, and then on
spiritual subjects. As we lived in the same room,
and had one table and one purse, he was my master
in spiritual things, giving me the means of raising
myself to the knowledge of the Divine Will and of
my own will. Finally, the union between him and
me became so great that we were as one in desire
and will, as well as in the design of choosing the
kind of life which we possess now, which will be
followed by all those who in the course of ages
shall enter this Society."

Thus we see, that before becoming the master of
these young men, Ignatius was to begin by being
not merely their friend, but their pupil. At the
end of his course of philosophy, which was probably
in the autumn of the year 1533, he began his theological studies and carried them on up to the end
of 1535. That was the ordinary length of time
devoted to them, and he always endeavoured to
make his disciples pursue the same plan, being of
opinion that theology could only be successfully undertaken if it had been preceded by serious literary
study, but that in its turn it ought to serve as a

foundation for the study of Eastern languages and for the interpretation of holy Scripture.[1] Our hero was to carry through all those labours with resolution and patience, and as a rule with success, as is proved by the official diplomas, of which the authentic text has been preserved to us. Nevertheless, difficulties were not spared him.

To begin with, there was his poverty. It is true that he had arrived in Paris with a tolerably large sum of money, given to him by Elizabeth Roser. But he had entrusted the larger part to a friend, who had used it for himself, and had then found it

[1] This last question had been eagerly discussed in the University of Paris in 1534. Should Hebrew be studied like any other tongue, or did the language which had received the deposit of Divine inspiration require for its proper comprehension that the light of the further teachings of the Church should be cast upon it ? This gave rise to an interesting scientific trial. Du Boullay has preserved for us the discourse or harangue delivered on the occasion by Montholon, speaking in the name of the king's procurator. Here is a passage from it, which gives us an idea of the point of the controversy, and also of that extraordinary style, a mixture of French and Latin, which was commonly used by everyone :—

" Le roi, princeps Christianissimus, simul et religiosissimus, n'entend que par telle profession de lettres étrangères puisse advenir inconvénient, ne minimum quidem, à l'interprétation des saintes lettres reçue et approuvée par l'Eglise universelle, ce que pourrait être si les interprètes de la langue hébraïque voulaient interpréter les livres de la sainte Ecriture qu'ils ne fussent bien fondés et entendus en la faculté de théologie ; car il ne suffit pas à bien interpréter et traduire d'avoir la simple langue et intelligence des mots, mais il faut prendre sensum medullarum et mysticum et non reddere verbum verbo seu adhærere cortici verborum, ut faciunt Judæi, nec verbum verbo curabit reddere fidus interpres."

out of his power to refund it. In this unlooked-for
state of destitution his biographers say that he was
obliged to seek admission to the hospital Saint-
Jacques, where at least he did not run the risk of
sleeping out of doors or of dying of hunger. But
the rules of the hospital were a great hindrance to
his studies; for the doors were opened and closed
at hours which did not allow its inmates to be
present either at the morning or evening lessons,
at any rate during the winter.

In order to extricate himself from his difficulties,
he sought for one of those domestic situations which
made it possible for a man to serve a professor and
the students who lodged with him, and in the intervals
of leisure to avail himself of the University lectures.
His piety, which took delight in imagery and liked
it exact, pictured to himself beforehand the professor
as standing to him in the place of Jesus Christ, and
the other pupils in that of the Apostles, so that in
serving them, he might say to himself: " I am doing
this for St John, this for St Peter." But he made
enquiries in vain, and in vain entreated a certain
Carthusian, as well as the monks of the abbey of
St Victor, to find him this humble post; quests and
applications were alike fruitless.

It was then that his countrymen advised him to go,
during the University vacation, and seek out the rich
Spanish merchants of Flanders, and appeal to their
generosity. It appears that more than one student
had already profited by it. Ignatius followed their
advice, and, in fact, for three years running, in 1528,
1529, and 1530, he went to Belgium, not to Brussels

(despite the conjectures of Father Bonheurs), but to Bruges and Antwerp. The third year he also went as far as London.

Recently published works[1] have cast light on some points of this part of our history. At Bruges the student-pilgrim met a noble Spaniard of great reputation, who, like many noblemen of that time, had devoted himself to commerce with considerable success. His name was Gonsalvo d'Aguilera, and he was married to Anne de Castro, probably related to John de Castro, a University comrade with whom we shall meet later on, and also connected with the family of another fellow-student, named Peralta. In the man who came to him—whether preceded by a recommendation or not we do not know—Gonsalvo perceived more than an ordinary petitioner, however interesting he might be. The author of the *Exercises* had a manner peculiar to himself, at once humble and dignified, both in accepting and in asking for alms. As the troubadours of preceding ages often paid for the hospitality bestowed on them in castles by songs and verses, so he gave the equivalent of what he received in pious assistance, instructions, and prayers. He was already animated by that spirit which he was later to display in his dealings with the great and with princes. " It is just," we find him writing from Rome, in 1549, to the Duke of Bavaria, "that those who sow spiritual things should gather those needed by the body." We are in a position to affirm that Gonsalvo estimated this kind of exchange at its real value. Brought

[1] *St Ignatius at Bruges.* By Canon Chambry, Bruges, 1898.

to Paris by the requirements of his important business, he would not go and lodge in a rich hostelry, but asked Ignatius to let him share his poor room, and he remained with him thus for several months, in order to the better enjoy his friendship. Later, he made great efforts to introduce the Society of Jesus into the town of Bruges.

It was in this same city of Bruges that our Saint made acquaintance with another Spaniard, the celebrated Louis Vivès, born in Valencia in 1492, who, after having experienced both favour and disgrace at the court of Henry VIII., and held a professorship at Louvain, was to end his days at Bruges. Louis Vivès is, together with Erasmus and Budé, one of the most brilliant representatives of what is known as humanism in the first thirty years of the sixteenth century. A less elegant writer than the two others, he excelled them in his scientific spirit and in some bold views rather in advance of his day; he, before Bacon, proclaimed the use of the experimental method. With regard to education it has been asserted that he had recommended many things which were soon entered to the credit of the Jesuit colleges; the physical care bestowed upon the children, the infrequency of punishment, the systematic teaching of Latin in a series of classes, the study of practical sciences, of history and geography in conjunction with the explanation of the texts, the use of note-books and the like.

Having invited Ignatius to his table he was inspired with esteem, and we may say admiration,

for his sanctity; he even foretold (the fact is
authentic) that he would in the future be the
founder of a religious order. Did he submit to
his guest's criticism his most cherished ideas?
did he offer them as set forth in his books for
his perusal?   We may reasonably suppose such
to have been the case without being able to prove
it.   Ignatius was certainly quite prepared to appreciate everything that was valuable in all talent;
but if he admired—though without the capacity
for imitating them—beautiful language and the art
of skilful writing, he made a great point of their
being regarded as a means, not an end. As we
have already seen, he disapproved of all species
of theories of art for art's sake, especially when
they strove to soar above doctrine, and professed
towards Catholic dogma an obedience more apparent than real, mingled with some irony.   .

Vivès had written a book on St Augustine's
"City of God," which, on account of various
passages on wars between Christians, on the
mendicant orders, on grace, on fasting, on aca-
demic degrees, and on the riches of the Church,
had been put on the index " *donec corrigeretur.*"
He had, alas! not without reason, demanded the
reform of the Church, and at this same period
(towards 1529) advised the summoning of a council, but he did it with a criticism so vigorous as
to go rather beyond due bounds.

It was in the same rather sceptical spirit that
when offering the hospitality of his table to the
errant and mendicant student he declared that, in

his opinion, abstinence from meat on prescribed days
and at certain seasons was not very useful, as far
as bodily penance went; "for," he would say, "so
many other dishes have been invented, and the art
of seasoning them is so well understood." Ignatius
did not relish this criticism of Catholic tradition.
"Doubtless," he replied, "you and all who fare
very daintily are far from making this abstinence
serve the end with a view to which it was ordained; but the Church has to think of the mass
of the faithful, who, enjoying less refined diet,
are very really supplied with an opportunity of
mortification and penance." His answer was
praised; but he did not retain, on his side, a very
pleasant recollection of this conversation. Later, he
thought it wiser to forbid his religious to read the
works of Vivès, as well as those of Erasmus, such
estrangement did he feel from minds more widely
opened to the impressions of nature than of grace,
and more inclined to minimise their own beliefs
than occupied with the duty of getting the utmost
possible profit out of them.

The journey taken to Flanders and thence to
England in 1530 was the last. The Spanish merchants made it a point of honour to spare him these
expeditions, and after this date themselves despatched
to him at Paris their yearly donations. By adding
these alms to those still sent him from Spain, he
had enough to defray the expenses of his studies,
and even to help his necessitous companions.

The scant use which he made of these resources
for himself and for his own personal convenience,

is sufficiently proved by the precarious state of his health and the weakness of stomach from which he almost constantly suffered. That was a fresh obstacle to progress in study, and was only to be overcome by courage like his. In the process of his beatification Father Lainez and Father Salmeron, who had known him early in life, made the following deposition: "As for his studies, though he encountered in their pursuit more obstacles than any of his contemporaries, and more, perhaps, than any person at any time, he surpassed, *caeteris paribus*, the other students in diligence. Thus he made considerable progress in the sciences, as is attested by the public examinations, and by the debates held between him and his companions."

Whence arose this difficulty, from which, despite his dearly-bought success, he suffered all his life? Certainly not from a lack of intelligence, taking the word in its general sense. It is superfluous to say that the man who composed the *Exercises*, organised the Society of Jesus, and dictated its constitutions was possessed of one of the most powerful intellects of his day. Had he embarked upon abstract and speculative studies too late? Had imagination, heart, and will got the upper hand too speedily and too completely in the ordering of his thought, and did his understanding, properly so called, find the task of conforming to the narrow rules of grammar, to the dryness and subtlety of scholastic philosophy, too hard? Obviously this was so, but the explanation requires

completion.   As at Barcelona and at Salamanca
so in Paris, he must needs repress his mystical
raptures and spiritual ardour in order to fulfil
conscientiously all his belated scholarly duties.
He has long been aware that when he yields to
this powerful attraction, ordinary work becomes
too difficult to him, and, since he has vowed to
himself that he will carry on his studies regularly
to the end, he refrains, throughout his whole
course of philosophy, from giving the *Exercises*.
He pretermits for the time different pious practices which were dear to him.   He and his room-
mate, Peter Le Favre, confine themselves to what
they consider strictly necessary; Mass every morning, and also, "as much as possible," examination
of conscience twice a day, and weekly Communion.

Not only in his interior life does he succeed in
conquering himself and in sacrificing temporarily
the consolations to which he is most attached, but
he knows, when the necessity arises, how to remove
to a distance every occasion of outward struggle
and contradiction.   A friend one day observed to
him that times were much changed, that he was left
in peace, that even his enemies covered him with
praise.   This was his answer: "Wait till my course
of philosophy is finished, and you will understand
the cause of this tranquillity.   I am silent, they are
silent; but directly I move, I am attacked on all
sides."

He was in truth attacked more than once.   The
dangers to which he was exposed in Paris were less
serious than those which he had braved in Spain.

Nevertheless we cannot pass over in silence the more or less important attacks which he had to undergo, either from the University or from the Inquisition.

His manner of life at first excited astonishment in the University; he was treated as a beggar, and the well-known fact that he belonged to an illustrious family did not contribute towards lessening the strangeness of his proceeding in the eyes of the majority. Nevertheless his masters do not seem to have shared the prejudices of his companions on this head. On one occasion, having been stung for the moment by the keen reproaches of a fellow-countryman named Madera, he submitted to several doctors, as a case of conscience, the following question: " Can a nobleman, who has renounced the world for the love of God, go and ask alms in different countries, without prejudice to the family honour?" Couched in these terms, the question of course obtained the expected answer, that there was no sin in it. That was enough for Ignatius.

Some professors, and among others the Portuguese Govea, took umbrage for a short time at his apostolate. A few literary exercises fixed, with some lack of discretion, for Sunday morning, were gradually abandoned by a good many students, who, following the instruction and example of their comrade of Loyola, frequented the offices of the Church more than was usual. It was then that occurred the incident of the *aula*, related in all the biographies. Provoked by what he characterised as an omission of scholastic duties, Govea determined to have inflicted on Ignatius the punishment which consisted in giving him the hall (*aula*), that is to say, having him publicly scourged in the common room. Everyone knows how, after an interior struggle in which his humility had been ready to resign itself, the sentiment of his honour as a Christian and the duty of not allowing himself to be discredited in the eyes of those who even thus early in his career entrusted the direction of their souls to him, prevented his accepting this kind of humiliation. The doors of the College were already closed, the bell was ringing to collect the students, the executioners were arriving, rod in hand, when suddenly, in the midst of a private interview with his pupil in his room, the master felt his anger evaporate. He did, indeed, bring back Ignatius with him into the hall, but in order to ask his pardon and assure him with tears of his esteem.

But not every one was clear-sighted, or even became so with time, like Govea. At Paris, as at Alcala, people were surprised to see a man still young, not in Holy Orders, not having even finished his course of theology, take upon himself the spiritual direction of his equals, and sometimes of his superiors, though it must be said that those who were brought into closer contact with him felt their distrust melt away, and more than one conceived a positive enthusiasm for him. "You give lessons to me, a doctor," said a member of the theological faculty to him one day, "it is not just that you should not be a doctor yourself." And he wished to have the degree conferred without further delay on Ignatius, who only prevented it by vigorous resistance. But the crowd who simply heard him talked about, and judged his method of action superficially, was biassed in quite a contrary direction. He was even accused of sorcery and denounced to the Inquisition, which, fortunately, was not at all the same thing in France as in Spain, but showed far more intelligence in its proceedings.

On the first occasion, the author of the *Exercises* had been summoned to Rouen under rather unusual circumstances. The Spaniard who had, as we have seen, made an unjustifiable use of his fellow-countryman's deposit, was now at Rouen, whence he was to return to his own land. Being seriously ill and oppressed by a melancholy into which some honourable remorse probably entered, he did not hesitate to appeal to him whom he had so grievously wronged. Ignatius, on his side, *did* hesitate a little, as though fearing that this journey would do him some fresh harm. At last, however, he made up his mind, and it seems as if during this absence, which of necessity interrupted his studies, he determined to give the ascetic and mystical part of his character, thus set free from its usual bondage, full play. Not only did he resolve to go on foot (any other method of locomotion would have been difficult for him), not only did he sleep the first night in a hospital, another on a little straw (all that was likewise planned beforehand), but he wished to traverse the whole way without either eating or drinking. In the early part of his journey, he felt himself, as it were, weighed down and held back by

an invincible weight, but after reaching Argenteuil,
whose church still boasts of possessing a tunic belonging to Christ, he no longer walked, he "flew,"
full of marvellous ardour, scarcely able to contain
himself for joy, and speaking aloud to God. At last,
at the end of three days, he arrived, had an interview
with the man by whom he had been summoned,
nursed him, consoled him, and ensured his departing
in a satisfactory state of mind. But in the streets
of Rouen itself Ignatius received a letter which had
followed him, and which informed him that his departure had been the signal for an increase in the
rumours ;concerning him, that his ambition and
spiritual rashness were blamed in all quarters, and
that in short he had been denounced to the holy
office. With that consummate and almost over-
minute prudence which, in his case, was coupled
with bursts of enthusiasm and the acceptance of
all necessary sacrifices, he went, accompanied by the
messenger, to the house of a notary in the town,
whom he caused to deliver to him, in the presence
of witnesses, a certificate declaring that he had
started back as soon as summoned. He then returned to Paris, and went without any delay to see
the inquisitor, whom he supplied with every possible
proof as to his never having contemplated avoiding
an inquiry. The inquisitor, a Dominican named
Matthew Ori, was quickly won over by such a
mark of simple and fearless submission. He left
the accused at liberty, assuring him that he had
nothing to fear.

Shortly afterwards, in consequence of fresh denunciations, the inquisitor was obliged to request Ignatius to make him acquainted with the *Exercises*. But he had scarcely gone through them before he asked the author to give him a copy for his own use, and he set no proceedings on foot. It is true that, despite all calumny, he must have been pre-possessed in favour of Ignatius, who had indeed often brought him heretics, but heretics whose conversion he had wrought, and whose reconciliation with orthodoxy and with the Church he was furthering.

Nevertheless the defendant thought it wise not to be satisfied with this remarkable proof of good-will, for he foresaw the day when he would be at a distance from Paris, and enemies, as yet in the future, would demand an account of his past life. He wished for authentic testimony, and as the good Dominican persisted in regarding it as useless, he himself sent for a notary and witnesses, and thus obtained, and had registered, declarations, the text of which it was his intention to keep. He therefore possessed a formal document destined later to attest that he had left the University of Paris, entirely untouched by condemnation, and even by prosecution.

Such were the principal difficulties against which he had to struggle, as Polanco expressly states, in the first and third years of his stay in Paris. In the second, given up to the study of philosophy, he had maintained on every head a reserve absolutely indispensable to the tranquillity of his scholastic efforts.

We learn, again, on the invaluable testimony of his secretary, that the experience gained by all these trials was very useful to his immediate disciples, and to all those who, year by year, succeeded them in the Institute. He desired—and he took measures accordingly—that the novices of the Order, although remaining poor, and accepting the rules of a society which was itself poor, should be secured against want. He recollected his own physical sufferings, and did not fail to take fatherly precautions against sickness, nor to have it cured when it had been by chance contracted. He even went so far as to order the selling of the furniture of the colleges or of incurring debt rather than deprive anyone of "necessary or desirable care."

But neither the trials of his struggle nor his temporary retirement had hindered him from exercising over those around him an influence, sometimes gentle, sometimes energetic, but nearly always irresistible. We have already seen more than one instance of it. We will not now speak of the victories gained, so to say, by the way, over certain sinners. One day, being asked to join in a game at billiards, he finally consented, staking the practice of the *Exercises*, beating his adversary, and by this means gaining an unexpected conversion—another time he succeeded by ingenious artifices in making a wretched man give up a design of suicide—now we find him going to confession to a bad priest in order to bring him back to the right path by contact with his own repentance—now putting himself in the way of one of the guilty parties in a case of adultery, and flinging himself, before the eyes of the hardened sinner, into frozen water, declaring that he would remain there till the criminal connexion ceased, gaining his cause this time also by this heroic intervention. It is time to pass on to the more prolonged and prolific intercourse which he kept up with a small number of friends destined to share the glory of his name.

CHAPTER FIFTH

IGNATIUS had always striven to collect young men round him. In Spain there had been three, and later, four, who had been very devoted to him, but who had dispersed at the end of some time. In Paris, about fifteen months after his arrival, he was sought out by three others, all Spaniards; they were Peralta, John de Castro and Amador. They had made the Spiritual Exercises under his direction, and then, on fire with noble zeal, had begged, in the parts of Paris where they were best known, in order to consummate the sacrifice of their pride. Factitious imitation, even when sincere, is not free from blunders; the attempt was not much appreciated, and the young men, being forcibly brought back to the University, abandoned their scheme. Thus it was not they, any more than those first mentioned, who were to form the foundations of the Society; although—as historians have been careful to tell us—all three led in the future good and Christian lives, and one of them, John de Castro, even became a canon of Toledo.

There were also others who held tolerably intimate intercourse with him, and who would have liked to attach themselves to him permanently, but, seeing that he did not found any Order, could not make up their minds to wait any longer, and entered the Franciscans, Dominicans, or Carthusians. Therefore, the predestined fellow-labourers of Ignatius were those who, when putting themselves under his guardianship, were willing to trust him. They, like himself, hoped to go and preach to the heathen, and then, with him, to die amongst them for the faith of Christ. Such, says Polanco, was one of the "human reasons which kept them," as compared with their friends, "in suspense."

This chosen band at first numbered six: Peter Le Favre, Francis Xavier, James Lainez, Alphonsus Salmeron, Simon Rodriguez, and Nicolas de Bobadilla.

Peter Le Favre, born in 1506 at Villaret in Savoy, had, as a young boy, kept his father's flocks. He had been at a very early age tormented, but at the same time preserved from serious faults, by an "inordinate desire of knowledge and learning." At ten years old he cried with longing to go to school, though at the same time he felt drawn, in his lonely shepherd's life, towards devotion and purity. His prayers had been heard. After having studied for nine years in his own country under the direction of a holy man, he had been sent to Paris by his family in 1525, made Bachelor of Arts in 1527, and, a few months later, licentiate. We have seen how he shared the same room as Francis Xavier and Ignatius, as pupil of the former and tutor of the latter. He had a thorough knowledge of Greek, and was always consulted by his Master, Peña, when puzzled by a passage in Aristotle. Being disposed, like all the saints, to exaggerate the account of his troubles and the public confession of his faults, he relates in his "Memorial" how frequently he sinned through his eyes, also by love of vain glory, and finally by want of temperance. He cured himself of this last fault by an absolute fast of six days' duration; as for his remorse or his scruples, he was in great measure indebted to his friend's company for their tranquillisation. Thanks to him also, he was enabled to concentrate his desires and obtain a clear insight into his own vocation; "for until then," said he, "without being able to settle upon anything, I wished sometimes to be a physician, sometimes a lawyer, sometimes a schoolmaster, sometimes a doctor of theology, sometimes a simple priest without any dignity, sometimes a cloistered religious; I was more or less disturbed according to the element then dominant in me." This prolonged state of agitation was to be ended by the practice of the *Exercises*. Nevertheless, for four years Ignatius had refused to allow him to make them,[1] whether because he wished to extend for his friend as for himself the period of absolute absorption in studies

---

[1] Genelli wishes to reduce these four years to two. It is incorrect. The "Memorial" (page 10 in the French edition of Father Benix) says positively: "He advised me first to make my general confession, and so on, for he would not admit me to the other *Exercises*, though Our Lord bestowed on me a great desire for them. Thus passed for us about four years in the relations and the state of mind which I have just described."

from which the intoxication of devotion would have distracted him, or because he thought it better to wait until the soul in which he was so deeply interested had by its own efforts unravelled the threads of its destiny.

At last, after a stay of nine months in Savoy, where his mother had just died, Le Favre, on his return to Paris, practised the *Exercises* for which he had longed, and almost immediately afterwards received Holy Orders.

Such was the character of the first priest of the Society of Jesus. Destined to die young (in 1540), he nevertheless had time successfully to defend Catholicism in Southern Germany, to be the Master of Blessed Peter Canisius, and to leave us a " Memorial," stamped with piety, which was at once touching and original. I am referring to his devotion (held in admiration by St Francis of Sales) to the angels—angels of particular places, angels of cities, angels of churches, angels of each of the faithful. He strongly recommended this devotion, not merely for the benefit of men, but for the sake of the angels themselves; for, he was accustomed to say, "they too desire to have some particular friends in this life, which is the state of merit." Such a man was likely to inspire sentiments of friendship in the minds of others, and the first historians of the Society tell us that, when he died, nothing short of the entrance into the Order of St Francis Borgia could have consoled his brethren, and in any degree made up for his loss. They add that St Francis

Xavier, being in a terrible storm on the Indian Ocean, invoked Le Favre as a saint.

The figure of the future apostle of China and Japan is familiar to everyone; everyone knows that this young Navarrese—whom, having regard to the period of his birth (1498), we may call a Frenchman—had at first felt less attraction to Ignatius than had the rest of the little band, and thus had required rather more effort on the part of the latter. His was a fertile and brilliant nature. One of his biographers, Tosellini, quotes from a contemporary writer, Navarro, the following passage concerning the early years of his hero: "There was no one to be compared with the boy; he was so gentle, amiable, polite, merry, even jocose, endowed with a singularly penetrating intelligence, anxious to learn, eager to excel in everything that becomes an accomplished nobleman. And, nevertheless, despite the entreaties of his brothers, who wished to draw him into the profession of arms, he preferred to every other glory the glory of learned men." He therefore came to the University of Paris, where he remained, without any break, from October 1525 to November 15th, 1536.[1] Licentiate of Arts in 1530, he soon became a professor, and gave a public commentary on Aristotle at the College of Beauvais. But, devoted as he was to learning, he was still fonder of "showing himself off," and strove to extend his reputation by his deportment and his manner of living, "spending far more

---

[1] The date is variously given by different authors, but Father Cros supports that quoted above by authentic documents.

than his income as a younger son." It was at this
juncture, apparently, that his father wished to
summon him home, but the eldest daughter of the
house, his sister Madeline, a Poor Clare, interceded
for her brother, declaring that he would some day be
one of the pillars of the Church, and the father
yielded. He was also rather vain : Ignatius, who
knew it, was careful to bring him listeners, not,
however, without repeating to him, by way of comment, the celebrated sentence of Holy Scripture :
"What doth it profit a man if he gain the whole
world and lose his own soul ?" At last the distance
between the two began gradually to diminish; the
handsome and proud Navarrese had to yield to the
"force of the spirit which spake by the mouth of
Ignatius" (*vim spiritus loquentis in Ignatio sustinere
non potuit*). In the days to come no Father of the
Society was to profess more deep, respectful and
tender admiration for the founder. He met with
his due reward, for Ignatius intended to leave to
him the government of the Society, and, as a matter
of fact, had recalled him from India, in order to prepare him for his new office, but when his letter
reached Asia, the great apostle of the Indies was no
longer in the world.

Ignatius had less trouble in winning the confidence
of James Lainez (born at Almazan in the year 1512),
for this young Castilian, who had heard Ignatius
much spoken of at the University of Alcala, had come
to Paris on purpose to see him. He had scarcely
dismounted from his horse when he met him in
the courtyard of the hospital where he was going

to lodge. Ignatius at once helped him with his advice, and with the little money at his disposal. A short time was enough to make him appreciate the intellectual resources of the new-comer, who was destined to become one of the greatest theologians of his age, one of the orators who commanded the deepest attention, and whose speeches carried the most weight in the Council of Trent, and a diplomatist capable of conducting satisfactory negotiations with Philip II. and Catherine de Medicis. If he was already, at least to some extent, what he was later, when he refused the sacred purple, and was even, it is said, very nearly elected Pope, he was the most scientific, and, as we should say, the most intellectual of the six. It was also he who gave most vent to his personal feelings, and who had a tendency to express his own will strongly. Of a less emotional piety than his companions—for he wrote to Ignatius in a well-known letter: " having said my prayers with tears, which rarely happens to me "—he sometimes had with his Superior slight disagreements, which his deep love for the Society and its Founder easily and completely disposed of. In after years Ignatius often reproved him, with deliberate—we may almost say studied—rigour and severity; he was of opinion that Lainez was too exacting with regard to others, and too prodigal of complaints, but he appreciated him at his real worth, and had a sincere affection for him. Peter Le Favre and Francis Xavier, the two real saints, being dead, we may be certain that he looked forward with confidence to Lainez becoming the

second General of the Society. Moreover, he had
offered him the succession at least on one occasion.

On his arrival at Paris Lainez had brought with
him two Spaniards still younger than himself (for at
the vows of Montmartre one was twenty and the
other eighteen). The first of the two was Alfonso
Salmeron, born at Toledo. He retained his youthful
appearance and good looks for a long time; in 1547
we find him described as "young and beardless."
Nevertheless he was an excellent Greek and Hebrew
scholar, and shared the work of Lainez at the Council
of Trent.

The fifth of the companions of Ignatius, Simon
Rodriguez, a Portuguese nobleman, a pensioner of
his king at the University of Paris, was always more
inclined to contemplation and asceticism than was
compatible with the requirements of the new Institute and its rules. Therefore it will often come to
pass that his master will find it necessary to stir up
his courage, to calm his fears, to make him give up
those dreams of hermit-like solitude, which were not
free from a certain degree of melancholy.

Nicolas de Bobadilla, a poor Spaniard from the
neighbourhood of Palencia, who had finished his
studies and begun to teach at the University of
Valladolid, had quite a different character. A com-
mentator on Bartoli, a writer of authority, has not
hesitated to say of him : " He was of an abrupt and
warlike nature, an enemy of compromise, dreading
no adversary of the Church. St Ignatius, wishing
to designate the solid virtue concealed under this
external independence, called him playfully the only

hypocrite of the Society." At Paris he helped him
to overcome the difficulties caused by his lack of
resources; later he helped him to conquer those
which he met with in his own temperament and in
the weakness of his health.

So much for the first six. But a short time before
their departure from France three others joined
them—Claude le Jay, of Savoy, likewise one of the
speakers at the Council of Trent, and one of the
first Fathers sought for, though in vain, by different
princes of Europe, to be promoted to episcopal
dignity; John Codure, of Embrun, whom St
Ignatius, when at Rome, saw going up to heaven;
lastly, Paschasius Bröet, born at Amiens, of whom
St Ignatius, at the time when he wished to send
him out as Patriarch of Ethiopia (1547), says in one
of his letters: "Goodness, learning, and exterior
dignity, together with physical strength and a suitable age—I do not see these qualities combined
to the same extent in any other member of the
Society."

How was it that all these young men, so different
in birth and disposition, but all equally full of ardour
and piety, all determined to serve God, remained
gathered round Ignatius, patiently waiting till a
definite future slowly opened before them? After
making due allowance for the mysterious attractions,
both of nature and grace, we must go back to the
kind of life which united them. Although they did
not all live together, they met almost every day at
the house of one or other amongst them, often took
their meals together ("according to the ancient

custom of the Saints," *veteri sanctorum more*, says Ribadeneira). They gave each other mutual help in their temporal and spiritual necessities, without neglecting, says Polanco, literary work, in which the talents of the most advanced and most highly gifted were at the service of all. They supported each other still more by pious observances common to them all, discharging their practices of devotion in the same way and on the same days. Lastly, a little sooner or a little later, the master was to stamp his influence on them by means of his *Spiritual Exercises.*

.   .   .   .

Let us then return to this book which has excited so much admiration and caused so much discussion. It is a distinguishing attribute of great works, that posterity, in studying them, constantly discovers in them fresh resources, and that everyone, drawing upon them according to his needs and his capabilities, comes upon treasures of infinite variety. We, who are following out to the best of our ability the evolution of the life of the Saint, naturally ask ourselves what place the *Exercises* occupied in his life and his relations with others from 1528 to 1535. Moreover, it may be that returning thus to them at different intervals will enable us to arrive, according to the measure of our capacity, at making them better understood.

We have already seen, as is now a fact recognised by everyone, that the *Exercises* were altered and completed several times. It seems probable that among the ideas set forth in his little volume

Ignatius, both at Montserrat and Manresa, had made an exhaustive study of three in particular— the service of Jesus Christ, placed above all that the kings of the earth can offer; the discernment of spirits, as he had acquired it itself on his bed of sickness when meditating on his past and thinking of his future; lastly, the choice of a state of life.

Whoever the friends might be before whom he was setting his *Exercises*, the author must have directed their attention to these three heads, the importance of which is obvious to all.   He must also have recommended to them the methods of meditation of which he made a point, such as the using of all the powers of the soul and the composition of place; but experience of the spiritual life, the knowledge he had acquired of the needs of different souls, the daily incidents of a constant struggle against the spirit of error and malice, and finally his theological studies, had of necessity enlarged the whole of his ideas.   If we put aside the last additions to which we have already alluded, on the use to be made of benefices and on the priestly life, we have the *Exercises* exactly as the author made his first fellow-labourers go through them.

What did they find in them?   Neither fully developed doctrine nor long exhortations, nor sermons.   The person who is making the *Exercises*, and who for the time has put on one side the agitations of the world, temporal cares, and even his ordinary work, has little to read.   In the course of the second period, he is advised to

make use from time to time of these three books,
the Gospel, the Imitation, and the Lives of
the Saints.   Thus there is nothing subtle or
recondite; nothing, in a word, but the simplified
essence of pure Catholic doctrine.   It was not
now a question of borrowing more or less from
Cisneros, and of mingling these loans with recollections of chivalry.   To friends such as his, and
after the works that he has accomplished himself,
he may quote authorities more worthy of their
mutual attention.   He may comment to them on
this striking passage from the Epistle to the
Hebrews:—

"Laying aside every weight of sin that sur-
rounds us, let us run by patience to the fight
proposed to us.

"Looking on Jesus, the Author and Finisher of
faith, Who, having joy set before Him, chose the
Cross, despising the shame, and now sitteth on
the right hand of the throne of God.

"For think diligently upon Him that endured
such opposition from sinners against Himself, that
you be not wearied, fainting in your minds." [1]

Yes, such indeed is the plan of the *Exercises*, a
sort of abridgment of all that the Christian ought
to cultivate when he can, in the depths of his
being, so as to be equal to all the works and all
the struggles of life.

[1] Father Soyer, one of the directors of the retreats at the Villa
Manresa, directed my attention to this text.   It was familiar to
the contemporaries of St Ignatius, since Ribadeneira comments
upon it, seeing in it, as it were, the programme of the action and
the destiny of the Society.

Let us resume the course of the *Exercises*. The first week[1] is devoted to preparation, by means of examinations of conscience, of confessions, repentance and penance. Thus the burthen is laid down, and the soul freed from the sins which enveloped it. As is said in one of the most important passages, one ought "to prepare the soul fitly, and dispose it to stripping itself of all ill-regulated affection, and then to seeking and discovering how God desires that it should order its life with a view to its eternal salvation." In the second and the third weeks the soul will meditate on all the scenes of the life and Passion of Christ one after another; she will take part in that Passion, following it with all her powers, each of which will devote itself to it in its own particular manner, the senses by images, the memory by the arrangement of all the recollections, the understanding by a just comprehension of the mysteries, and above all the will by the resolutions it forms. From the very beginning the soul will know what inspiration is of the Good Spirit, and thenceforth she will be capable of rising from dejection, and causing all her life to profit by the joyous energy which she will have stored up in these moments of consolation. Lastly will come the fourth week, in which the regenerated soul will rest in contemplation and love.— Is not the plan of the apostle fully carried out?

A sketch so slight, even when added to that

---

[1] This word *week* must not be taken quite literally; it is a period of days, longer or shorter, according to what is required or allowed by the particular circumstances of the retreatant.

already drawn at the beginning of this memoir, is still far from giving an adequate or exact idea of the method of the *Exercises*.

Despite many superficial or malevolent interpretations the practice of the *Exercises* is absolutely opposed to the passive state, and the self-abandonment of Quietists of every kind. It is an active art; it proceeds methodically and by degrees of course (as is necessary in every kind of exercises, from exercises on the piano to military exercises), but in the most important part of its action it remains a free art. I am now speaking (in order to avoid all misconception) of the person who is making or receiving them still more than of him who is giving them.

Certainly, I do not vouch for the discretion of all those who have given them from the beginning, nor for the strength of soul of those who have received them. Nothing is more likely than that there have been among the first some imperious natures addicted to high-handed measures, and among the second some weak souls ready to let themselves go, or to allow themselves, as has been said recently, to be hypnotised. But I am speaking here of the spirit of the founder and of what he transmitted to his chosen disciples.[1] The notion that the *Exercises* were invented in order to turn men into professed Jesuits, or into coadjutors of the Society, is absolutely untenable. We have just seen that Ignatius had waited four years be-

---

[1] In order to understand it, we have only to study the spirit breathed by the *Directorium*, a collection of instructions designed for those who " are giving the *Exercises*."

fore letting Peter Le Favre make them, and that Francis Xavier had not yet done so when he pronounced his vows at Montmartre. Do we not know, moreover, that the first general of the Society was far more anxious to send away subjects than to seek for them? And have not his successors frequently been reproached with aiming at endless variety in the social duties of their pupils, and of not sufficiently fostering priestly vocations in their magnificent colleges?

Moreover, can anything be more simple and of more universal application than this short fundamental meditation with which all begin?

Every Christian, despite all the weakness of nature and the snares of the world, must of necessity admit that to remind himself of the last end of man, to condemn as inordinate every affection which leads him away from it, to strive thenceforth to get rid of, or, to speak more exactly, to direct such affection aright, next to regard with indifference everything which is not calculated to tend towards his final end, is the very essence of his belief and his religion.

But when the supreme object of desire is once fixed upon, the means remain to be chosen. Here the efforts of the faithful soul begin, and his responsibilities increase. The person who gives the *Exercises* does not suggest, far less enjoin them; he may be said rather to superintend them. Why, may we ask, does he even do that? In order to give explanations, to answer questions by a *resumé* of the tradition which he has received, that is, of course, one reason; but also, as Ignatius himself

has told us, to moderate, if necessary, unreflecting
fervour, to hinder rash vows, finally to hold the
balance equal, by means of his own observations,
between the two decisions, either of which the retreatant is perfectly free to make.[1]   But, lastly,
who is to make for the retreatant either his general
examination or those particular examinations undertaken with the specific object of decreasing a
particular fault or sin — which the enemies of
Ignatius, with rather singular logic, ridicule in him
and admire in Franklin? Who is to make for him
the choice à propos of which the author constantly
says: "We begin by asking of our Lord and God
what we desire. The second prelude consists in
asking what I wish for and what I desire. . . ."
These formulas recur in every "week." . . . It is,
of course, understood that what the soul thus asks
for is not a favour in a human sense, but a grace
with which it must correspond by its efforts. He
who is the petitioner knows what he is undertaking; it is not for him to sit down and wait with

---

[1] These are the words of the fifteenth note : " He who gives
the *Exercises* must not try to induce him who receives them to
choose one state of life more than another. . . . At the actual
time of making the *Exercises*, whilst the soul is seeking to know
the Divine Will, it is more fitting and much better that the Creator
and Lord should Himself communicate Himself to the soul devoted
to Him, drawing it to His love and praise, and disposing it to
follow the way in which it will for the future be best able to serve
Him ; thus he who gives the *Exercises* must neither lean nor incline one way or the other, but maintaining his equilibrium like a
perfectly balanced pair of scales, allow the Creator to act immediately with the creature and the creature with its Creator and
Lord."

sighs. He has no manner of doubt that God will be faithful, and, for that reason, in St Ignatius the Christian soul is, to a certain extent, more free with God than with man, and more liberty is allowed her in her spiritual existence than in the ordinary conduct of life. But once she has made her request to God, it is for her to be faithful and to watch over herself in order that she may remain so; for a man who really desires a particular virtue and implores its bestowal ought to begin practising it at once.

It may be asked how it is possible while in retreat to practise so many virtues which require outward action.—Is it not in social life that we are to be really tried and exercised? Undoubtedly retreat is only a preparation for life, but is a very valuable preparation. One of the most profound maxims of the *Exercises* is that in making a good resolution we must not wait for the moment when the difficulty arises, and inevitably offers the temptation of taking the pleasantest or easiest way, but that after mature reflection we must have seen with a "clear eye" the resolution to make and have made it. We see ourselves, we look at ourselves in the future, as we should regard another man on the point of action, and we make up our mind as we should advise that other man to do, thus creating within ourselves a strength, which, in the actual moment of trial, will not allow the will to be taken unawares.

Nevertheless, it is not at the end of the first week that the retreatant is to arrive at what is called the

election.[1]   In order to ask himself in a practical
manner whether he is going to belong to Christ or
to His Enemy, to range himself under one standard
or the other, he must have been purified by the
exercises of this first week, and must also have
been enlightened by the meditations of the second.
Lastly, in order to settle upon his choice, with all
its consequences, it is not sufficient to see clearly;
the will must come in.   There are doubtless many
sacrifices to make, ties to break, restitutions to
accomplish, desires of ambition to abandon, or at
any rate to subordinate; in fact, all kinds of things
have to be done.   Here we may foresee many
struggles between different feeling and inspirations.
How are we to find our way?   How are we to discover what is an indifferent matter or what simply
arises from nature and what comes from without,
that is to say, from the good or the bad spirit?

Here again we may conjecture that the author of
the *Exercises* had brought his work to singular perfection.   Doubtless he had long ago perceived at the
first glance this primary truth, that the bad spirit
casts down, and the good strengthens, but the store-
house of his knowledge of souls must have gradually
taken in one by one many fresh rules.   There are
those who take delight in ridiculing this array of
fourteen rules for the first week, eight for the
second, and so on.   In this quantity of subdivisions

[1] I do not forget that the election is demanded of those who are
held fast by indissoluble bonds, just as much as from those who are
still free from any tie.   They may have entered on their state of
life with evil intentions, or they may be fulfilling its duties badly.
Thus one always needs to choose a better way of life.

St Ignatius is obeying two principles. First of all he loves clearness above everything. We shall find him writing in 1536 to a nun suffering from her lack of knowledge and disturbed by the rather vague advice given to her; "I share your opinion, and like you I think that a person who does not go much into detail has little capacity for enlightening and directing souls." Then he knows that the essence of every exercise is to take the difficulties, in order the better to settle them, each in turn, thus making ourselves more easily master of the partial difficulties contained in them. The ardour which characterises our efforts and the feeling we have of progress made are sufficient to guard against dryness.

Indeed once we are inspired by this lucid and deep psychology it would be strange if we did not make progress. How trustworthy are its views about dispositions, causes, about the various phases, either of consolation or desolation, and the profit to be drawn from both. How bold are the outlines, and how vivid the colours of these pictures: "Our enemy is like a woman, he has her weakness and her obstinacy. . . . His conduct is that of a seducer; he demands secrecy, and dreads nothing so much as discovery. . . . It is a distinguishing mark of the evil spirit to begin by entering into the sentiments of the pious soul, and to end by inspiring it with his own."

It may be asserted that when the "election" is decided on by the light of these counsels the most difficult part has been accomplished, and the remainder of the *Exercises* will effect the transforma-

tion of the Christian gently by means of love. Therefore that was the culminating point; the most holy
of Ignatius' disciples were well aware of the fact.
Peter Le Favre, in the many passages referring to
the *Exercises*, recurs constantly to the link which
connects them with the "discernment of spirits."
He comments on St Ignatius, as Malebranche does
upon Descartes, and we recognise that his experience has been drawn from the fountain-head,
when we read the passage explaining how many
good, and even pious, souls are unacquainted with
the variety of these impulses, as long as they are
restricted within the limits of an average task, but,
directly they are confronted with the effort of
attaining a more perfect life, the struggle begins
anew. Then it is easy to see the action of the two
conflicting spirits, "the spirit which fortifies and
the spirit which casts down, the spirit which illu-
minates and the spirit which sheds darkness, the
spirit which justifies and the spirit which defiles; in
a word, the good spirit and the spirit which is contrary to good." Like his illustrious friend, he returns
again and again to the art of distinguishing empty joy
which ends in sadness, from the sadness whence
the good spirit will draw us in order to carry us to
that which is solid, and to console us truly. He
always lays stress upon the joyous, captivating,
trustful, character of the good spirit, and upon the
"abundance" of his inspirations, and likewise upon
the discouragement, the lack of confidence, the
" penury " of the bad spirit.

"As for you," he says to himself, "when you

consider what you are, and when you look at things that are to be seen outside, you often think that you can do nothing, that you know nothing, and that you have nothing to hope for the advantage of your neighbour; but the Lord, on the contrary, leading you by His spirit, shows you countless things which seem to you easy to do with His help. He gives you, moreover, hope, affection of heart and love for a greater number of things than all men together could be able to accomplish, so that in this way you may feel your ardour for good works excited, and you may not despair." [1]

Certainly Genelli is right when he says that the *Exercises*, thus understood, produced real reform, because they tended to reform life, which always stands in need of it; to reform it without error of mind, without illusion of heart, without corruption of morals, and without revolt against dogmas. It involved neither deception, nor violence, nor war for the maintenance of a privilege; it was simply a return to manly and courageous piety. We cannot refrain from adding that such a "counter-reformation" was peculiarly opportune, as confronted with Luther and Calvin's chilling and disheartening tenets concerning predestination, enslaved will, and the uselessness of good works.

It is true that in the *Exercises*, besides the principles and the methods, there are the preliminaries, and that this word alone, applied to matters of piety, is enough to awaken in many minds an unfavourable prejudice. It is obvious that every one will not

[1] "Memorial." French Edition, pp. 173, 309, etc.

easily submit to these meditations in a room apart, to this variety of postures and attitudes, of which the book advises the adoption during the prayer. But to begin with, it must be observed that these preliminaries are only an accessory, and an accessory left at the disposal of individuals. The main point is that each should notice what distracts him or helps him to recollect himself, what chills his devotion and what touches him; he will then repeat what has been successful and avoid what has been indifferent or harmful. If anyone prefers for any particular part of his exercises, morning to evening, the sight of a landscape to that of a bare wall, he is free to choose as he wills. In no case is a new mechanism to be created, but the adaptation of that which exists in all of us, whether we will or no, is recommended, as also the turning it to the best possible account.

.   .   .   .   .   .

Such, then, was this method, a copy of which the good Dominican, to whom Ignatius had been denounced, desired for his own use. Such was it as practised by almost all the companions, formed of their own free will into a band by their brotherly adhesion to the ideas and views of their friend. Their "election" was made; all they had to do was to consecrate it. It was at Montmartre, on the 15th of August, 1534, that they did so. Let us here allow the witnesses, or rather, the very actors in this ceremony, to speak; it was as hidden and as simple as it was destined to be prolific of far-reaching and long-enduring results.

"In that same year, 1534," says Le Favre, "on the feast of the Assumption of the Most Blessed Virgin, all those among us who then shared the designs of Ignatius, and who had all already made the spiritual *Exercises* except Master Xavier, who had not yet made them, went to Notre Dame de Montmartre, and there we took a vow to serve God, and to start on the appointed day for Jerusalem, and to abandon kinsfolk and everything else on earth, only taking with us our fare.   Moreover, we formed the resolution of going, after our return from the Holy Land, to put ourselves under the obedience of the Roman Pontiff.   Now, those who were at this first meeting were Ignatius, Master Francis Xavier, then Le Favre, Master Bobadello, Master Lainez, Master Salmeron, Master Simon Rodriguez.   Father Le Jay had not yet come to Paris with the intention of joining us, and Master John Codure, as well as Master Paschasius Broët, were not as yet won over. In the two following years, that is to say 1535 and 1536, we all went on the same day to the same sanctuary to confirm the resolution that we had taken, and each time we experienced a great increase of spiritual life.   Master Le Jay, Master John Codure, and Master Paschasius Broët were with us in these two last years."

Another companion, Simon Rodriguez, has filled up this rather bare accouut.   With a little hesitation, on which I shall touch presently, he adds more than one tender touch to this picture, in which, be it observed, Le Favre seems to have forgotten himself. "They had decided that this vow should be made in

the chapel of St Denis, half-way up the Martyrs'
Hill, about a mile from the town, a solitary place, far
removed from all noise and all intercourse with the
crowd. Le Favre said Mass. Before giving the Holy
Eucharist to his companions, he took the Host in his
hands, and turned towards them. Then, with their
hearts fixed on God, kneeling on the pavement of the
chapel, all, without leaving their places, pronounced
their vows in a clear voice, so as to be heard by all,
then they communicated. On returning to the altar,
the Father in his turn, pronounced his vows in a
clear and distinct voice so as to be heard by every-
body, then he communicated.[1] When all was over we
went to the fountain of St Denis to spend the rest of
the day there."[2]

[1] This, if accurate, would involve a liberty with the rubrics as
they now stand.—ED.

[2] From the acccount of Father Simon Rodriguez, addressed
to Father Mercurian, General of the Society, July 15th, 1577.
Father Clair, who gives various drawings of the place, may be
consulted for additional details on the local memorials of
Montmartre.

Some authors have thought that the presence of St Ignatius at
this first meeting is open to doubt. They take their stand on an
obscure and contradictory sentence in the narrative of this same
Rodriguez. But Father Clair seems to have explained this passage in the most convincing fashion. After the few lines quoted
above, and after having said that all the Fathers (*cuncti Patres*)
having taken the Blessed Virgin for their advocate, and having
implored the intercession of St Denis, resolved . . . and so on, he
adds : "But at this vow, which they confirmed the two following
years, on the same day, and in the same place, in the same chapel,
with the same ceremony, Father Ignatius, in consequence of
certain causes, was not present, nevertheless, everything was
done by his advice and decision. I doubt equally whether in
the second year Father Le Jay were present." It is more than

With this memorable day, and especially with the last renewal of the vows, their student life seemed to end. At least the time had come for them to say good-bye to Paris, to its University, to the memories,

likely that Rodriguez, in his rather involved Latin sentence, meant that Ignatius was not present at the confirmation or renewal of the vows in the years which followed 1534. In any case, this obscure text, accompanied by dubitative formulas, cannot withstand either the expression that Rodriguez himself uses further back, "all the Fathers decided," or, above all, the extremely explicit text of Le Favre, who, being the only priest of that little company, alone was qualified to receive their vows, and who, as we have seen, counted them so exactly one by one.

Lastly, an extract given by Edouard de Barthélemy (*Bulletin of History and of Archæology*), July 1883, from the records of the Abbey of Montmartre, adds valuable testimony to that of Le Favre (supposing that the latter stood in need of it).

"In the year 1612 died, at the age of a hundred, the good Mother Perrette Roudlard, who was prioress when Madame de Beauvillers came to Montmartre. . . . She was very much devoted to the rule which she followed most exactly by night and day, going every day without fail to matins, till she was eighty-eight. Now, as she had been a long time in the house, she often talked to Madame of the remarkable things that had happened there in her time, and in that of the elder members; besides, she was under-sacristan when the blessed Ignatius of Loyola, founder of the Society of Jesus, came to make his vows in the chapel of the Holy Martyrs, and so she had the happiness of seeing him and of giving him the keys of the said chapel, as it was then never opened, except with the permission of the abbess." (*Manuscript of the National Library*).

If we are to believe this same document, it was not the holiness of the monastery at that date which had attracted Ignatius, for there were irregularities which had to be looked into. Evidently it was the traces of St Denis of which the companions were in quest. They were more enamoured of great memories and of really holy traditions than troubled by the calamities of the day, granted that they knew of them.

—saluted by Le Favre in his "Memorial"—of St Denis, of St Géneviève, of St Marcellus. Ignatius is suffering tortures from disease of the stomach, and is advised by the doctors to seek rest in his native air. He is about to start for Spain, provided with a horse, bought for him, despite himself, by his companions, with whom he arranges a meeting in Venice, which they are to reach by way of Lorraine and Switzerland. A letter of St Francis Xavier, recommending him to the attentions of his family, informs us that he must have started towards the 25th of March 1535, or, at any rate, shortly afterwards.

CHAPTER SIXTH

WHEN he again set foot on the soil of his native land, Ignatius had neither fixed upon all the outlines, nor still less upon the final shape of the design that he had in his mind. Nevertheless, he made a great point of its being known at once that these eight years of study at the University of Paris had only consolidated the intentions of the pilgrim of Manresa. His brothers and his nephews were expecting him, and had sent men charged to escort him, and to bring him with honour to the family castle, but, despite all the efforts of his relations, he had determined to lodge at the hospital and to live upon charity.[1] Those amongst his companions who were, like himself, Spaniards, had charged him to go and settle and conclude in their name certain pieces of business; he did so, without accepting on their behalf any money. As for himself, who belonged every day more and more, body and soul, to the Church at large, he wished, if I may be allowed the expression, to liquidate all his national past. The next year, when at Venice, we shall, it is true, find

[1] Maffei, nevertheless, says that he consented at the very beginning of his stay to spend three days at the castle of Loyola.

him writing that he has a keen desire to come back and announce the good word in the towns of Spain, and especially at Barcelona. But in this month's stay at Loyola, and at Azpeitia, he seemed to be really bidding a kind of farewell to the land of his childhood.

Although he was not a priest, he began resolutely to preach, and nobody made any objection, except his relations, who decidedly always regretted the nobleman in him. It was impossible, they asserted, that anyone should come to hear him. Nevertheless, people *did* come, and came, moreover, from afar and in great crowds. The church being too small, he preached upon the hillside, and some, in order to hear him better, climbed into trees. It was at this period that he chose to confess aloud and to expiate certain sins of his youth. He and several comrades had in those days robbed a garden, and, not having given themselves up, had been the cause of the condemnation of an innocent person. Ignatius related the fact, begged pardon of the victim of his prank, and, as a reparation of the injury, though it had meantime been forgotten, gave him some acres of land which still remained to him.

His lay-preaching produced other results mentioned by himself a little later in a letter to the faithful at Azpeitia. Not only did he convert great sinners of both sexes (some of the women went on pilgrimages, or devoted themselves, in the hospitals, to the care of the sick), reconcile enemies, bring about the marriage of people living in sin, but he exercised a sort of public influence for good.

He got a prohibition made against games of cards, which had at that time become a great abuse, he was instrumental in the establishment of the custom of ringing a bell three times a day, in order to call the faithful to offer special prayers for those in the state of mortal sin.   He also succeeded, and the fact is worth notice, in getting the town to take upon itself the care of its poorest inhabitants in order to hinder them from begging (*ne mendicare cogerentur*).   He, who had imposed on himself a prohibition against gaining anything for himself by his preaching, had recourse without any scruple to what he called " holy mendicancy," which simply allowed anyone willing to do so to give him the fair remuneration for his labours.   But this mendicancy ceased to be holy in his eyes when it was a case of poor people, undoubtedly anxious to earn their living and unable to find the means of doing so.   He founded, with the produce of some property that had fallen to him, a charitable institution, the management of which he entrusted to the magistrates of the town. Finally he put an end to a scandal which has been explained to us in plain terms by his first biographers.   It was the fashion for girls to go about bareheaded, as long as they remained single; they only covered their heads when they married. Now many women, living in illicit union either with clerics or laymen, had adopted the custom of covering their heads like those in lawful wedlock. Ignatius begged that they should be forbidden to do so, and the abuse ceased.

At the end of a few weeks, filled, as we have seen
with good works, he started again, as he had done
before, after receiving his wound. He was compelled
to accept the gift of a horse, but he only rode it as
long as he was on the family estates, giving it away
directly he was out of them. We are told that in
memory of him the animal was left all its life at
liberty in a meadow, without being set to any work.
Moreover, he was everywhere regarded as a saint;
the sick drew near him in order to be healed, many
marvels were related about him, such as that his
head had been seen surrounded by a halo, that he
had been heard to prophesy the destiny,—which had
later been accomplished according to his predictions,
—of some of his interlocutors.

Whatever may be the truth of these stories,[1] he
quickly escaped from the enthusiasm of his fellow-
citizens, and went on foot, without any money, as far
as Valencia, whence, after a visit to the Chartreuse
of Vallis-Christi, where he consulted his old pro-.
fessor of the humanities at the University of Paris,
John de Castro, about his plans, he set sail on a
ship, which, after a very bad voyage, brought him to
Genoa. Thence he went, again on foot, to Bologna,
which he did not reach without crossing a mountain,
on which he lost himself, where he ran the greatest
danger and experienced the keenest anguish of his
whole life. As a culmination of misfortune, he fell,

---

[1] His different secretaries, Gonzalès, Ribanedeira, Polanco, say
nothing of these facts. Was this because they had taken their
notes at his dictation, and he had concealed from them everything
that was miraculous?

just as he was entering the town, into a muddy ditch, and on extricating himself was treated as an object of derision by the passers-by, nor did he find anyone to give him the smallest alms.   In spite of this unfortunate beginning, we see by one of his letters that he at first desired to stay there at least a year in order to " finish his studies." Elizabeth Roser had sent him a fresh sum of money to help him, but he was so consumed by fever that he did not think he could remain there any longer; he decided to go without any further delay to Venice, where he was to wait for his friends.

He waited for them nearly a year, occupying the time mainly in the propagation of his *Exercises.* They procured for him the lasting friendship of Peter Contarini, nephew to the Cardinal of the same name; they obtained for him three new companions, two of the brothers d'Eguia, whom he had known at Alcala, and who had then just come back from Jerusalem, also a licentiate of theology, named d'Hozez, of a noble family in Cordova.

It is at this same period that took place his meeting, not with Gaëtan de Thienne, but with John Peter Caraffa, and that he made acquaintance with the order of the Theatines.   It is well known that there is a tradition, which has been closely scrutinised by historians, to the effect that at one time Ignatius must have been received amongst the Theatines.   Such an assertion is utterly contrary to the independence and originality of the ideas of his whole life, and is, moreover, absolutely gratuitous, resting upon the authority

of no document whatever. The resemblance of
the dress, and in many points the temporary resemblance of certain pious efforts, caused the common
people to confuse the two groups for some time; that
is the principal foundation of the tradition. Nevertheless there is ground for supposing that Peter
Caraffa made advances to the new-comer, and that
he slightly resented their not having been better
received. A Protestant work, "The Encyclopædia
of Religious Knowledge," suggests a reasonable
hypothesis when it says: "The Theatines called
his attention to the abuses which defiled the Roman
Church, as well as to the moral degeneracy of the
West, and invited him to a field of action as wide
as it was fruitful." That may be granted, but, after
all, Ignatius was not to be behindhand with his
interlocutor, and he was able, in his turn, to give
some prudent counsel. The chronicle of Polanco
does not cast any more light than the earlier
accounts on these episodes. It is most expressly
stated that the saint would never relate what had
passed between him and Caraffa, though giving it
to be understood that there had been incidents
of some importance.

A piece of business, speedily brought to a termina-
tion honourable to him, with the Venice Inquisition
(to which he had been denounced on the strength of
vain rumours) filled up the rest of the leisure of
Ignatius.[1]

On the 6th of January, 1537, he at length saw

---

[1] Genelli departs from the earlier traditions and puts this
incident further back. Polanco assigns it to this date.

his friends arrive. In vain had Francis Xavier been named Canon of Pampeluna; in vain had the brother of Rodriguez pursued him with the intention of calling him back; both had been faithful. They had started on foot, dressed in their long cassocks, a rosary round their necks, and carrying on their shoulders a bag filled with their University books or manuscripts. At intervals they discussed in common some point of sacred knowledge; then each one made his prayers and meditations in private. Seeing them pass along thus people asked each other, and asked them, who they were. Those who knew French best answered: "We are students of the University of Paris." One day, near Melun, they met a peasant, who answered for them in a patois which Lainez has handed down: "They are going to reform some country" (*Ils vont à reforma quoque pays*). Of reformers of all kinds there was indeed no lack. Wars and religious struggles were at their height; hostilities had just begun again between Francis I. and Charles V. Nothing stopped them, neither the illnesses resulting from their labours and austerities nor the torrents of rain which they had to endure in Lorraine, nor the snowstorms in Burgundy during an exceptionally severe winter, nor in the towns of Basle and Constance the public disputations which began, on the part of their adversaries, by invitations to banquets, and ended, on their refusal, by threats of imprisonment.

As a general rule it is true, especially when Lainez spoke in defence of Catholic tradition, they

gained the admiration and even the sympathy of
their auditors, although these last might have been
Lutherans. Three of them were priests, since Le
Jay and Broët had joined Le Favre, and thus they
never lacked spiritual help. The day on which they
reached, and were about to cross, the French
frontier they had all gone to confession and communion, by way of bidding a religious farewell to the
country which had sheltered them.

" Having thus reached Venice safe and sound,"
says Le Favre, " we went, with hearts full of joy,
to lodge in the hospitals—four in the hospital of St
John and St Paul (where Ignatius was living), and
three at that of the Incurables. There we had to wait
till Lent to go to Rome in order to ask the Sovereign
Pontiff Paul III. for leave to go to Jerusalem."

They did, in fact, go to Rome, but on this first
occasion without Ignatius; the prudence, which
never forsook him, made him afraid of compromising them by a meeting in the Eternal City with
those who had scattered injurious reports concerning him. Ortiz, who in Paris had always
regarded him with suspicion, was among them, and
he was now at Rome charged, as ambassador of
Charles V., with the duty of protesting to the Holy
Father in the Emperor's name against the repudia-
tion of Katharine of Arragon by Henry VIII. As
for his prejudices against the future general of the
Jesuits, which had excited such alarm, they no
longer existed, for he willingly placed himself at the
service of the pilgrims and himself introduced them
to the Pope.

Their journey from Paris to Rome must have rather resembled that from Paris to Venice. They walked this time in several groups, three and three, the French always mixed with the Spaniards, and each band having a priest with it. Everything was decided by plurality of votes, a custom which they preserved until the regular constitution of the Society. People seeing their bags, which really contained nothing but books, imagined that they were carrying money in them, which nevertheless did not hinder charitable souls here and there from giving them the small coin necessary for the crossing of a piece of water, so as to avoid, said the donors, their changing their gold pieces for such a trifling matter. Again they were tried by the weather, they walked in continual rain, often wet up to their waists. But such was their joy of soul that they took no harm, and John Codure was even cured, during these forced marches, of an affection of the feet from which he suffered.

Moreover, their reception by Paul III. would have sufficed to put heart into them. He welcomed them with paternal benevolence, made them discuss theological propositions in his presence, and summed up his impression of them by telling them that he was really edified to see so much learning joined to so much humility. He granted them the leave they sought, and though he declared to them, " I do not believe that you will be able to go to Jerusalem," he gave them 150 golden crowns, which were soon increased by the alms of rich Spaniards. Lastly, he gave to those among them who had not yet obtained the priesthood permission to receive it.

They availed themselves of this immediately after their return to Venice—Ignatius was ordained. None of them notwithstanding was in a hurry to say his first Mass.   Neither their past trials, nor the intensity of their desires, nor episcopal consecration was enough for them; they wished, in addition, to impose upon themselves a special preparation of some length.   That of Ignatius was destined to be prolonged for a whole year, perhaps because he cherished the hope of saying his Mass at Jerusalem, perhaps because humility and a sort of fear of the holy mysteries still kept him back.

It was not that his soul was then in what he has so often called the state of desolation.   The mystical ardour and the flights towards God, which he had successfully, by force of will, repressed within himself during his course of study, were henceforth set free from the hard necessity of former days, and he no longer thought of checking their impetuosity, but allowed them free play.   The extraordinary bodily agility which he had experienced during his few days' journey from Paris to Rouen, undertaken in order to help a sick friend, was again his portion when he had to go and minister to both the soul and body of Simon Rodriguez.   According to the witness of different persons, all very exact and in perfect agreement, to it was added the gift of second sight.   He foresaw and confidently predicted to his comrade on the journey (who with great difficulty followed him in the distance) the cure of their suffering brother.

Being anxious that their time of preparation

should likewise be profitable to other souls, and
seeing that the war and the difficulty of communication by sea hindered their going to Jerusalem,
they had scattered themselves all through the duchy
of Venice, at Bassano, at Vicenza, and at Verona.
Each one of them in these different towns practised
works of humility and charity. They preached in the
open air, after having summoned the inhabitants
from a distance by waving their caps. The language
which they spake must nevertheless have been rather
curious; as they were but imperfectly acquainted
with Italian, they interspersed it with expressions
borrowed from two or three languages; but they
succeeded all the same in making themselves understood. They atoned for their incorrectness by the
vigour of their discourses, for, in their efforts to con-
vey their meaning and to convince their hearers,
their words, says Ribanedeira, were like a hammer
breaking stones.

It was Vicenza that St Ignatius, with Le Favre
and Lainez, had chosen as his abode. The two
latter went every day into the town to beg their
bread; as for Ignatius, whose eyes were affected
by the abundance of his tears, he remained at
home to soften and boil down the hard and mouldy
bread which constituted the staple of their alms and
their food. They lived in a forsaken monastery without doors or windows, and their bed was composed
of a little straw. The health of all three was much
tried by this kind of life, and, although the inhabitants of Vicenza had quickly manifested generosity
towards them, they had, says Polanco, plenty to test

their patience and their spirit of prayer for forty days.

This time of retreat having elapsed, they all met at Vicenza, and, with the exception of Ignatius, who still delayed, the newly-ordained offered the Holy Sacrifice for the first time. They then deliberated as to the course they were to pursue. They perceived that they were still prevented from going to the Holy Land, and that there was nothing for it but to distribute to the poor the gifts that had always been put on one side for that journey. The time that they had fixed for taking it, if possible, had gone by. After having taken their vows of poverty and chastity at the hands of Verelli, the Papal legate, they resolved to go separately into the towns of Italy, and especially into the University towns, in order to continue their apostolate; they would then, in conformity with the last part of their vows at Montmartre, betake themselves to Rome, and put themselves at the disposal of the Holy Father. Whilst the larger number scattered themselves through the towns of Padua, Bologna, and Vicenza, Ignatius, still accompanied by Le Favre and Lainez, went straight to the Eternal City.

On their journey, about six miles from the town, took place the celebrated ecstasy and vision of La Storta. The three biographers, Gonzalès, Ribanedeira, and Polanco, all three relate them, with similarity of detail, which is a proof that their blessed Father, on almost every other occasion so sparing of the marvellous, had given them an exact account of them.

We have seen that he was already the recipient of all kinds of spiritual influences. He was again, as he had formerly been at Manresa, between Heaven and earth, with this difference, that this mystical ardour seemed to increase the importunity of a scheme which each day took more definite shape, and in which he wished to make the companions, who were one with himself, participators. However intimate was his intercourse with God and divine things at that time, what took place in him at La Storta was still more solemn.

He had entered a little chapel which was on his way. Scarcely had he begun to pray than he felt a deep change take place in his whole soul (*animum suum moveri mutarique sensit*, writes Gonzalès—*mutatum prorsus cor ejus est*, says Ribanedeira). He beheld "in spirit," the eyes of his understanding being suffused with light, the following scene. The Eternal Father was looking with love upon himself and his companions, and was recommending them to His Divine Son, Who was bearing His Cross. The Son in His turn said to them: "In Rome I will be favourable to you." The vision, on its disappearance, left him full of strength and confidence; he immediately went to relate it to Le Favre and Lainez, and, according to the confidences gathered up later on by Ribanedeira, he expressed himself to him in the following manner: "What will happen to us at Rome? Shall we be crucified or put on the rack? I do not know. But what I do know, and what I am certain of, is that whatever may be the final result, Jesus Christ will be favourable to us."

And he revealed to his two friends, in order to excite their zeal and courage, everything that his mind had just seen.

It is easy to understand that such a recollection possessed extreme importance in the eyes of the first Fathers of the Institute, and that they devoted considerable attention to it. It has been objected that Rome had not "recognised" this vision, which means that, without in the least denying it, she has not placed it in the number of authentic miracles. She only acknowledges and proclaims solemnly as facts those of which others besides the saint whose process she is drawing up have been eye-witnesses. But, putting this on one side, the reality, if not the complete and absolute nature of this great event, cannot leave room for doubt in anyone's mind. Ribanedeira, having put several questions on the subject to the Father, he answered: "Ask Lainez, I told him all about it before, and I told him exactly; there are details which I do not recollect very well now." This is how Lainez related the occurrence:

"What especially made our Father decide on choosing this title (Society of Jesus) in preference to any other was especially, it seems to me, the event that I am going to narrate. We were coming to Rome by the road from Siena, the blessed Ignatius, Le Favre and I, and at that time Father Ignatius was more than ever favoured with spiritual inspirations and heavenly gifts, especially when he received Communion; for Le Favre and I then said Mass, but he did not as yet. Now, when we came to a certain place on the road, he told me that God

Himself had imprinted deeply on his heart these words; 'I will be favourable to you at Rome,' of which he did not yet understand the full meaning. 'I do not know,' he said, 'what will happen to us at Rome. Who can say? Perhaps we shall be crucified there!' Then he added that he had seemed to see our Lord with a heavy cross on His shoulders, and near Him the Eternal Father, who said to Him, 'My Son, I wish Thee to take this man as Thy servant,' and Jesus, pressing Ignatius to Himself and to His cross, said: 'Yes, I desire that Thou shouldest be my servant.' "

All these accounts appear to me to be in perfect harmony. No doubt, if it were a question of a common man, or even of a worldly hero, we might think, as has indeed been asserted, that there is a contradiction between the idea of possible torture and the certainty of a benefit about to be received. " That is precisely," it might be urged, " the confusion, at any rate, in outward seeming, belonging to either a natural or a hypnotic dream in a man filled with the hopes and fears which always accompany the preparation of an important scheme." But here we have to do with a saint, that is to say with a man in whom the idea of martyrdom is very far from excluding confidence in Divine favour. Therefore, the conjunction of these two anticipations need not astonish us, even from the point of view of a natural explanation. Thus, when Lainez says that his master did not yet clearly understand *all* the meaning of the words; " I will be favourable to you in Rome," there is no need to seek for subtle and ingenious explanations in the disciple's statement.   Ignatius did not understand in what way Christ would be favourable to him, and how He would make him, for the good of souls, a partaker in the glorious burden of His cross; but he knew that this favour would be granted to him. That was enough for him; and it is not surprising that his project of calling the Society, whose foundation he was contemplating, the Society of Jesus, thenceforth became in his mind a fixed and ineradicable idea.

Despite the continuity which binds together, without sudden breaks, the whole life of St Ignatius, from his conversion to his death, it may truly be said that at this point a whole period of his existence ends and another begins.   The man whom Rome is about to receive within her walls is no longer either the ascetic, or the pilgrim, or the student, or even we may say the apostle, he is above all the founder, for if the Society of Jesus is not yet constituted, it is certainly now only a question of days.

CHAPTER SEVENTH

ROME—FOUNDATION OF THE SOCIETY

A "visionary" usually goes straight before him, pursuing through unknown obstacles the object which fascinates him. Such was certainly not the behaviour of Ignatius when he entered Rome after his ecstasy and his vision of La Storta. His biographers tell us that he was very anxious about finding "closed windows," that he advised his companions to be extremely prudent, and that for his own part he had begun to look about him right and left with the greatest attention.

In a letter of the 19th of December to his benefactress Elizabeth Roser, he thus gives an account of his beginnings. "More than a year ago we came, three of us that is, to Rome, as I remember having written to you. My two companions began to teach gratuitously at the *Sapienza*, one positive theology and the other scholastic theology, and that by order of the Pope. For my part I occupied myself solely in giving the *Spiritual Exercises* in Rome and outside the city. Our object was to find less opposition among people in the world, and to be able to preach with more liberty the Holy Word of God, for judging by appearances we are labouring on a land barren in good works and fertile in bad."

This last brief verdict on the city of Rome is not flattering. It is obvious that a soul such as that of the author of this letter must have taken a good deal of exception to the paganism of the place, intermingled as it was with all the allurements of the Renaissance. On the other hand the See of Peter was undoubtedly beginning to be purified from its contact with Alexander VI., even the martial ardour and the dangerous prodigality which had distinguished the pontificates of Julius II. and Leo X. were visibly declining, but a good deal of the poison which had for a long time been creeping into the veins of the body of the Church still remained to be eliminated. Italian society as yet answered only too well to the description given of it in the writings of Burckardt, "Holiness, the ideal of Christian life, had been replaced by that of historical grandeur; faults which had not hindered a man from becoming great were regarded as indifferent. And moreover, what was the idea formed by men of this same greatness? How strangely abused was the word *virtu* which meant, it seems, what we call *virtuosity*, virtuosity in elegance and in the worship of the beautiful of course, but also in pleasure, no matter of what kind, in the contempt of prejudices and in the art of getting rid of enemies. By means of the court of Naples and of the frequent "visits" paid by the Imperial armies to the peninsula, Spain had grafted a few shoots of her own on the Italian trunk, but the son of Loyola found little consolation for his piety in the loans made by his countrymen. What he saw was not the chivalrous spirit of his ancestors, but rather a certain sloth coupled with a love of empty titles, and with regard to passions a strongly-marked inclination to the spirit of vengeance and hardness. As for the "most Catholic" or "most Christian" kings, the help which they occasionally gave to the Church was rather dearly bought. Charles V., as we have already seen, was quite willing to defend by energetic means the integrity of traditional dogma, but he did not like his power or even his vanity, to suffer the slightest loss thereby. When the hostility which he so often displayed against the Sovereign Pontiff gave place to an understanding, the diplomatic arrangements which sealed this apparent renewal of friendship were not always very edifying. What, for instance, could the general morality gain by seeing Pope Paul III. (who had been married before entering holy orders) secure the succession of Parma and Piacenza to his posterity by marrying his grandson Octavius Farnese to Margaret of Austria, natural daughter to Charles V.? The father of Octavius had been assassinated in Parma in consequence of his licentiousness, and Margaret's first husband, Julian de Medicis had likewise been assassinated in Florence. The cruel misfortunes of that brilliant period were not then yet over.[1]

And nevertheless, despite this remnant of nepotism, which his relations repaid by ingratitude and evil conduct, thus embittering his last days, Paul III.

[1] It must be acknowledged that Margaret of Austria was a most noble and a most pious woman, and a remarkable benefactress to Ignatius and the Society.

was destined to usher in the line of reforming popes. For a long time he had been expressing a desire of seeing a council called in order to resist the Lutheran heresy. "Immediately after his succession he opened the sacred college to several distinguished prelates, who were, like himself, convinced of the necessity of prompt and energetic action: Peter Caraffa, who had in 1532 co-operated in a scheme of reform, the Venetian Contarini, well known for his hostility to the abuses of the pontifical court and the propagator of a liberal movement in the Church of Italy, Pio di Carpi, Reginald of Paris, James Sadolet, John Morone, bishop of Modena, John du Bellay, bishop of Paris, Jerome Aleandre. From this chosen band he selected a commission, whom he charged with preparing the reform of the Church, and whose work, drawn up in 1537, was published at Rome in 1538."[1] A little later Contarini was sent to Germany, but his concessions (which were, it may be said, excessive) at the diet of Ratisbon did not disarm his adversaries.

We may safely state that neither the desires of the Pope, nor the help, sometimes feeble and sometimes imprudent, of his great dignitaries would have been sufficient to transform the Church, if God had not bestowed upon it the heroic initial movement and the pure zeal of His saints.

The commission nominated by the Pope was not itself very confident in the efforts of the congrega-

---

[1] It was entitled : *Consilium delectorum cardinalium et aliorum praelatorum de emendanda ecclesia.*—*Crénon, General History,* already quoted, vol. v.

tions.   It had declared, in the course of its report, that the professors at the university publicly taught doctrines contrary to the Faith, and that great scandals existed in religious houses, Consequently it proposed the suppression of all the monasteries, or at least the temporary check of their increase by their being forbidden to receive novices.   The old community once having disappeared, an attempt would be made to train a new generation in the spirit of the primitive rule.   The Pope had not adopted this rather singular means to his end, and contemplative Orders like the Carthusians and Carmelites, mendicant Orders like the Franciscans, Orders devoted to study like the Benedictines, or to preaching like the Cistercians and Dominicans, continued to exist. The chivalrous and military Orders now only survived in memory.   But the movement which at all periods of history urges the Church more or less strongly to create for herself new armies by concentration and by action was as powerful as ever.

We have on our way already met the Theatines, whose existence was approved by Clement VII. in 1524.   The object of their institution was to bring back the clergy to perfect poverty by making them depend for their subsistence upon the free and unsolicited charity of the faithful, to restore solemn functions and ceremonies, to encourage the frequenting of the sacraments, to reform preaching, to visit the sick, to assist those condemned to death.   These new religions had scarcely had time to spread before the name of Theatine (derived from the fact that one of their first superiors was bishop of Theano), had become synonymous with a strict and zealous priest. Thus one historian declares that when the Jesuits began in Italy the people often called them Theatines. A short time afterwards the Clerks Regular of Somasco had been established in that town (whence their name) for the instruction of the Italian and foreign universities. They were approved as a congregation in 1535 by Clement VII., and Paul III. was to make them into an Order in 1535. Two years later Angela de Merici founded the Ursulines, and the same Pope Paul III., who had sanctioned them, was to see before his death in 1548 St. Philip Neri lay the foundations of the congregations destined to become the Oratory.

By all this we see how the principal currents of the ecclesiastical world were divided when St. Ignatius arrived at Rome. If there are still in existence people who fancy that one fine day he and the Pope suddenly resolved, as in a council of war, to let loose the new army, fully organised, against Protestant Europe, they are far from the truth. Like all great institutions, the Society was formed little by little. Paul III. beheld in these young men arriving from the University of Paris first, pious pilgrims, then, good theologians and good priests well fitted for training others, and, finally, men at whom he could not possibly take umbrage, since they had made a vow to put themselves at his disposal in order to do simply what it should please him to enjoin. But what did they themselves, at the exact point which we have reached, think of their vocation and their future? St. Ignatius and Polanco shall tell us.

St Ignatius had been to spend forty days on Monte Cassino. He had there given the spiritual exercises to Peter Ortiz, the famous ambassador of Charles V., as he had given them in the city itself to Cardinal Contarini. We may here take up again the letter, already quoted, to Elizabeth Roser: "After having, by these *Exercises*, with the help of God, won over to our side some people of importance on account of their rank and knowledge, we resolved, four months after our arrival, all to meet in this same town. As soon as we were all collected we asked leave to preach, exhort and confess. The legatè gave us very extensive powers in these matters, though in truth attempts were made, by means of evil reports, to hinder the granting of the faculties sought for. As soon as we had attained them some of us began to preach in different churches on Sundays and feasts, and in other churches to instruct children on the commandments of God and on mortal sin. The two lessons in theology at the *Sapienza* and the confessions were continued. All my companions preached in Italian; I alone in Spanish."

Thus he only, as he admits, had found the learning of a new language too difficult. He used, therefore, to speak in a church frequented by his compatriots, which was called by a name which must have been dear to him—Our Lady of Montserrat. Many came to hear him, and it was acknowledged at once that he was a man having " power over souls."

As for the intimate meetings that he and his friends had at this time, he says very little about them to his benefactress. ⹁ He regarded her with affection, he was sincerely grateful to her, and as he himself writes to her in this letter, if he had forgotten he should have thought himself "forgotten by God." But for all that he treated her rather like a woman. He relates to her at length their visits to the Pope, the cabals of which he has been the object, the simultaneous and truly providential presence in Rome of all the men best able to bear witness to his past life in the countries where he has been, and the like. But as to the important deliberations which had been the cause of his meetings with his friends, this is all he says to her: "One of the things with which we were and are reproached is wishing to found a society without the authorisation of the Holy See. Although we do not as yet live in common, we are nevertheless all united in heart, so as to understand each other for the future. We hope that our Lord and God will not delay making known His designs upon us, for His better service and greater glory."

At this point Ribanedeira and Polanco come to our help. As both of them are in perfect agreement, I confine myself here to translating this passage from Polanco.

"In this year 1538, at the beginning of spring, all our Fathers assembled at Rome. They had not yet formed in their minds the scheme of founding a permanent congregation or a religious order; they only intended, with the concurrence of those whom the Lord should give them as helpers, to devote themselves to the service of God, and to give aid to souls. It was no longer possible for them to go to Jerusalem, but a wide field was open to them, not only in the different towns and provinces of Italy, but outside; for, the good odour of their virtues having spread, many claimed their assistance, and it seemed that the Holy Father encouraged this by sending our men to preach in more than one place. It was then that all began to think that it might perhaps be the will of God for them to form among themselves a lasting society which, at their death, would continue to offer to God the same ministry, and would be increased by people desirous of following the method which they should have instituted. Therefore, before separating to go into different lands they, who, though born in various countries, had been joined together by the Lord in the same spirit and vocation, began to occupy themselves with the kind of life which they ought to observe. And, as at the outset the ideas of each were different, they resolved to offer to God their Holy Sacrifices, and then carefully to seek out what might be the will of God. They were confident that if they did everything in their power to enlighten themselves, God Himself would inspire them with what was to be most pleasing to His Sovereign Majesty. Thus they met every night, and the reflections that each one had made were put at the disposal of everyone, so that all might follow the votes and reasons of the majority."

This expressive and clear passage is undoubtedly one of the most important in our possession with regard to the beginnings of the Society. The Bollandists of the present day have added the weight of their authority by making on it a commentary which runs as follows in their *Analecta* :—

L 5

"Thus although Xavier, Le Favre, Lainez, Salmeron, from the day when they joined Ignatius, . . . always desired to work for the salvation of their souls, neither they nor Ignatius had before 1538 entertained an idea of founding the religious company that we call the Society of Jesus. When on the point of separating, perhaps for ever, they are struck with the results they have obtained, . . . they ask themselves whether they ought not to remain united by enduring ties. This idea emanated from several among them, and Polanco says nothing to indicate that it must be attributed specially to Ignatius.[1]   It was only in 1539 that it was decided to lay the foundations of a social body; and after various attempts Ignatius laboured, from 1547 to 1550, at erecting the edifice of the Constitutions."

Let us return to these first deliberations. If they took place at night, it was because it had been resolved that, far from retiring to a monastery as some had proposed, they would avoid any interruption of the work begun. In the second place, each one was to consider the matter in private, without consulting or advising any of his brethren; each one was, as far as possible, to remove from himself all his affections, all personal considerations, and picture to himself that he was working for other men, and

----

[1] In his French edition of the *Letters*, Fr. Bonix gives a self-styled allocution or circular from Ignatius to his companions, which does not seem to possess any guarantee of authenticity. It is one of those "speeches after Livy," such as the Jesuits themselves have reproached Bartoli with composing only too often.

had to give them for their benefit perfectly disinterested advice.

Guided by this method, they speedily decided on founding a society in which they would be for ever united to each other, however far parted they might be on earth by the missions entrusted to them by the Sovereign Pontiff.

They held more lengthy discussions in order to settle whether they should add the vow of obedience to the vows of perpetual poverty and chastity which they had taken at the hands of the apostolic legate. The reader may perhaps feel surprised at their greater hesitation over this point, but the reason has been very clearly explained. When this third vow was pronounced, they became by that very fact *religious*; and then they asked themselves whether they should not be bound to a sedentary life, to office said in choir, and to the other observances then in use amongst all monastic bodies? Now they desired to guard jealously a freedom of conduct which should allow them to widen and to vary their plan of action. But when they had satisfied themselves that the obligations which they had determined to decline were not in the least essential, their objections disappeared. It seemed to them plain that obedience would be effectual in consecrating the victory over pride, in maintaining an enthusiasm always ready for heroic actions, and in strengthening for ever the unity of the Society.

It was this extreme desire of unity which caused them to vote unanimously for choosing as head one of their number, to whom they should promise obedience—subject, however, always and everywhere, to the approbation and confirmation of the Holy See.

These preliminary deliberations on fundamental points lasted from the middle of Lent to the feast of St John the Baptist (the 24th of June). According to the distinct statement of Polanco they began again towards the end of the year. Then, he says, were laid down, at any rate mentally, a great many rules which, completed and arranged in better order, were to be reproduced by St Ignatius in the text of the Constitutions. They arrived by mutual consultation at decisions as to the admission and "probation" of the new members who were to be employed at first in the Spiritual Exercises and in the care of the sick in the hospitals, as to the poverty to be observed in the houses. . . . It is still more plain from Polanco's text that they then drew up that declaration which, after having been submitted to Pope Paul III., was by him inserted in its entirety in his Bull of the 27th of September 1540. We shall therefore only be anticipating a little by extracting from the Papal Bull that important document which was to wait nearly two years before being thus reproduced and approved.

First of all we must notice that the Pope, when mentioning the application addressed to him, distinctly mentions all the signatories: "Our beloved sons Ignatius Loyola, Peter Le Favre, James Lainez, Claude Le Jay, Paschasius Broët, Francis Xavier, Alphonsus Salmeron, Simon Rodriguez, John Codure and Nicolas Bobadilla, who, guided by the inspiration of the Holy Ghost," and so forth, "and after

having practised in many countries all the offices
of charity, have settled upon a plan of life; now,
this is," the Bull adds, "this way of life as it has
been conceived."

"Whoever shall wish to bear arms for God in
our Society, which we desire to be called the Society
of Jesus, and to serve only Jesus Christ our Lord
and the Roman Pontiff His Vicar on earth, must,
after having made a solemn vow of perpetual
chastity, set before himself that he is going to
belong to a Society principally instituted to work
for the advancement of souls in Christian life and
teaching, for the propagation of the Faith by public
preaching and the ministry of the Word of God
by the spiritual *Exercises*, and by works of charity,
especially by teaching the Catechism to children
and to those who are not properly instructed in
Christianity, and by hearing the confessions of the
faithful for their spiritual consolation. He ought
also to act in such a manner as always to have
before his eyes in the first place God, and then
the form of this institute which he has embraced.
It is a way which leads to God, and a man should
use his utmost efforts in order to attain the end
that God Himself sets before him, though always
in proportion to the measure of grace which he
has received from the Holy Spirit, following the
peculiar degree of his vocation for fear that anyone
should let himself be carried away by a zeal not
according to knowledge. The General or Superior,
whom we shall choose, will decide upon the degree
fitted to each one as well as the offices, all of which

shall be in his hands, that due order, so necessary in every well-ordered community, may be observed. This General shall have authority to make constitutions agreeable to the aim of the Institute, with the consent of those who are associated with him and in a council where everything is to be decided by the plurality of votes. As to important things which are to live on into the future, this Council shall consist of the greater part of the Society whom the General shall be able conveniently to gather together, and as to the smaller and temporary matters, he shall consult all those who are in the General's place of residence. As for the right of commanding, it shall belong altogether to the General. Therefore let all the members of the Society know and remember, not only in the first days of their profession but all the days of their life, that this whole Society and all those who compose it are fighting for God under loyal obedience to our most Holy Father the Pope and of the other Roman Pontiffs, his successors. And although we have learnt from the Gospel and from the orthodox faith, and though we profess to believe firmly that all the faithful of Jesus Christ are subject to the Roman Pontiff as to their Head and the Vicar of Jesus Christ, nevertheless, in order that the humility of our Society may be still greater, and that the detachment of each one of us and the abnegation of our will may be more perfect, we have thought that it would be very useful, in addition to that bond common to all the faithful, to bind ourselves also by a peculiar vow, so that, whatever the present Roman

Pontiff and his successors may command us concerning the good of souls and the propagation of the Faith, we may be obliged to carry out instantly, without evasion or excuse, in whatever country they may send us, whether to Turks or any other infidels, or even to the Indies, or to heretics and schismatics, or to any of the faithful. Therefore, let those who wish to join us seek carefully to discover, before taking this burden upon themselves, whether they have sufficient spiritual foundation to be able, according to Our Lord's advice, to finish this tower; that is to say, if the Holy Ghost, who is urging them on, promises them sufficient grace for them to hope that with His help they shall manage to bear the weight of this vocation; and when, by the inspiration of the Lord, they are enrolled in this army of Jesus Christ, they must be always ready, night and day, with loins girt up, to pay this great debt. But in order that we may neither seek after these missions in different countries, nor refuse them, each and all of us will pledge himself not to present to the Pope on the subject any solicitations, either directly or indirectly, but to abandon himself in the matter entirely to the will of God, of the Pope as His Vicar, and of the General. The General, like the others, will himself promise not to solicit the Pope about the destination and mission of his own person, except with the consent of the Society. All will make a vow to obey the General in everything that concerns the observance of our rule, and the General will prescribe the things which he is aware are calculated to accomplish the end which God and the Society have had

in view. Let him always, in the discharge of his
office, remember the goodness, gentleness and charity
of Jesus Christ, as well as the humble words of St
Peter and St Paul; and let him, together with his
Council, be careful never to depart from this. Let
all likewise have greatly at heart the instruction of
children and of the ignorant, teaching them Christian
doctrine, the Ten Commandments, and other like
elementary truths, according as shall be fitting,
having due regard to the circumstances of persons,
places and times. For it is very necessary that the
General and his Council should watch over this point
with great attention, both because it is not possible
to build up the edifice of the Faith in our neighbour
without any foundation, and because it is to be feared
it may happen among us, that, in proportion as we
are more learned, we may refuse this office as being
less distinguished and brilliant, although nevertheless
there is none more useful, either to our neighbour
for his edification, or to ourselves for the practice
of humility and charity. As for the inferior brethren,
both on account of the great advantages which result
from order, and to ensure the constant practice of
humility, which is a virtue that can hardly be sufficiently praised, they shall be bound always to obey
the General in everything which concerns the Institute, and in his person they shall seem to see Jesus
Christ, as if He were really present, and shall revere
him as much as is fitting. But as experience has
taught us that the purest life, and that which is
most pleasing and edifying to our neighbour, is that
furthest removed from the contagion of avarice and

the most in conformity with the poverty of the Gospel, and knowing that Our Lord will supply with necessary food and clothing His servants who only seek the kingdom of God, we desire that all our members and each one of them should take a vow of perpetual poverty, declaring to them that they cannot possess individually nor even in common for the support of the Society, any of the rights of a citizen to real property, or to any sort of income or revenue; but that they must content themselves with the alms given to them in order to procure what is strictly necessary.

Nevertheless, they shall be able to have in the universities, colleges possessing revenues, rents and funds applicable to the use and the needs of the students; the General and the Society keeping all administration over the said property and the said students in regard to the choice, refusal, reception and exclusion of the superiors and students, and as to the rules concerning the instruction, edification and correction of the said students, the manner of their food and dress, and every other subject of administration and government, in such a way, nevertheless, that the students cannot make a bad use of the said property, nor the Society itself turn it to its own use, but that it should only be used for the needs of the students. And the said students, when their superiors are satisfied with their progress in piety and learning, after a sufficient trial, may be admitted into our Society, of which all the members who are in Holy Orders, although they have no ecclesiastical benefices or revenues, shall be bound

to say Divine Office according to the rite of the
Church, each separately and in private, and not in
common and in choir.   Such is the sketch that we
have been able to make of our profession under the
good pleasure of our Holy Father Paul III. and of
the Apostolic See.   Which we have done with a
view of giving information by this written summary,
both to those who are now making inquiry about our
Institute, and those who shall succeed us in the
future, if it happen that by the will of God we ever
have imitators in this kind of life; which, since it
offers great and numerous difficulties, as we know by
our own experience, we have thought it advisable to
command that no one shall be admitted into this
Society except after having been most carefully tried
for some time, and that it is only when a man has
made himself known as wise in Jesus Christ and
has distinguished himself by learning and purity of
Christian life, that he can be received into the army
of Jesus Christ, Whom may it please to be favourable
to our little undertakings for the glory of God the
Father, to Whom be glory and honour for ever and
ever, Amen."

The above is a full and complete plan of the
Society, with that *esprit de corps* and that love of ·
discipline in which the devotion of each member to
the good of the Church was to find manly and discerning satisfaction.   The Constitutions, which we
shall soon have to study, will not do more than embody in a code what the friends of Ignatius had settled
of their own free will in harmony with him.   The
Pope left them full leisure to write these constitu-

tions.   For after this long extract he contented himself with adding: "We approve, bless and endow
with perpetual stability the preceding manifesto, both
as to its whole and its details, and as for the associ-
ates themselves we take them under our protection,
granting them leave to draw up with perfect right,
and according to their own will, the constitutions
which they consider fit for this Society, to the glory
of Our Lord and the edification of our neighbour."

Up to now the ascendency of Ignatius had certainly
been very great; but neither his humility nor his
desire to lay at the base of his foundation a complete,
unanimous and perfectly free consent were for that
reason any the less.   For that reason we always
find his name in the autograph documents mixed up
with the others.   Nevertheless, if we do not know
exactly everything which in these deliberations was
drawn up or inspired by him, we know that it was
certainly he who made such a great point of the
Society being definitely called the Society of Jesus.
When they were preaching in the Duchy of Venice
one of them had said one day: "But if we are asked
what we are called, how shall we answer?"   And
another—we do not know whether it was Ignatius—
"We will answer that we belong to the Society of
Jesus." He said it with a very general meaning, and
perhaps with a smile, without thinking that this desig-
nation was to continue.   What is absolutely certain
is that after the vision of La Storta Ignatius had
made up his mind.   He was resolved, he used to say,
to defend this name, unaided, if necessary, against

everyone, and only to yield it to him who had the power of asking it from him under pain of mortal sin.

It has often been said that reserving the honour of such patronage for himself argued a certain amount of pride.   Such was not Ignatius' own feeling; he did not wish his followers to be designated by his name, and to have people say the "children of Ignatius," as they say the "children of St Benedict" and the "children of St Dominic."   As to the word "Company" or Society, it was in his mind a metaphor taken from military life, "company" being synonymous with battalion or regiment.   His disciples were to be not the favoured and privileged companions, but the soldiers, always armed and always ready, of Jesus Christ.

.   .   .   .

By the simple fact of the fresh dispersion of the greater number of his followers, Ignatius of necessity beheld the gradual increase, I do not say of his real influence, which had always been very great, but of the outward and visible part played by him.   It was he who had to steer the bark in the midst of the storm which had arisen in Rome against him and his work.   (He had recognised in it the handiwork of a certain Dr Navarro, who had already wished to assassinate him in Paris.)   It was he who went to the Pope and obtained one by one the authorisations destined to open the ways.   It was he who wrote to distinguished personages in order to announce to them that justice was obtained.

On the 23rd of September 1539, Paul III. consented, at Tivoli, to give his verbal approbation to the plan that had been submitted to him. It is even related that on reading the pages he exclaimed: " The finger of God is here." But it was necessary for the approbation to be confirmed by letters apostolic, and here began fresh difficulties. The preparation of the Bull was entrusted to a commission of three cardinals, of whom the most influential happened to be Cardinal Guidaccioni. Now this prelate, very learned and very pious as he was, was ill-disposed towards any congregations, old or new. He was of opinion that there were too many of them, and had written a book to prove this. The line of argument attributed to him, which was founded on an experience, only too real, of the decay of religious Orders, was as follows: " All Orders are, in their beginnings, full of fervour, but become relaxed with time, and when they have grown old they do more harm to the Church than they have done good at their foundation." Ignatius, in order to conquer his opposition, had recourse both to prayers and reasoning. He had several thousands of masses said, and devoted himself personally to the task of producing on the mind of the cardinal an impression calculated to soften his refusal. He succeeded in his aim, for, without giving up his theory, Guidaccioni owned that he could no longer take upon himself to hinder the existence of the new Congregation, and at last on the 26th of September 1540, appeared the bull *Regimini militantis ecclesiae*, which comprised in its approbation and eulogium the whole scheme submitted to him by the founders, the text of which has been given above. Nevertheless, there was one restriction which alarmed neither the prudence nor the patience of Ignatius: the number of the professed members was provisionally limited to sixty.

The Society was thus in existence. It remained for it to be formed in the spirit that had just been consecrated. In order that the body should live and do its work it required a head. The Fathers did not delay long in assembling to settle the election of their first General.

In reality, Ignatius had all the authority of the office in consequence of the universal confidence of his brethren, and he exercised all its functions. Before having received the Papal Bull, he wrote to his brother, Dom Bertrand of Loyola (the 16th of March 1540), a letter beginning thus:—" Considering the extreme press of business upon me, having to despatch all at once some of our religious to India, Ireland, and different districts of Italy," and so forth. And he announces in a few words the departure of Francis Xavier for Portugal and thence for India.

The sending out of the missionary destined to such great glory had not merely preceded the official constitution of the Institute, it had greatly helped it. Ribanedeira relates all the circumstances in a truly charming fashion. John Govea, the professor of by-gone days who had wished " to give the hall " to Ignatius, had retained for him all the esteem with which he had so soon felt himself inspired. He had heard the congregation which Ignatius was forming spoken about, and he had persuaded John III. to ask him for six missionaries to evangelise the new empire of the Indies. The request was made, and answer was at once given that it was for the Pope to give the order, and that as a matter of fact it would not be very difficult to obtain from him the despatch of two Fathers, but that, as for a larger number, it would be no easy business. And as the King's ambassador persisted, Ignatius answered him with a tranquil air: " If for one province you take six out of the ten that we number, what will you leave us, good Jesus! for the remainder of the world ? "

Finally, the Pope left the solution to the judgment of Ignatius, who decided to send Rodriguez and Bobadilla to John III. Then, as Bobadilla fell seriously ill, he sent for Francis Xavier and said to him with that simplicity which we gladly recognise in the style of his confidant: " Bobadilla's health prevents him from going, and the ambassador is in too great a hurry to be willing to wait. It is for you, Francis, to take his place." And, without any more talk, Xavier joyously answered, " I am ready." Two days later, the apostle bade farewell to his friends, embraced his brethren, and, dressed in an old patched cassock, started with no luggage except his breviary for the spiritual conquest of China and Japan.

Rodriguez had arrived at Lisbon before him. Being anxious wherever they were not to lose time, they began by exercising their ministry in the kingdom with so much zeal and such abundant results, that for a time there was a question of keeping them both in Portugal. In order to settle things satisfactorily Rodriguez remained there and Xavier set out alone, with the title of apostolic nuncio, on the 14th of April 1541. During this time, the ambassador of John III. was making use of his great influence with the Holy Father to hasten the publication of the expected Bull.

It was in this same month of April that Ignatius and his companions, who had remained in Italy, met together in order to proceed to the election of the General. They were obliged to lose no time, for the Pope himself was in haste to send some to preach in different places. Broët came from Siena, Lainez from Parma, Le Jay from Brescia. Those who were present had to devote three days to prayer and meditation, and then arrive with their vote written beforehand. Peter Le Favre, then in Germany, Simon Rodriguez and Francis Xavier had sent theirs; Bobadilla alone voted neither *vivâ voce* nor by writing. They assembled in the house which they had rented, a small building already all tumbling to pieces and destined to disappear with the old church which adjoined it. There the votes, both of those absent and those present, were counted up; Ignatius, as might have been expected, was elected by the unanimous choice of his friends.

Some, namely the absent, and a fourth, John Codure, on the eve of setting forth in his turn, had given a name with a view to the possible death of Ignatius; Peter Le Favre was thus mentioned as a second choice by John Codure, Simon Rodriguez and Francis Xavier; as for Peter Le Favre himself, he had given his second vote to the last-named.

Ignatius had not chosen to propose anyone by

name. He excluded himself, and declared that he would give his vote to the man among the others whose name was most frequently written.

What spirit was he obeying in this matter? He had desired above everything that the Society should exist, that it should be granted to him to live in community of feeling and action with those whom he had collected together; it was indifferent to him whether he himself or another ruled, or rather, if I am not mistaken, he would have thought that he was committing a sin of rashness or pride if he had not left himself out as far as was in his power. Indeed, must we not go a step further? In his desire no longer to find so many occupations and so many temporal works between God and himself, no longer to see his supernatural visitations disturbed by the necessities of government, as they had been by those of study, must he not really have dreaded the burthen and made sincere efforts to avert it?

He certainly did so, alleging that being incapable of directing himself he could not direct others. He demanded a fresh voting, which produced exactly the same results. As he manifested the same repugnance, Lainez rose and said firmly to him: " My father, yield to the voice of God, or the Society will break up, for I have quite made up my mind not to acknowledge any head but him whom God has chosen." There was nothing for it but to yield to such words; nevertheless, Ignatius asked to consult his confessor, and it was not until his spiritual guide. had united his entreaties to those of the others that he definitely yielded.

M 5

A few days later, on the 22nd of April 1541, in the church of " St Paul-without-the-walls," he received the vows of all those who were present, and at the same time repeated his own aloud at the moment of Communion, as had been done at Notre Dame de Montmartre.

CHAPTER EIGHTH

FIRST WORKS AND MISSIONS OF THE SOCIETY—THE INSTRUCTIONS OF THE FOUNDER

THIS time the perilous strait is safely crossed; the famous Society is founded. Its life, its action, its relations with the outside world are not yet settled in a definite fashion, for ten years have yet to go by before the text of the Constitutions is laid before the professed Fathers assembled in Rome. But progress continues and will not grow slack for a single day. However important for the future of the Society the date of 1541, which we have just passed may be, we shall not in future see more than the gradual, and so to say imperceptible, development of the principles already laid down, accepted and practised by the founder and his faithful adherents.

We have before us a space of ten years. We do not bind ourselves to follow its chronological divisions from year to year; but let us see how the new General filled it up:—by his works of charity in the city of Rome;—by his efforts to get his Institute accepted, at the same time specifying more and more clearly its original nature;—by the more or less distant missions which he caused his Fathers to give, and which he directed at least in the beginning;—lastly, by the relations which he himself kept up with the principal personages of the day, in order to organise and to defend his first foundations.

Scarcely was he elected when he began to devote himself specially to two objects; first to guarding personally the simplicity and humility necessary for his interior perfection, secondly to using his authority for the " greater glory of God," a formula which constantly recurs in his letters and in his actions.

At the outset he insisted upon filling for some time the post of cook, and he added to it the lowest offices in the house.   Then he made a great point of consecrating by his own example an obligation, the only one among many, which had for a short time excited slight opposition: he gave religious instruction to little children for forty-six days.[1]   A great many of their relations and a goodly number of persons of all ranks profited by the opportunity of hearing him. Not that he expressed himself elegantly; despite

[1] This was, according to Maffei, the way he usually spent his time. On rising, he meditated for an hour and then prepared to celebrate holy Mass, which he said every day, unless hindered by his infirmities.   If any outside business required him, he went out with a companion; if not, he received the people in the house. It was never necessary to consider his mood or to seek a better time before discussing anything with him or obtaining a favour from him.

After dinner, he rested his mind by talking of edifying and instructive subjects.   When recreation was over, he occupied himself with the various details of his office, signed his letters, looked over his correspondence.   In the evening, after supper, he prepared the business of the next day and held a conversation with his secretary.   As soon as he was alone, he recollected himself thoroughly, walking up and down his room, leaning on his stick, for, after his wound at Pampeluna, he always limped.   At last he went to rest, but never to sleep more than four hours.

the admonitions of his secretary, who was commissioned to draw up for him every day a list of his solecisms and barbarisms, he never succeeded in speaking Italian correctly.   But his speech was so vigorous, his tones inspired his hearers with such burning charity to their neighbour, such hatred of vice and such love of God, that he exercised great influence over them, and drew them which way he would.

His actions naturally increased his prestige in the minds of all those who were not blinded by prejudice or jealousy.   No sooner had he arrived in Rome than he saw the town overwhelmed by all the consequences of a terrible scarcity of food.   To privation succeeded hunger, and to hunger sickness.   Ignatius and his companions had multiplied themselves in order to collect alms, open public refuges, get beds for the worst cases and provide at least with a couch of straw, in some kind of a shelter, those who felt their poverty press upon them even more hardly than usual, in consequence of this exceptional distress.

When this crisis was over, the Saint proposed to devote himself to works relating to more lasting needs, and to wretchedness that was always in danger of spreading.   He occupied himself specially with the Jews, women of bad life, and orphan children.

His aim with regard to the Jews [1] was evidently to convert as many of them as possible.   He knew very

---

[1] [When we remember that Ignatius was imbued by education with all the feelings of a sixteenth-century Spaniard in regard to the Jews, we may well be surprised that his attitude towards them, however narrow in some ways, was so relatively wide compared with that of many Catholics of our own day.—ED.].

well that with all men, and no less with Jews,
anxiety about eternal life does not put an end to
all care about the present life.   He therefore desired
that a house of refuge should be opened for the
young catechumens who were the children of converted Jews, where they could live during their
period of instruction, and in order to endow the
house better he conceived the idea of raising an
annual tribute from the synagogues, which, to use
the language of public law at the time, were *tolerated*
in Italy.   He employed both speech and action to
secure for the catechumens the retention of their property, which, until then, had been in great danger,
both from ecclesiastical authority and from their
own families, when these last were still Jews and
could not forgive them their conversion.   By his
counsel it was decided that a Jew should have no
right to disinherit one of his children who had
become a Christian.   Nay, beneficence to these new
converts was carried even further; Ignatius bringing about the regulation that the sums recovered
from usurers should be assigned to them, at anyrate
in cases when, the injured borrower being unknown,
it was impossible to have the money restored to him
from whom it had been extorted against the rules of
Christian justice.   Thus the goods of the Jew who
had remained a Jew were more respected than before,
and yet the Christians had the wit, if the expression
is admissible here, to make them serve in a reasonable degree the necessities of the baptised Jews.

As for the apostles, who could only use the capital
at their disposal, they used the most valuable of all,

that is to say, sincere charity and the knowledge of religion. More than one Israelite of low extraction might be drawn on by the allurement of certain advantages; others richer, enjoying high rank among their co-religionists, were convinced by the interpretation of the Scripture. Ignatius did not disdain to intervene and to employ the effect of the peculiar charm of his speech. One day a Jew was brought to him, who, after having shown the intention of receiving baptism, had gone back to a state of hostility reaching the point of extraordinary fury. Hardly was he inside the saint's room than Ignatius, with these few words, " Isaac, stay with us," instantly conquered his resistance, and secured his conversion.

It has been frequently said that Rome had long been one of the favourite abodes of the Jews. The reader will feel more surprised at learning that in Ignatius' days the city numbered " a great multitude "—so Ribanedeira expresses himself—of women of bad life. The General of the Jesuits acted in this case much as he had done with the Jews. He realised that the difficulty of finding honest means of existence, and the penury resulting therefrom, were various obstacles to these " unfortunates " regaining their footing, for, as his secretary tells us, from the fact that many desired to leave the worst of all ways of life, it did not follow that they were in a condition to embrace the " best," that is to say, to enter a convent. In those days the " working-woman " was unknown, and those miserable creatures who were " on the streets," did not possess the valuable resources (however we may regret their abuse) of the hard-working woman of our times. Our ingenious reformer resolved to secure his "penitents" against want by providing them with an asylum, and he was not afraid to take them thither himself through the streets of the city. Naturally, he desired to effect their lasting conversion, but in answer to the scepticism expressed by some people, he replied that he should consider himself fortunate if, for the honour of Christ, he saved his "refugees" from even one night of sin. In this asylum they waited till they were reconciled with their husbands (if they were married and had left their home) or till they succeeded in making a suitable marriage; or lastly, till some, more deeply touched by grace than the others, became nuns. Failing any of these different solutions, the house kept them if their conduct was irreproachable.

When he wrote to Francis Xavier in the Indies, he delighted in relating all these details, both about the work for the penitents and that for the Jews. He even told him of the marriages which he had blessed among this first class, and of the respectable god-mothers whom he had found for the children who sprang from these unions. The last venture had cost rather dear and the difficulties were for a short time very great, for the Society engaged in the attempt was very poor. Its General had secured the first funds by a lucky transaction; he caused to be sold for a hundred golden crowns old stones which his disciples had dug up from the ruins of ancient Rome. The impulse once given, rich families were induced to bestow substantial alms and the future of the foundation was secured.

He to whom the credit of it was due then began to think, not of curing, but of preventing the evil by providing poor and friendless young girls with an asylum in their turn; he had built for them the house known as St Catherine's. A corresponding refuge was erected for the orphan boys.

All these novelties were not carried through without provoking resistance and calumny; sometimes a man was infuriated by seeing a woman for whom he had conceived a mad passion, "illegally detained," as he said; sometimes people attributed to the saint extravagant schemes of reform. I will let Ignatius speak for himself; "Barbaran," he wrote in the October of 1540, "has brought an action against 'St Martha's house.' His Holiness has ordered Cardinal Cressenzi to look into the matter, and I heard from him yesterday that the complaint has no foundation. To give you an idea of the frivolity of the things imputed to us, he told me that we were accused of doing what we did for the house of St Martha without the authority of the Holy See, of wishing to reform the whole world, and of enacting Statutes with the object of shutting out from Rome all married women who had failed in their duties, and other things of the kind, which are absolutely absurd."

St Ignatius set to work with his accustomed prudence to reduce all these annoyances to an unavoidable minimum. This is how he proceeded. When he had conceived the idea of a foundation of this sort, he spoke about it to a few serious, enlightened and charitable friends, and with them settled the fundamental principles of the institution. For its completion he applied to some benevolent people possessed of fortune and authority, finally he begged a cardinal to be the protector of the undertaking. When the work was set on foot, with regulations, method and resources of its own, he retired, delighted to feel that it no longer needed him, and from that moment he began to turn his attention to some other equally useful venture, "for his charity could never remain idle and he was always planning something fresh for the salvation of his neighbour."

Such an inventive spirit must necessarily have brought him on to the borderland and even on to the peculiar domain of other institutions already in existence. But he understood avoiding all conflict quite as well as retaining his liberty of action. We may note that in the beginning the Society of Jesus was to devote itself to the care of the sick, to country missions, and to the relief of prisoners, but that even during the life of its founder it gradually resigned to other orders some of the very numerous responsibilities that it had at first taken upon itself. It was, of course, in later times that St Vincent de Paul and St Alphonsus Liguori were to establish on a secure footing *missions* properly so called. But in 1540 St John of God had opened his first house for the care of the sick, and when he died, in 1550, the existence of his Order was secured.

Whilst busied in the work of making his followers thoroughly well-instructed priests, and at the same time leaving them free and ready for the numerous tasks which so far had found no workmen to under-take them, St Ignatius had to reject more than one offer of such and such a congregation to amalga-mate with his own.   He had declined the advances of the Theatines; he declined in 1547 those of the Clerks regular of Somasco, who from that date joined the first mentioned community.   Later, he was likewise to refuse to be united with the Barnabites.   He gave the same answer to all these requests, that it seemed to him more for the greater glory of God that each of the two Societies should remain constituted as God had allowed it to be up to that date.

Amidst all these refusals there was one which, more than any of the others, put his wisdom, quite as much as his charity, to the test.   It will be re-membered that he had, at an early date, in Spain especially, excited in a great number of pious women an interest which had never flagged.   After having helped him for so many years at Barcelona and Paris Elizabeth Roser had also sent him supplies at Bologna.   When it was a positive and well-known fact that he was to take up his abode at Rome, she wished to come and live near him who had so often called her, and with good reason, his sister and his mother.   Other Spanish women joined her.   Ignatius received them, undertook their spiritual direction, and it is clear that they contributed generously to the endowment of some of his foundations.   But at this juncture he began to experience some of those difficulties of which he was by no means fond; for, however ready he might be for useful sacrifices, he did not like his time wasted.[1] Certainly he was under great obligations to Elizabeth Roser, and he was quite willing to discharge them, but always provided that it was not to the detriment of his present or future undertakings, with which he was always of opinion that women could not be directly or actively associated.   The reasons are easy to guess.   —

In the present case, Elizabeth Roser was an elderly woman, whose friendship with him had always been above the least suspicion.   But he may have feared the contagiousness of example and the making of a precedent, whilst we know that he desired to remove from his followers all hesitation, and we may say all reflection on this head, not even contemplating the possibility of their being tempted by the occasion of sin.   The day when he entered Rome with his companions he had in general terms exhorted his friends to prudence; then he had said to them: " Let us avoid all intercourse with women unless they are of the highest rank " . . . a few years afterwards he was able to add " or of the lowest and most abject," which formed a fitting and saintly completion to the wise counsel.

He therefore considered it allowable for women,

---

[1] He used to recommend, and always used himself, an ingenious method of getting rid of those importunate visitors who return without any necessity, namely, to talk to the intruder of nothing but mournful subjects, such as death, the last judgment, the pains of hell, and the like. Thus, he said, either they will not come back, or, if they really enjoy such conversation, we must have patience in consideration of the good that it must do them.

either those who were alone or who lived with others—whether in a family or a religious community—to seek his advice. Even then he contented himself, as a rule, with sending them the *Spiritual Exercises* and recommending them to make them carefully, uniting themselves to the prayers and merits of the Society.

He went a little further when there was a question of co-operating in the reform of one or several convents. But what his eager and persistent countrywomen desired was, in plain words, to become members of the Society. Among them was Dona Juana de Cardona, who, having been left a widow by the assassination of her husband after a very short period of married life, had displayed extraordinary courage and activity in tracking the murderer, and then had given herself up with passionate devotion to nursing the sick in the hospitals.

" My most reverend and dear father," she wrote from Valencia to Ignatius in 1546, " I have never had, nor have I now any other feeling in our Lord, but that I am called by Him to enter the camp and serve under the standard of the Society of the Name of Jesus. Thus my heart is ready, my most dear father and lord, my heart is ready. Humbly prostrate at your feet, I will not rise, and, like the woman of Canaan, will not cease to cry out till you have given me the salvation of my soul, typified by the daughter of the Canaanite. Command me to go to India, or to stay here, or to go anywhere you please, I will obey you till death.

She who, yielding to the vehement impulses of her soul, has journeyed more than a thousand leagues to demand justice, will not fear to go quite as great a distance again, and even to travel as a pilgrim for the remainder of her life so as to obtain mercy, and that only out of love and for the love of Him to whom she has given herself entirely, soul and possessions," and so forth.

The whole letter is really beautiful, and the receiver could not fail to be touched by it. But after all he must have considered Dona Juana's opinion that to "obtain mercy" and secure "the salvation of her soul" it was necessary for her to be admitted into the ranks of his Institute, rather exaggerated. We do not possess the answer that he gave her, but we have the letter that he then wrote to Elizabeth Roser, on the 1st of October '1546, to let her know that he could no longer "retain her under his obedience," nor admit that she was bound to him by vows; once more, that he regarded her as his good mother, which she had been for a long time, but henceforth not as his spiritual daughter. In consequence of this discussion his relations with his benefactress threatened to become seriously disturbed. There were disputes, and he was within very little of having a lawsuit about the residue of certain sums of money deposited or expended. The consummate skill and the gentle firmness of Ignatius at last calmed the storm, and he resumed his friendly intercourse with Elizabeth. Meantime, he had not merely got the Pope to relieve him from the direction which he had at first taken upon himself, but, in order the better to defend himself for the future against a recurrence of similar requirements, he obtained from the Holy Father a prohibition against the Society having any special bond with any religious Order of women. Later he inserted in the Constitutions a clause distinctly forbidding his disciples to undertake the ordinary direction of a convent of nuns. Ribanedeira, who had been a near spectator of this little contest, summed it up in these short, but suggestive lines: " It is astonishing to what amount of worry and annoyance the management of these three good women (*trium muliercularum*) has exposed him in the course of a few days."

If the head of the new Society had a few disappointments in this direction he was abundantly compensated by the public and solemn tokens of brotherly esteem offered to him by the heads of two great religious Orders, the Carthusians and the Dominicans.

.   .   .   .

By what arts and diplomatic skill did the new Institute succeed in conquering its enemies and obtaining an ever-increasing popularity? Edgar Quinet, in passing judgment on the character of St Ignatius, wrote a sentence which is noteworthy as one of those which, coming from an enemy, is valuable; for in its rather studied incoherence it contains a certain effort of impartiality. " In him," he says, " Machiavelli did not stifle St Francis of Assisi." We have seen " St Francis of Assisi " in the penitent, full of the love of God and the love of all those whom Christ desired to save; in the pilgrim, who for himself is contented with beggary, but who wished to make that state needless for those of humble station; in the friend of sinners; in the man deeply concerned about the intelligent relief of all distress; in the priest ready to help courtesans. Has the time come to search for Machiavelli? If Edgar Quinet only chose this name in order to bring to mind an unparalleled knowledge of men and wisdom of government he was not far from the truth. If he intended, as is probable, to make an offensive remark (in the full sense of the word) about a scheme of policy more remarkable in his judgment for skill than scruples—well, let us try and examine the matter a little more closely.

One reflection at once suggests itself; namely, that the policy of Machiavelli is essentially individualist, and that it seeks success especially in division, whilst the policy of St Ignatius is essentially Catholic, and aims always at the union of souls. Now, does it seek to attain this end by means which savour of contempt of men, and which do not respect their natural dignity? Let us allow our hero to answer here for us.

To begin with, let us read through the instructions, given by him on very important occasions, to those among his followers whom he is entrusting with missions.

With regard to Francis Xavier, he appears to have confined himself to a perfectly simple expression of absolute confidence. He sends him, then he writes and gives him news as to what is being done in Rome and throughout the rest of Europe for the development of the Society. Xavier answers him as a friend answers a friend. What strikes one most in the letters is the absolute conformity of ideas and the liberty of soul secured by it equally to both.

The first mission which the master really had to guide by his inspirations was that which sent two of his companions to Ireland. That unfortunate island was suffering from serious troubles caused by the religious policy of Henry VIII. Whereas the English landlords had followed the king in his schism, the native population remained Roman Catholic, but its relations with the Holy See were attended with the greatest difficulty. For this reason, one of the Irish bishops had asked the Pope to send an apostolic nuncio to look into things and to grant to the faithful the dispensations and favours which the situation seemed to require. Paul III. had decided to entrust this mission to the little Society which had just sworn obedience to him. It was Codure who was at first chosen for the business, but he died before the day of departure was fixed, and the task then devolved on Salmeron and Broët, to whom was added a young novice, named Zapata, who, having still his fortune at his own disposal, wished to defray the expense of the expedition.

It was of necessity difficult and even dangerous. The envoys simply held their lives in their hands, orders having been given by the English government to arrest them as agents of the Court of Rome. A price was set on their heads, and, as they were sought for everywhere, they were obliged to change their place of residence constantly. They were only able to remain a bare thirty-six days in Ireland; nevertheless, this short stay was sufficient for them to strengthen the Catholic Faith by the display of their courageous and disinterested conduct.

Such was, briefly, the nature of their mission. We must not lose sight of it if we would rightly appreciate the instructions given to them by their master. The text which has come down to us says nothing of the special difficulties which they would encounter, of the danger which their personal security might run. On the other hand, we feel that the founder, when for the first time laying down the rules of diplomatic behaviour, made a point of having them sufficiently broad and high to allow of his followers applying them indifferently to all circumstances, easy or difficult, to those which involved a risk of life equally with those which required defence against offers of honours and dignities. We shall soon see that he was not fond of going into details of which his subordinates, from being in immediate and prolonged contact with the events, would be the best judges; but the fact that his orders referred to the most general obligations did not prevent their being distinguished by remarkable precision.

To begin with, we are at the period when the sale of indulgences and the traffic in holy things brought the Church into discredit. Thus the true reformer says, with as much prudence as sincere love of poverty; "as for money, do not even touch that which may be assigned to the dispensations which you have to grant; have it distributed among the poor by other hands, or use it in good works, so that you may be able, if the necessity arises, to declare upon oath that you have not received a single farthing during the whole course of your legation." [1]

Was there anything exaggerated in the prudence which dictated those words? Is it not clear that their aim was to pacify men's minds by taking away every pretext, both from the intemperate accusations of those who disagreed with them, and from the raillery of sceptics? And were not the following words concerned rather with the appeasing of strife than with the tranquillity of the missionaries to whom they were addressed? " Never lose sight of the fact, not merely in your sermons, but also in your private speeches, more especially when you are reconciling enemies to one another, that all your words may be published, and what you say in the darkness brought out into broad daylight."

Next comes the art of speaking to people so as to bring them back to the right, or to obtain their co-operation. In all times, but in preceding ages even more than in our own, it has been very necessary to make a distinction between the manner of speaking to the great, and of speaking to the lowly. Neither dogma nor moral varies, but the art of making them acceptable necessarily varies with the state of mind, the habits, and the prejudices of those with whom

[1] He himself practised what he recommended, always keeping an exact account of what he received and spent.

we are dealing. Ignatius was a past master in this art, more so, perhaps, than would be desired by those who value above all things the equality and liberty of the Gospel. His excuse, if he had to make one here, would be that outbursts are not generally good for anything, except for the satisfaction of the person who ventures on them. In the instructions that we are analysing, he confines himself to the following piece of advice : " When it is a case of speaking to the great, let Broët undertake it." We know that Salmeron looked quite young, and that Broët had " more presence."

Next comes the intercourse to be held with the generality of men. Here the master of diplomacy is much more explicit, and is worth quoting. " I counsel you to be with everyone in general, but especially with your equals and inferiors, temperate and prudent in your speech, always ready to listen and patient in doing so, lending an attentive ear, until people have revealed to you their inmost feelings. In this way you will get a hold over them, but you must take great care not to allow them to do so over you. When you are thus enlightened you will then give them a clear and brief answer, which shall anticipate, as far as possible, the occasions which may arise; you will then dismiss them in a courteous manner."

Is this advice to be considered Machiavelian ? Before passing judgment let us see what ends it was to serve. The man who dictated it has told us himself: we must find means of gaining confidence by using language appropriate to the particular disposition, and by prudently seizing the opportunity of praising any good we may see in it; then, confidence being once gained, we may apply the most effectual remedy to the evil which we have perceived. This two-fold end once stated, I do not believe that we shall consider advice like the following as being otherwise than prudent and worthy of attention. "After having studied the disposition and the moral nature of each person, you will strive to conform to it as far as duty will allow, so that if you are dealing with a lively and eager nature you must avoid all wearisome lengthiness; on the other hand, you must become rather deliberate and cautious if the man to whom you are speaking shows himself more circumspect and slow in his talk." That is to say, that he who is thus prepared to accommodate himself to the spirit of his interlocutors is a man who has become master of himself, who has bid farewell both to anger and weakness, who is, in a word, strong with real strength. Ignatius desires that in every case where there is question of acting for the good of another his sons should manifest in the most unmistakable manner promptitude and anxious fidelity about keeping their word. "In business, anticipate rather than put off or delay. If you promise anything for to-morrow, do it to-day."

Thus, then, we have a general method, but no imperative edict, no resolutions imposed beforehand on a passive agent. "Deliberate among yourselves as to all points as to which your opinions happen to be divided; do what two or three have approved. Give an account of your mission every month."

I do not know whether this latitude as to actions—properly so called—allowed to the deliberations and resolutions of those sent out will excite astonishment. It is perfectly consonant with the habitual practice of Ignatius, and is easy of comprehension in a body in which the final end does not vary, is known to each member, and each is always ready to devote himself to it with equal love and an equal spirit of sacrifice. It is when a state has no fixed policy, none recognised even by itself, or when it seeks aims that cannot be acknowledged, that it is obliged to dictate daily to its delegates the action destined to serve the adventure or the passion of the moment. It is when it possesses a traditionary and clearly marked line of action that it can best find satisfaction in choosing its servants well, and in leaving to their initiative the care of forming, as occasion arises, the resolutions most suitable to the glory and interests of their country. Still more will this be the case in a society which has only in view universal and eternal interests.

When Ignatius gave these instructions to Salmeron and Broët, he had been General only a few months. We might perhaps be inclined to think that his authority was not yet very secure, but we should certainly be greatly mistaken. Moreover, if we open the instructions which he gave five years later to that same Salmeron and to Lainez, when delegates at the Council of Trent, we shall indeed find that some of the directions are more positive, because the circumstances are both more important and better known, but the spirit is, in the main, the same.

When several of them are engaged upon the same work, the initiatory spirit must not engender division. For that reason he says to them: "Although you ought never to forget what specially pertains to your Institute, you must nevertheless recollect before everything else to preserve among yourselves the closest union and the most perfect harmony of thought and judgment. Let no one among you trust to his own unaided wisdom, and as in a few days you will be joined by Claude le Jay, whom the Cardinal of Augsburg is sending to the Council as procurator, you will fix a time each day for deliberating in common." Moreover, it is not always sufficient to deliberate just before an event; there are tasks which demand preparation for a long time beforehand. "Therefore," writes the master, "I am giving you some counsels which may be useful to you in the Lord, either by retaining them just as they are, or cutting them down, or adding to them others of a like nature." Here is the summary of this advice, gathered up by himself in a *résumé* as clear as it is definite: "You will never lose sight of these three principal points; 1st, in the Council, the greater glory of God and the good of the universal Church; 2nd, out of the Council, your old rule and method of helping souls; 3rd, the special care of your own souls, so that you may not come to neglect and abandon yourselves, but may strive, on the contrary, to make yourselves daily more worthy of filling your office."

This office was neither commonplace nor easy, seeing that the life of the Church was at stake and that the two Jesuits were charged with defending it as theologians of the Sovereign Pontiff. Now, it is noteworthy that the General of the Society goes into no details either about the claims of the Protestants, nor about the difficulties of the dogmas which have to be reconciled, nor about the line to be taken in the midst of the disputes of every kind which divided, according to their apparent interests, the Pope and the temporal princes, the Emperor and the King of France, the nations of the north and south, the religious Orders and the secular clergy, and the like.[1] Ignatius leaves everything which is to be brought under discussion to the Holy Ghost, and afterwards to his two sons more than to himself. Had he already inserted in his *Exercises* the second part of what is now to be found in them concerning the "rules of orthodoxy"? Let us suppose that he had done so. The two eminent theologians would in that case have found in it nothing irrational, nor anything whatsoever of a nature to limit the freedom of their researches, for it lays down the rule that they must never, by treating too much of predestination, of grace and faith, run the risk of weakening belief in free-will and in the necessity of good works. From the doctrinal point of view this single warning was like a light-house enabling them to avoid the most dangerous shoals of the new doctrines; for we must not forget that subjects which seem to us now-a-days almost trite were in those days argued about

---

[1] Polanco says that the Spanish prelates had at first regarded the two Jesuits in an unfriendly light, and were at no pains to conceal their sentiments.

with vehemence which threatened to put all Europe
to fire and sword. Lastly, the special instructions
contain positively nothing concerning the problems
to be elucidated and the solutions to be recommended for overcoming difficulties. On the other
hand, the advice given about the art of intervening
and of discussing excites our admiration by its calm-
ness, good sense, and charity.

" In the Council you should be backward rather
than eager in speaking, prudent and charitable in
expressing your opinion about things which are done
and are to be done, quiet and attentive in listening,
striving to catch the spirit, the intention, and the
desires of those who speak, so that you may know
when it is most opportune to speak or to be silent.
In the discussions which arise you must always set
forth the reasons for both views, so as not to appear
attached to your own judgment. *You ought always,
to the best of your power, to act so that no one may
depart less inclined to peace after your speech than he
was at first.*"

How keenly we feel that here the Saint is on the
ground which belongs to him, and of which he is
undisputed master ! He concerns himself about the
behaviour of his followers outside the Council. We
all know that every assembly, of whatever kind, has
its lobbies and rooms behind the scenes, where men,
who will always be men, sift and examine the small
reasons, frequently more powerful than the great,
and strive to settle questions rather by what is not
said than by what is openly avowed. How does
" Machiavelli " speak here ? Has he overlaid " St

Francis of Assisi" with a thick veneer of his own?

" Outside the Council, neglect no means of deserving well of your neighbour.   Nay, even seek for opportunities of hearing confessions and preachings, of giving the *Exercises*, of instructing children and visiting the poor in the hospitals, so that the grace of the Holy Ghost may descend with more abundance on the Fathers of the Council, in proportion as you draw it down with more fervour by these works of humility and charity."[1]

Such then, according to the Father of the Society of Jesus, was the real way to take part in intrigues and to ensure the triumph of his own personal ideas. Will he be looked upon as over-prudent for repeating to the two theologians what had been said to the two legates in Ireland ?   " Consider that everything you say to your penitents may be published on the house-tops.   When giving the *Exercises*, and indeed always, speak as you would in public."   What was the object of this circumspection ?   We have seen pretty clearly, I think, that it was peace.   And if prudence was required, as was only too evident, in dealing with the great ones of the world and of the Church, the " St Francis of Assisi " desires more

[1] This is what a book, recently published, more full of epigrams than of facts, and especially of accurate facts, calls " sending his disciples into the furnace, and giving them minute, childish, and bigoted rules."   I am amazed at the conviction with which the author (whose pseudonymity I do not intend to remove) reproaches St Ignatius for having *forgotten* that the reform of ecclesiastical morals was the great question of the Council, and that it alone could save the Church and put heresy to confusion.

freedom with the lowly. " You will visit the hospitals in turn every four days, at hours which are not inconvenient for the patients; you will alleviate their sufferings, not merely by words, but by bringing them, as often as you can, little presents. Finally, while it is necessary that our words should be brief and well considered in answering and settling questions, we should, on the contrary, speak with a certain prolixity and in a kind manner when it is a case of stirring up devotion."

We have thus made acquaintance with the diplomatic manual of Ignatius of Loyola. Lainez and Salmeron, his true disciples, or rather his true sons, drew their inspirations from it. It is beyond our purpose to relate the brilliant part which they both played in the great discussions of the Council, especially on justification. Their striking success was then obtained by their personal talents and their own knowledge. But the spirit of their Father showed itself most plainly in their behaviour outside the Council, for they admirably fulfilled the whole programme sketched out for them as to their dealings with the poor and sick. Both had refused the hospitality of cardinals, and lodged at the hospital. Out of the money which the Pope and the Cardinal of Augsburg had insisted on giving them for their maintenance they provided for the relief of many necessitous persons. In one day they clothed from head to foot seventy-six, who had come in procession to a church, after which they gave them a meal in common, and then sent them back to their homes.

Such conduct not merely acted upon the deliberations of the Council by bestowing upon the arguments of the theologians that authority which makes itself felt in the depths of the soul, but a great number of foreign prelates thus learned to hold the Society in esteem, and begged from it missions, colleges and universities, at the same time offering the means necessary for their maintenance.

.   .   .   .   .   .

Meantime, the influence of the General naturally increased, and heightened the importance of the relations which he had with princes. He had already had occasion to intervene in very delicate negotiations. A rather serious difference had arisen in 1542 between the Pope and John III., King of Portugal, the latter reproaching the Sovereign Pontiff for having disposed, without his authorisation, of an important benefice in the kingdom. Now, as both were great benefactors to the Society, Ignatius must have been in a dilemma, but with singular prudence he suggested to the Roman Court an arrangement, allowing it to satisfy the king without seeming to go back or retract. On the other hand, without writing directly to John III., he caused such delicate explanations to be put before him that his anger was entirely appeased.

A few years later, in 1548, a quarrel had arisen between the citizens of the town of Tivoli and the inhabitants of the stronghold of Saint Angelo, which belonged to Margaret of Austria. They were on the point of coming to blows, when Ignatius succeeded in persuading them to submit the solution of the difficulty to arbitration.

Meantime, there was no lack of opportunity for negotiating with princes concerning the interests of the Society and those yet greater interests which it ardently desired to serve. Many requests were addressed to its head, but were far from all meeting with the same reception. Some wished to make such and such a Father a bishop, and to entrust to him an important diocese in their dominions; others begged for the religious in order to found universities or colleges. He was quite as ready to accede to these latter demands, and even to skilfully evoke them, as he was at pains to discourage the first. The brother of Charles V., Ferdinand I., King of the Romans (that is to say, sovereign of Austria, strictly so called), was very anxious to give the bishopric of Trieste to Le Jay, with whose work at Ratisbon, Ingolstadt and Nuremberg, and at the diets of Spires and Worms, he was well acquainted. The cardinals favoured this scheme, the Pope sanctioned it, and Le Jay was on the point of being nominated, when, through the intervention of Margaret of Austria, Ignatius managed to obtain a delay, and then took upon himself to make Ferdinand give up his plan. The entreaties and energetic remarks by which he succeeded in persuading him (December 8th, 1546) ran as follows:—

"The greatest benefit and the most remarkable favour with which you can honour us is to help us to walk sincerely and faithfully in the way of our Institute. Now, in our opinion, honours are so contrary to it that, if it were necessary to invent a means of destroying it utterly, the most efficacious would be forcing us to accept ecclesiastical dignities. Those who first entered this Society resolved to go for the cause of religion, and at the least sign from the Sovereign Pontiff, to all parts of the world; so that the first and true spirit of this Institute is to go in all humility and simplicity for the glory of God and the salvation of souls, from town to town and from province to province, without limiting its sphere of action to any province in particular. This little Society has made tolerably rapid progress through holiness, humility, and poverty. If people were to see us enjoying honour and riches they would have reason to be scandalised at our alteration, and they would form an opinion of us which would render all our works useless. . . . We entreat you, by the Blood of Jesus Christ, to vouchsafe in your mercy and piety to remove such a danger from us."

It seems to me that the almost passionate tone of this letter can leave in no mind any doubt concerning the sincerity of its author. I will make only one concession to those whose suspicious turn of mind induces them always to look for something in the background; the petition says: "Our spirit is to go in all humility and simplicity," and we freely admit that it might have added "and in all liberty." Ignatius had the full right to think so, and would have even been justified in saying so. This spirit of freedom showed itself in all the efforts which he subsequently made in order to avoid the conferring of a bishopric on Canisius, the purple on Lainez and on Francis Borgia.

No one could be more vigorous than he was in warring against heresy by means of making foundations. In order to understand the dispositions, the arms, the policy, that he brought to bear upon this work, we have only to read the lines written in 1549 to the duke of Bavaria. "This college (which was to be founded at Ingolstadt) is to direct all its studies, all its cares, and all its attention and labour to one end only, namely, to the reformation of the depraved morals of this age, to the conversion of hearts by example, by the sanctification of souls, by knowledge and learning founded on the pure and true faith and the holy precepts of Jesus Christ, to the bringing back of men from the pernicious seductions of pleasure to a blessed and Christian life, from flesh to spirit, from the world to God."

In the course of all these works and negotiations the Institute had (in 1546) experienced a great loss. Father Le Favre, whom the Pope had caused to be recalled from Spain in order that he too might be sent to the Council of Trent, had died at Rome in the arms of Ignatius. But, at that very moment, valuable compensation was awaiting it in the shape of the vocation of Francis Borgia. Francis Borgia, Duke of Gandia, had, even in the life-time of his wife and in the midst of all his honours, been a man of extreme piety. In 1545 he made Ignatius accept the gift of a college, ready built and endowed, which was

soon to become a university, the first belonging
to the Society. The two were well calculated to
understand one another, for the great nobleman
had no less humility and ardour in the service of
God than the man whom he was to succeed at
a future date. He was firmly determined not to
remain, as he himself wrote, "an unprofitable servant, doing nothing but eating his bread without
earning it." Let me quote another speech of his
which must likewise have found an echo: "What
we specially lack here is men; those who possess
talent and learning want good-will, and those
who have good-will want learning." Ignatius conceived for a man of this stamp—for he was in
truth one among a thousand, and moreover was
prepared with the means of training others—a
friendship such as is experienced and created by
sanctity. The nobility and greatness of the witness
borne to it by his letters of that date are unparalleled. Soon, at the death of the duchess, the
duke, despite his eight children, desires to join
the Society, and with the persistent firmness of a
Spaniard, who finds it easy to be hard on himself,
he practises extremely severe penance. But the
Master checks him; he will not receive him till he
has married his daughters and settled his sons in
a way of life, and meantime he marks out for him
a plan of study. "As you possess a solid preliminary knowledge of literature, your best plan will
be to raise on that foundation the sacred edifice
of theology." Then he orders him to give up a
great number of his bodily mortifications, to re-

place those which are exhausting, by those which deliver from bondage, so that soul and body may be better fitted to serve God by thoughts, words, and works, which are no longer cold, disturbed, and confused, but "ardent, clear, and exact." Few words are sufficient for the mutual understanding of such souls, especially when they possess such fulness of nature.

Thus the master was able to say in his own pious language that he had provided his Society with powerful protectors, both in Heaven and on earth. One by one the favours of the Church had been conferred on him. A Bull of 1543 had done away with the limit at first put to the number of professed. Another in 1545 had given the Jesuits power to preach and administer the Sacraments. In 1546, a fresh Bull had granted to the Society the right of enrolling temporal and spiritual coadjutors with participation in the privileges of the Order. In 1548, at the request of the Duke of Gandia, Paul III. had the *Exercises* examined, and declared that they were full " of the Spirit of God."

This was one of the last acts of the Pontiff to whom the Society and the whole Church were greatly indebted. It is not my purpose here to go into the question of whether his successor, Julius III. was, as has been said, an indolent Pope, indifferent to great European interests. What is certain is that the Society lost no time in obtaining from him the confirmation of its existence. At the Council of Trent it had experienced his good-will and had received marks of his esteem. From the beginning of the new reign it found that its petitions were granted, nay, often exceeded. For instance, in the extension of the Jubilee to the Christianised districts in India, Japan, and China, it received for its missionaries special rights and privileges which it had not demanded. Then came the confirmatory Bull. It simply and exactly reproduced the Bull of Paul III., containing the statement which, as we have seen, was presented by the first Fathers themselves.

Henceforth Ignatius was able to gaze with confidence and consolation upon the finished work. In the beginning of the year 1550 this was the condition of the Society: it had as yet only created three provinces—Eastern India, with Francis Xavier as provincial; Portugal with Simon Rodriguez; Spain with Fr. Araoz. France, Germany and Sicily were not yet formed into provinces, but in each of these countries were some of the Fathers, whose Superior corresponded with Ignatius; he, besides being General of the whole Society, filled the place of Provincial to them. The Society now numbered twenty-five fixed residences and a tolerably large number of temporary missions.

Many colleges (or, to speak more properly, schools) already existed in India, and the Fathers were beginning to go out to the Congo and Brazil. The houses of Coimbra, Gandia, Padua, and Messina had obtained fixed revenues. The house at Rome contained fifty novices. The Institute was no longer in its childhood but had almost reached adolescence, having its future before it. It expected contradictions, difficulties, and persecutions: it possessed the strength necessary for resisting them.

He who had created and sustained it thought that the time had come when he might, and perhaps should, leave its government to another. In 1547 he had already tried to abdicate and to put Lainez in his place. In 1550, after the Bull of Julius III., he assembled all those who were able to come to Rome, and set forth to them in writing his desire of resigning office. This missive has been preserved, and it seems to me difficult to discover in it anything theatrical or stereotyped. " Having regard to my sins and my faults, my bodily and spiritual weakness, I have frequently thought, and indeed, I think from the bottom of my heart, that I am a long way removed from the degree of strength necessary for supporting the burden which the Society has imposed on me. Consequently, I earnestly desire and I beg of you that, having examined the matter carefully from every point of view, you will choose someone who will acquit himself better, or at any rate less badly than I, of the general government of the Society. I may even go so far as to say that I do not merely wish to transfer my responsibilities to a better than myself; I am ready to give it up to anyone who would do neither better nor worse. Therefore, in order to proceed regularly, in the name of the Father, the Son and the Holy Ghost, I simply and absolutely lay down the generalship; I lay down and abandon the whole office. With all the strength of my soul, I entreat in Our Lord all the professed, and those whom it may please them to associate with them in this deliberation, to accede to my just desiré. Lastly, I beg you all to take in good part the supplication which I make to you."

How are we to " discern the spirit " in which these words were written?   Was it an act of weakness due to physical weariness, and, as it were, a natural and perfectly human yearning after well-earned repose ?   Was it an act of pure humility ?   Was it an aspiration towards contemplative life, the sweetness of which seemed very long deferred to him who beheld himself thus involved in so many negotiations and so much business ?   No doubt there was a little of all that in the desire once manifested by St Louis to abdicate the throne and retire into a monastery, and perhaps the motives of St Ignatius were equally complex.   In a man so accustomed to conquer himself the simple love of rest would not have been sufficient.   The same may be said of the desire for supernatural " visitations," for if his scholastic studies, if grammar and dialectics had required him to repress his mystical raptures, neither active life nor the work of administration and government demanded of him, as we shall see presently, such a sacrifice.   Lastly, it does not seem as if even humility can have played an exclusive part in this case, since it is enough for him, he writes, that someone should be found neither better nor worse than himself.   In order to unravel all these different motive-springs a conscience as perfectly trained and as unerring as his is required.   Nevertheless, let us observe that it is always a mistake to suspect the sincerity of the remorse of these great souls, just as it is to mock at the complaints of men of genius about their imagination or their memory. The more we have the more we seek, and the more liable we are to suffer from not meeting with all we desire. The greater a memory we have, the more recollections do we possess which strive to become complete by calling up others; and it is then that we complain, like Montaigne, when we perceive that many among the number do not immediately respond to the appeal. Such is the humility of those whom we esteem perfect, when we only compare them with what we are ourselves.

However this may be, Ignatius saw his demand unanimously rejected, and there was nothing to be done but resign himself. He did so, and immediately resumed the work, which he had already begun, of the Constitutions. The final drawing-up, the commentary, and the application according to rule, of these Constitutions, almost entirely filled up the last period of his life from 1551 to 1556.

THE CONSTITUTIONS DRAWN UP, COMMENTED ON,
APPLIED—LAST WORKS AND DEATH

JULIUS III., when confirming the existence of the
Society, had, like Paul III., authorised it to exist
and to guide itself by its constitutions; but, although
these constitutions were living in the mind of the
founder, the complete text of them, far from being
published, had not even been decided upon.

Nevertheless, in 1550 a first edition had been submitted to those amongst the Fathers who, although
summoned to Rome, had not been able to get there.[1]
From this first text, considerably modified in consequence of these deliberations (I am now taking my
stand on the Introduction to the great Madrid folio
edition, 1892), arose a second text, known as the
autograph text. St Ignatius wished to send it everywhere, even to the Indies, so that all the members
of the Society, without exception, might freely make
observations on it.[2] And this began to be done in

[1] What was communicated to them was probably not the text
written by the hand of Ignatius, for that text was in Spanish; it
was the Latin translation of it made by Polanco and reviewed by
several collaborators, among them, doubtless, by Fr. Frusius,
who had already translated the *Exercises* into Latin.

[2] They had been specially requested to judge of the different
articles from the point of view of the necessities or difficulties

1552. After this text had been put in circulation, and then compared with the result of this universal consultation, it was again amended, either by St Ignatius or, after his death, by the first "congregation" or assembly of the Order. The result of this was a third text which, carefully reviewed by Polanco, was final, in the sense that if the fourth "congregation" retouched it later, it was simply with regard to the form, in order to correct the copyist's errors and the slips of the pen. In fact the Constitutions drawn up by Ignatius underwent, at the hands of his companions, nothing but modification of detail, conformable to his views, inspired by his spirit, almost all approved by himself. It may safely be affirmed that the work is his.

Our labours would be enormously prolonged were we to analyse it in all particulars and compare it with the constitutions of other Orders. We are here chiefly concerned with the stamp of the great saint's personality. Let us try to acquit ourselves of our task, without being too brief, and without losing sight of our real object.

Let us begin by what has always most keenly excited the attention of men, more particularly of the French, who are so fond of plans of government. This one has changed far less than those of their country. Ribanedeira's *résumé* shows the main outlines as well and clearly as possible.

"Such is the form of our government, and such is its system; the whole Society has at its head

belonging to their province, for it was necessary that all the rules of the Society should be applicable everywhere.

one General invested with supreme power. He is elected by the suffrages of the Provincials, to whom are added two professed Fathers, nominated and sent by each province with its Provincial to the General Assembly.

"The General is elected for life. By virtue of his great knowledge of the men and things of the Society it is he who nominates the rectors of the colleges, the superiors of the houses; he who creates the provincials, the visitors, and the commissioners. It is a method well calculated to preserve peace, modesty, and humility, for it suppresses or weakens the passions, dissensions, jealousies, and enmities which almost always follow the election of superiors when dependent on the appreciation and will of the majority.

"It is also the General who himself or through his Provincials governs the colleges. It is he who grants to his brethren the permissions and privileges bestowed by the Holy See, limiting, qualifying, taking away the enjoyment of them as seems fit to him. He has full powers as to admitting people into the Society, excluding them from it, convening the General Assemblies, over which he presides. In short, everything in the Society depends on his judgment and decision.

"In order that he may not abuse this power, those who elect him, not satisfied with the extreme care with which he has been chosen, elect at the same time four of the most worthy Fathers, who are called his assistants and who form his

Council. The General Assembly, which represents the whole Society and which is even above the General, may be convened by the assistants. It may depose the General, if the case demands it, and even pronounce upon him a sentence more serious still. . . .

"This form of government borders closely upon monarchy, but has still more in common with an oligarchy, for it avoids everything faulty in each of the two systems and borrows its best points. The government of one man, provided he is temperate and wise, possesses elements of stability. Nevertheless, it is to be feared that being puffed up by this honour he may follow fancy rather than reason, and that he may abuse, to the ruin of a great many persons, that power which was entrusted to him for their salvation. And even granted that this misfortune were spared him, that he were perfectly wise, one man cannot know everything; and consequently the salvation of others requires multiplicity of advice, each letting the others profit by what he happens to know better than they do. But then arises the danger of there being as many opinions as there are heads, and that what ought to constitute the unity of a society or an assembly, will be broken up and scattered. It is in order to avoid both these dangers that our Society has taken from the monarchy its unity, from the aristocracy the existence of a council, thus modifying each one of the two systems by means of the other, in such a manner that the General may command

every one, and at the same time be subject to every
one (*praesit et subsit*).   Such is the constitution,
such is the method of government in our Society,
planned by St Ignatius and bequeathed to us."

Since the sixteenth century the absolute power of
the General of the Society has given rise to much
discussion. It has sometimes been asserted that
Lainez had, by means of intepretation or otherwise,
extended and strengthened this supreme authority.[1]
Without entering into the subtleties or the ten-
dencies of these controversies, we may agree upon
this point, that the very growth of the Society, the
testing of its rules, the intensity of its outward
struggles, and the regularity of its internal development, in short, its whole existence, presenting as it
does the remarkable contrast of great peace within
and unintermittent war without, must, as a matter
of fact, have necessarily tended towards the increase
of the powers of the head.   It is none the less true
that the founder had very carefully limited, where it
was necessary, the authority of which he was to be
the first guardian.   The later text is on these later
points quite in agreement with the original.

(1.) The Council regulates the dress, food, and
expenses of the General, who must " conform to
what the Society has thus ordered."

(2.) As to the care of his body, the limit to be
observed in work and mortification, he will be " at
the orders of the Society."

(3.) As to the care of his soul, his confessor or

---

[1] Against this opinion see *Scholia in Constitutiones* of the contemporary Fr. Jerome Natal, first published in 1883, Prato, p. 257.

anyone else appointed by the Society will admonish him either concerning his duties towards himself or his office.

(4.) If any dignity in the Church is offered to him —unless the Pope lays it upon him under pain of mortal sin—the Society must forbid his accepting it.

(5.) If it were to happen that he neglected the duties of his post, either through sickness or old age and there were no hope of improvement, a co-adjutor or a vicar would have to be chosen for him.

(6.) Then come the serious cases: mortal sins committed by outward and visible acts, failure in the vow of chastity, blows and wounds, appropriation of the revenues of the colleges, alienation of their goods, false doctrine; if one or other of these facts is proved against him the Society must depose him, and if necessary expel him from its midst.

His authority is also restrained in other ways.   In the great majority of instances he is the supreme arbiter as to the admission as well as the dismissal of each of its members.   Nevertheless, if the postulant belongs to his family, if he is so closely connected with the General, either by nationality or kinship, as to give rise to some suspicion, if he is his spiritual son by confession or by the making of the *Exercises*, in each of these hypothetical cases the decision is to be left to the majority of the Council.

But it may be urged that all this rather resembles these countless political constitutions in which everything is theoretically perfect, but that as nothing is worth anything till it has been tried, we cannot judge by what is only on paper.   In truth, the most valuable part of any constitution is the spirit both of those who direct it and those who allow themselves to be directed by it. Now, in the first place, the constitution of which we are speaking has one merit not to be despised, it has endured, and those directly interested in it have never revolted against it.

Is this because the Society has successfully kept them down, moulded and fashioned them as dead bodies (to use the authentic words of the text), which allow themselves to be carried, directed, moved about, put in a place, taken away from it, by Providence, as represented by their superiors; or as "the staff held in the hand of an old man, and used according to his good pleasure"? That is an objection which we hear repeated on all sides. And it is certain that the rules would lose their virtue to a considerable degree if the individual members of this living body deserved nothing but indifference and contempt.

"The inmost principle of the Institute," says Genelli, "lies in the *Spiritual Exercises*. It is indeed by means of them that each particular religious receives the stamp which the Society, in accordance with its aim, desires for all its members." Let us clearly understand this assertion. Does it mean to say that the object, the end, the normal result of the *Exercises*, is to induce every good retreatant to become a Jesuit? We have, at an earlier period of this history, successfully convinced ourselves of the contrary. Ignatius maintained that the *Exercises* were fitted for the reform of every kind of religious order, and he considered them not less suitable for reconstituting every kind of existence, from the humblest to the highest. But there is this much truth in Genelli's statement that every retreatant is called to the choosing of the virtue which he desires and asks for. Therefore, he who after the *Exercises* (whether he has made them expressly with that object or not) elects to enter the celebrated Society knows what he is doing. He knows the end to which he is tending; it is the greater glory of God, and he knows the means which are to lead him to it, the first of all being the absolute renunciation of himself in favour of the body which he is entering. But if this is the first means it is evident that it is not the only one.

In their theology the Jesuits have always defended free-will, and their head, though no dialectician, set them an example in this respect. Free-will is designed for use as long as a man is in this mortal life. What is asked of him is not to annihilate himself, but to deliver himself, in proportion to his strength, from the limits which confine and contract him. The sole object of the sacrifices required of him is the removal of the obstacles which hinder him in his ascent to a life tending to greater and greater perfection. This perfection implies actions of two kinds. There are those which are accomplished in common with other members of the social body, and for them all, in conformity as complete as possible with the spirit which animates, moves, and directs the whole body; then there are those accomplished *for* oneself and *of* oneself. It is hardly necessary to add that these two lines of virtue are inseparably

connected, and that if the part cannot get on without the whole, neither does the whole get on without
its parts, all of which are called upon to give the
fulness of that which they are fitted to give.   But
the Jesuit, like every other religious, forms part of
a body, the constitution of which is presided over,
not by chance, nor birth, nor strength, but by free
choice; and with regard to himself, it is likewise
free choice which has brought him where he is.
Therefore he cannot be astonished at being asked to
abstain henceforth from all temporal ambition and
from every worldly occupation, to accept beforehand
all the affronts that men of the world may offer him,
to allow himself to be kept or sent wherever those
whose subordinate he has chosen to make himself
may consider desirable, to devote himself entirely
to the office entrusted to him without of himself
aspiring to any other.   Finally, he cannot be surprised that in order that he may be satisfactorily
used for the good of the community he should be
required to make himself fully known, with his good
qualities, his faults, his virtues, his weaknesses, his
temptations, his trials, and likewise his particular
graces.   It is not a case of a body in which each
member for ever fills the same place and perpetually
discharges the same duties.   For the greater glory
of God each one ought to be always ready for everything; but, in order that those who dispose of him
may place him at his right post, they must know
him thoroughly.   Napoleon never engaged in any
battle without reading through his muster-roll,
always kept carefully up-to-date.   In the monastic

army the strength or weakness of the forces lies not in their numbers but in their moral fitness, the greater part of which is usually hidden in the conscience, for in this case virtue counts for more than talent. Therefore, the conscience of the Jesuit must be known to his superiors. Every system has its requirements and may also have its excesses, and it is possible that this system with which we are concerned, being entrusted to men, who are only men, may have sometimes given rise to a few of these last-named. But we may safely believe that the spirit of the founder was more calculated to forestall them than to call them into being.

If the novice of St Ignatius thus knows all the sacrifices and all the devotion which he has to offer to the Society, he knows, on the other hand, all that the Society does for him. He knows that she sets him free from all care, that she watches with maternal interest over his health, better perhaps than he could do so himself. He knows that she sets him free with much wisdom and consideration, at least in practice, from the authority of some outside superiors whose decisions too often depend upon human considerations and necessities described as political. He knows that she does not cramp his piety by rigid forms and minute practices. " I see," wrote Polanco of his master, "that he prefers our striving to find God in everything we do, to our spending a long and continuous space of time on prayer." Therefore each member has to take care that his horizon is not shut out. It is for him to advance in virtue, according to his capabilities, by the combined action

of moral liberty and grace.   He will merely be asked
to manifest with all simplicity what he has thus
acquired of himself, and to bestow it entirely on the
works entrusted to him.   In short, he neither can
be free, nor does he desire to be so as to the part of
his being which he has sacrificed, but in that which
he retains and for which he has made that sacrifice,
nothing interposes between God and himself; that
is enough for him.

It will be said that the general spirit and the
teaching of the Society must be considered.   There
must of necessity be a general spirit, but nothing
proves that it is imposed by a kind of external
tyranny; it is a thousand times more probable that
those who freely enter such surroundings already
possessed that spirit in the degree necessary to their
vocation, and that the certainty of finding it in its
fulness and peculiar perfection was one of the most
powerful factors in their decision.   It remains to
deal with the teaching, and here it seems to me that
two kinds of considerations present themselves.

St Ignatius was neither a metaphysician nor a
learned man, nor even, in a certain sense, a theologian.
Not that he hindered his sons from becoming such,
on the contrary he urged them towards it; nevertheless, as far as he himself was concerned, the especial
object of doctrine is its utility, and he caused this
to be written down in the Constitutions.   Certainly
it must be useful by means of its truth, and he
desires that this truth should be put in the clearest
possible light, both for himself and for others; but
he also desires that in their onward journey his

sons should take their stand on the most common, the most approved, and the most certain teaching. It is true that he draws a distinction between those who are beginning their course of study and those who have finished it. He advises the first to abide by the solutions approved by the Society and peculiar to the Society, whereas he evidently leaves the others liberty in their studies, and is always careful to reserve the rights of evidence. He only enjoins them to take heed that the diversity of opinions may not hurt the bonds of charity, and recommends them to act so as to restrain, as much as possible, dissension within the Society. "Even on the points about which the doctors of the Church have different or perhaps contrary opinions, we should be careful to secure uniformity in the judgment of the Society." "Let us all think in the same way," he says again in the third part of his Constitutions, "let us all speak in the same manner, *as far as is possible.*" "Diversity of opinions, which is the mother of discord and the enemy of union of will, ought to be avoided, *as far as is possible.*"

So much having been said in order to throw light upon the personal genius of the Master, let us ask ourselves whether the existence of doctrine held in common is calculated to crush the freedom of those who accept it. It has been the fashion of late years, in some factions, to try and transport the methods of the Catholic Church and her religious Orders into lay society; I say advisedly the methods, for the spirit is left on one side; the mere bark is taken without any thought of getting

P 5

possession of the sap that made it. Thus, an Italian who prides himself on being bold and advanced, Scipio Sighele (Psychology of Sects, page 89), quotes with approval this saying of Bagehot's: "The most important problem is how to obtain from men blind obedience. What use will you make of that obedience? That is a question of secondary importance, which it is not necessary to settle at once." And here Scipio Sighele adds on his own account: "A rigid, exact and concise law is the first necessity of human nature." Well, we are bold enough to say that this theory is considerably less liberal than that of St Ignatius, for he does indeed exact obedience, but from people who know beforehand what will be asked of them, that is to say, the reign of Christ, of His doctrine, and of His moral teaching. Therefore, the doctrine professed in a body which one enters by choice is not designed to make subjection harder, but on the contrary to lighten it, by letting everyone know why he obeys, and what is the end in view of which his superiors are obliged to dispose of him.

What, then, is the obedience of the *perinde ac cadaver*? There is no evading the fact that it is due whenever it is demanded; but is it demanded every moment? Is it even often demanded? That is the question. It would be speedily pushing things to an absurd and impossible conclusion to imagine the members of the Society as being all their lives and at every hour of the day automatons without will or conscience. Nothing is further removed from the spirit of the Constitutions than demanding that its workers should be inert and passive. Finally, why not believe what one of the most distinguished members of the Society, Father Genelli, says? " In no case," he writes, " have so many precautions been taken that the mediation of reason should intervene between the command and obedience, in order that in the occupations, the orders, the commissions that are given to the religious, superiors may always consult, not only the strength, the talents and the disposition, but also the taste of the individual. Moreover, St Ignatius desires that for the good of the individual and of the whole Society the religious who has received any command should not merely be allowed, without violating obedience, but be obliged to set forth, after having consulted God in prayer, any doubts that he may have concerning the opportuneness of the order or commission that is given him."

Such are the Constitutions as to their main outlines. Let us now try to understand how their author set about the work, how, even in drawing them up, he stamped them with the peculiar impress of his own character. Then we shall see how he commented on them and used them, in the course of the last years of his life, in the government of the Society.

. . . . . .

All his biographers have told us that the drawing-up of the Constitutions was with him a slow work, prepared for by very long meditations, which he was careful to embody in language as brief and as comprehensive as possible.

As a rule, when it was fine, he went into the

garden which a rich Roman of the neighbourhood put at his disposal. There a table, paper, ink, but no book of any kind, were brought to him, and he wrote about the subject on which his thoughts were then fixed. Before concentrating themselves they had passed through many hesitations and scruples, or rather they had allowed themselves the time necessary for making quite sure of the spirit by which they were inspired. When he was uneasy about any particular point he made it the object of his constant reflections, and offered Mass with the special intention of obtaining absolutely clear light, and he persevered in his prayers until he felt within himself, without any possible doubt, an irresistible force tending in one particular direction. Long extracts from the journal, in which he noted down from day to day his supernatural impressions, have come down to us. These fragments correspond with the period when he was debating within himself whether the houses of the Society should or should not accept endowments.

He frequently repeats what he experienced and what cannot be explained either by memory, understanding, or words. Nevertheless, he strives to note down these sensations as accurately as the insufficiency of human language will allow. Sometimes he heard inward speech, which echoed like heavenly music. Sometimes also, but more rarely, he speaks of visions, and in one of these cases, he adds: "with much interior enlightenment and understanding." Every instant he shed such abundant tears that his eyes suffered from it, and that he lost his voice.

But the prevailing and dominant characteristic in what remains to us of these intimate notes,[1] is the record of his upward soaring, of his movements of tenderness "and loving humility," of the fire which consumed his soul and his whole being, of his strong conviction without special opinions, without discursive reasoning, but full of strength, peace and security. Security, calm, sweetness, "interior peace, tranquillity accompanied with certainty," and withal possession of himself and energy, those expressions recur in every line. Here are a few passages from these revelations, the greater portion of which has been lost. The wonderful combination of spiritual vigour and of physical emotion will be appreciated as they deserve.

"To-day, feeling of great devotion with tears, during morning prayer and preparation for Mass, as well as at the altar, without uttering a word. As far as possible I kept myself in a frame of mind hostile to any enthusiasm. For an hour and a half or even more, I worked at the 'Election,' considering what in this question appeared to me dictated by reason or indicated by the inclination of my will. Now, whilst I was begging the Mother with her Son to help me before the Father, and whilst I was afterwards imploring the Son with His Mother to intercede for me, I felt myself borne before the Father; my hair stood up on end, and I felt a shock and burning heat throughout my whole body; then followed tears and ardent devotion."

[1] They are found in the large edition of the Constitutions, which I have already quoted.

What were the inspirations drawn from the recollections of such states of mind, when he resumed the
drawing-up of his Constitutions, when he retouched
them in order to make them more clear and complete?   We can discover by reading the Madrid
edition, where the words and clauses, added by his
own hand in the authentic copy, have been carefully printed in small capitals.

Anyone, who picks them out page by page, will
say to himself that after having, with his intensely
accurate mind, dictated the first text, Ignatius,
wished, when reading it through again, either to
make it still more accurate, or, more frequently, to
satisfy a desire of his heart.   If the text enumerating
the groups of religious who are to form the Society
names first the professed, Ignatius has inserted with
his own hand: *propriamente y primero*.   In the
passage stating that the novice must declare that
he wishes to live in the Society, he has added "and
die there *y morir*."   If he has read in his own
text that the religious must content himself with
what is given him from the common store for his
use, "without superfluity," he has thought that
sufficient stress was scarcely laid on this point,
and he has written with his own hand "without
any superfluity."   But far more often he added words
that came straight from the heart, breathing per-
suasiveness and warmth, impregnating with goodness,
so to say, the somewhat dry and imperative text of
the rule.   If the first edition speaks of the duty of
maintaining obedience, which is binding upon the
superior, he considers that a counterbalancing state-

ment is necessary, and he subjoins that, on his side, the superior must practise "all possible love, moderation, and charity in Our Lord." It is unnecessary for me to say that he has, on more than one occasion, again written the formula so dear to him, "to the greater glory of God." But we often also see that he has chosen to translate it into another language, in which the most suspicious critic cannot accuse him of forgetting humanity, for instance, either "for greater edification," or still better, "*for the common good.*" Lastly, in a passage, reminding the professed Fathers in charge of a college, that they must not take any of the income intended to supply the needs of the students, and that this fact was for them a means of living with greater purity (*con mas purexa*), the master's hand has again taken up the pen in order to add these words, which are almost untranslatable in their brevity, but which admirably sum up the lucid enthusiasm of his vocation, "*y con major espiritu.*"

. . . .

This last phrase also sums up his correspondence, including the letter to the Jesuits at Gandia, and especially the famous letter to the Jesuits in Portugal, which has to be read every month by all the members of the Society. Anyone who reads them attentively easily distinguishes in them two sets of maxims, one destined for inferiors, the other for superiors, without, nevertheless, dividing the members of the Society absolutely and for ever into two separate categories, for there is no superior, whatever degree of authority he may possess, who has not to obey; and there are very few inferiors who may not have some power in their hands.

Obedience, in the eyes of St Ignatius, is not only a duty to be strictly fulfilled, by abstention or inertness, but a science and art to be excelled in; and there is "no exercise more suitable for the Society than the ardour of obeying with all desirable perfection." For anyone to know how to govern others well, he must, as a preparatory step, have " used all possible care" in obeying, and have become " a master in this faculty." What is it that mars obedience and weakens its efficaciousness? The division of forces, which, instead of being united as they should be, allow themselves to be impaired and disunited by doubt. If men discuss a question, they are tempted to prefer themselves to their superior, and then "the vigour and dignity of obedience disappear, in order to give place to sadness, sluggishness, murmurs, excuses, and other serious imperfections which rob obedience of all its value and all its merit."

Merely from a purely social and utilitarian point of view it would be difficult to dispute the truth of these maxims. Whether we like it or no, the superior and the inferior, the man who commands and the man who obeys, are workmen collaborating in the same undertaking, and their harmony is essential to final success. It is, if not necessary, at anyrate extremely desirable, that a plaintiff should be at one with his counsel, a patient with his doctor, a contractor with his architect, an officer with his general, a foreman with his master, a workman with his

foreman, an apprentice with the workman whose
business it is to teach him; and that if the subordinate gives a piece of good advice or offers a useful
piece of information, unity should be maintained,
or should, by means of the habit of discipline,
be promptly restored. This principle is, I believe,
generally admitted. But we run a great risk of
destroying all its results if we hold the opinion
that the superior ought to justify confidence by
arguments in which he allows his judgment to be
discussed. Every doctor may make a mistake,
but the patient, as a rule, runs far greater risk
of making mistakes, and very gross mistakes, if he
insists upon carping at everything; and, meantime,
the state of things grows worse and worse, because
his doctor gets weary of attending him. Thus, while
on the part of the inferior energy is slackened, the
superior little by little loses his sense of responsibility, his watchfulness, his spirit of initiation and
foresight—that is to say, just what he ought to have.
Therefore, it is quite certain that if, instead of letting
an order be justified by success, it is allowed to be
fettered by premature discussion, the amount of
useful consideration and of understanding demanded
by joint work is diminished. The danger is all the
greater, as nothing is more catching than mistrust,
and the crowd of fault-finders speedily make havoc
of actions on the lower plane, after having paralysed
those on the higher.

No one was more thoroughly persuaded of this
truth than Ignatius. Did he compromise it by ex-
aggerations? Many have thought and even said

so, probably because they doubted whether they themselves could be subjected to such discipline without protesting.   But that is a bad way of putting the question.   We must not forget that the saint was legislating for religious, given up wholly and without reserve to the service of the Church, and that they therefore had to accept in all circumstances of their lives what every one of us accepts without difficulty in his own special career, in a regiment for instance.   But, to leave generalities, what it behoves us especially to say here is that Ignatius, in the management of the temporal and spiritual interests of his Institute, contrived, better than anyone else, to complete the law of obedience by making provision for just and necessary initiative.

His correspondence in many different instances bears witness to this.   He recalls to the minds of those who are at a distance, and have to judge on the spot of the fitness of such and such a measure, their great duties from his point of view, but he respects their judgment to the point of refusing to reply to some of their questions.   For instance, here is a letter which he wrote on the 31st of January 1552 to the Portuguese Provincial, James Miron; everything with regard to this delicate subject is said in few words but with great shrewdness, and at the same time with most accurate appreciation of every grade of authority.

"It belongs neither to the office of a Provincial nor of a General to descend into every little detail. It is more worthy of their office and more calculated to ensure their tranquillity of soul, that they should commit these details to their inferiors, on the condition of making these latter give an account of them. That is the plan of conduct that I follow in my own office, and the advantages obtained by it grow daily greater. Therefore, I advise you to direct your chief thoughts and care to the spiritual profit and prosperity of the whole province. Occupy yourself personally with everything that you have to order and see carried out; and take counsel with men whom you consider capable; but, after that, leave the actual execution, the management and the concern of the business, as a rule, to your inferiors. Remember that the first superiors ought to be like the *primum mobile*, which, by a never-varying movement, keeps all the other heavenly spheres in motion. By acting in this manner you will exercise greater influence, and one more in harmony with your office; moreover, you will have this advantage, that if your orders are ill carried out, you will be able to rectify what has been done amiss; whereas, if you have succeeded badly at first, to which you would be very liable by wanting to have a hand in everything, it would not be very creditable to you that your inferiors should have to repair your mistakes."

Thus, when he sent one of his sons to fill any post, even for a time, he would use a familiar expression of which he was very fond: "Cut your coat according to your cloth." Next, he required that he should be kept informed of things, but only, as Polanco writes, of the "more important and difficult matters." It is true that before making his choice, he took every precaution to assure himself that the person he was about to select was really the man for the work, that he was prepared for it by his tastes and aptitudes; he questioned him delicately, or got some one else to question him. But when these investigations were completed, if the man whom he had in his mind seemed to fulfil the desired conditions, secondary considerations were worth nothing in his eyes.

" In the allotment of offices and functions, he did not take into much consideration either age or nationality, or the number of years spent in the Society, as long as his religious had the qualities necessary for fulfilling their duties properly.   By his orders and with the approval of the whole Society a Frenchman was named first rector of the Roman College, a Spaniard named rector at Paris, a Belgian at Perugia, a Frenchman at Padua. Scarcely a year after his noviciate Father Michael Torrès was named visitor of a province.   Father Oliver Manare, a few months after his noviciate, was director of the house of the professed Fathers at Rome, shortly afterwards rector of the Roman College. Father Leon Henriquez was, by apostolic dispensation, ordained priest at the age of twenty-three, and immediately sent, as confessor, to the great college of Coimbra." [1]

It may perhaps be urged that, in all these cases, we are dealing with authority, delegated or partial maybe, but still authority, and it may be argued that after all it cannot be denied that obedience, destructive of all personal activity, is imposed upon the

[1] Father Michel, *Notes on Bartoli*, II., 306.

greater majority.   The reply is easy; all subjects, whether they are confessors, professors or lay-brothers, have a post entrusted to them upon their personal responsibility.   It is for all of them that this law of the Society is made: "Let the rector take care that each man is fitted for the office confided to him, and let him give each a rule of conduct, but, after that, let him not interfere with the business."   Therefore, all the members of the Society are destined to experience the benefits of the advice given to Father Miron.

·   ·   ·   ·   ·   ·

The society being now thus constituted, formed, and directed, it was necessary to give it sustenance. Despite all difficulties, it grew and prospered; it was imperative to employ the zeal of its members, and enable them to supply the great needs of the Church.

We have seen how the foundations of new colleges followed each other from year to year, and it may be thought that this would be a fitting place for passing in review the educational system of the Jesuits.   Nevertheless, I shall not do so, for the *Ratio Studiorum* was subsequent to St Ignatius, and it appears that the founder, who laid the foundations of almost every part of his building, did not in this particular department take an initiatory or a reforming part.   It is evident from the documents published on this head by Father Genelli, that he preserved almost in its entirety the methods ordinarily used in his day by Catholic schools.   He considered, we know, the study of the classics as the foundation of everything else, and he did not desire that they should be learnt as a science, entirely by means of formulas, but that the boys should become familiarised with them by spirited and varied exercises. "The professors," he wrote, "must not confine themselves to giving their lessons, but they must be careful to practise their pupils in written compositions, in discussions and conferences, which are perhaps more useful than the explanations of the master." Here we have the whole system of classical and liberal studies, which alone can satisfactorily prepare the young for any others.

St Ignatius also expressed a desire that the editions of pagan authors which are put into the hands of boys should be free, as far as possible, from all passages dangerous to morals. He wished, in short, that the masters of his choice should be esteemed as much for cultivating the character as for training the intelligence of their pupils. With that well-balanced combination of a practical spirit and of kindness, which is to be found in all his conduct, he did not forbid the use of corporal punishment for the naughtiness or inattention of the younger ones, but he advised the masters never to strike with their own hand, and to have a person hired for this purpose. Moreover, they were not to have recourse to this means till others failed, and rather than continue in it, they were simply to send away pupils who appeared incorrigible.

Despite the similarity of names, we must not confuse these colleges properly so-called, houses of

" secondary education " which sprang up in Italy, Spain, and Belgium, with establishments like the German and Roman Colleges, in which "higher education" in its strict sense was given. The master did not regard this education as less important than the other.

"As for studies and knowledge," wrote Polanco,[1] "he desires, generally speaking, that all should lay a solid foundation of grammar and literature, but especially those who, on account of their age and particular bent, were to devote themselves to them. Next, he rejects no kind of approved learning, neither poetry, nor rhetoric, nor logic, nor physics, nor ethics, nor metaphysics, nor mathematics, particularly in those whom their age and particular aptitude drew towards those studies. Certainly, he applied himself above all things to the forming of ecclesiastical vocations, as much in the interests of the secular clergy as of that of his own Institute. But here he did not separate intellectual culture from preparation by means of piety; he worked simultaneously at both these aims without injuring either of them by a separation to which others have resigned themselves only too willingly.

This training of the clergy was one of the most pressing needs of real reform. Directly after the first Session of the Council of Trent, Lainez, inspired by St Ignatius, or at any rate with his approval, had counselled the bishops to establish houses of training or seminaries, in their dioceses.

[1] Letter of June 1st, 1551, included in the collection of Father Bouix.

But they had to wait for the Session of 1563 in order to obtain a favourable decree from the Council. In the interval the Superior of Lainez had acted.

This he had done first of all by founding the Roman College, which soon received a far more suitable name, that of Roman University. "There," Father Clair says most truly, "the greatest theologians whom the Church has had since the Council of Trent have been professors, Mariana, Vasquez, Suarez, de Lugo, Bellarmin, Maldonnat, and Cornelius a Lapide. There the learned Kircher founded his celebrated museum, just as in our own age the astronomer Seechi did his observatory. There, amongst other eminent personages, eight Popes were brought up—Urban VIII., Innocent X., Clement IX., Clement X., Innocent XII., Clement XI., Innocent XIII., Clement XII. There, also, the zealous Father Leo established the first congregation of the Blessed Virgin, whilst St John Berchmans, Saint Camillus of Lellis, St Leonard of Port-Maurice, bequeathed to the Roman College the perfume of their virtues and the memory of their examples. It was well named the *seminary of all nations*, to which men flocked from all quarters of the globe. Fourteen colleges sent their pupils there, among them being the German, English, Greek, Scotch, and Maronite Colleges. The students' register for the year 1584 bore 2,107 names.

It was not long (1552) before the German College was grafted on this stem. Its members, in common with many other people, were not blind to the deep

decay caused by the Reformation, both in religion
and in that famous "culture," which Prussian policy
in our day hoped to use as a successful weapon
against the Church. If there is a fact well-established now-a-days it is that Luther's Reformation
had put an abrupt ending, throughout the whole of
Germany, to the progress of arts, letters and philosophy. When Leibnitz was pursuing his studies at
the University of Leipsic, in the middle of the next
century, he found the teaching retrogressive to an
extraordinary degree; indeed it is not easy for history to realise the extent of this backwardness. It
is hardly necessary to say that the authorities would
have nothing to do with what we call the Renaissance, but they were equally hostile to scholasticism,
regarding it as a work of pride and intellectual paganism. They thus rejected ancient literature and philosophy, because they considered that their adoption
would imply slavery to the Pope and to Aristotle,
who, in the Universities of the 13th, 14th, and 15th
centuries, had brought about the licentiousness of
the 16th. We might, however, have thought that
they would have turned towards the future with free
confidence and have laboured earnestly at the task of
self-enlightenment. But by no means, seeing that the
Protestant masters of Leibnitz fought with equal
vigour against English philosophy and the philosophy
of Descartes, and that their pupil was obliged to go
to Paris in order to become acquainted with the
latter. Finally, after having been the correspondent
of Malebranche, Arnauld and Bossuet, it was in
correspondence with a Jesuit, Father des Bosses,

that he evolved his important theory concerning substance.

In the time of Ignatius the ruins increased in number in Germany, and nothing was built up to replace them. To cure the sensuality of the Renais- sance monastic vows were suppressed, and the theorists of the new Church, with ingenious subter- fuges, sanctioned the bigamy of princes. In order to cure the pride of scholasticism the understanding was emancipated; each one of the faithful became a priest, interpreting the Bible for himself, simply by reading the sacred text. Faith without works was sufficient, but faith in its turn dispensed with proofs, as it was fitting that philosophy should do; and that was the remedy by which tyranny of authority was to be cured. Where, then, was true and real reform to be found, save in the work of those who by word and example preached humility and poverty, and who had the wisdom to find a middle way between the blind and easy literal interpretation from which they had themselves suffered, and the interpretation aban- doned to individual fancy, in study made as wide as possible, with all the means that the learning of their day found in its present as well as its past?

Once more, these are well established truths, but it is as well to mention them here, because that was what constituted the value and originality of the foundation of the German College at Rome.

Whilst uniting his resources with those of Cardinal Moroni, who, having been nuncio in Germany, had been a close spectator of the miseries and needs of the country, and, whilst collecting on the spot, after

numberless difficulties, the necessary funds,[1] Ignatius wrote (July 30th, 1552) to Father Le Jay, then
at Vienna : " All those who desire the salvation of
Germany have come to the conclusion that the most
efficacious and perhaps the only human means of
supporting religion in countries where it is tending
to its decline, or of setting it up again where it has
fallen completely, is sending as many capable men
as can be found belonging to the same nation and
speaking the same language, so that, fortified by
the example of laborious life and of sound doctrine,
they may, by preaching the Word of God, tear away
the veil of ignorance and vice which binds the eyes
of their compatriots.   Therefore, those who come to
this college, founded for the good of Germany, will
find masters to teach them Latin, Greek and Hebrew.
Those who have already finished their humanities
will be instructed in logic, physics, and other higher
sciences, then afterwards in theology, by means of
public lectures and constant exercises."   In another
letter he adds exegesis, of which Luther had written
that it must be " avoided like poison."

Many other documents bear witness to the care,
even in minute details, which Ignatius, having regard
to the importance of the object, displayed in his
new foundation.   He wrote about it to Blessed Peter
Canisius, whose apostolate in Germany has been
fully made known in our own day.   He wrote about
it to all those among his sons who were at Vienna,
Ingolstadt and Louvain, asking them for boys of

---

[1] Father Shraeder, *Monumenta quae spectant primordia collegii
germanici*, Rome, 1896.

about twelve years old, who would be able to remain at Rome till the age of twenty-two. He wished, says Polanco, that those who were chosen should be possessed of some natural gifts, and have received some sort of training in literature and virtue; all were to be of good appearance, strong and healthy, able to endure the fatigue of study, and to be of a good disposition. The more satisfactory their education had been, the more easy it would be to send them out with a real hope of seeing them occupy useful posts in the ranks of the clergy, and even of the episcopate. Lastly, it was desirable to take rank into account (for among the nations to whom they were to return this advantage would give them more authority); in default of nobility of birth they were to have greatness of soul.

It is to be supposed that his correspondents chose people answering this description, for the college made rapid progress in a short time. The young men had a house of their own, under the direction of the Jesuits; but to the special lectures organised for them in their own residence were added several others, for which they went twice a day to the Roman College; in short, nothing was neglected which was likely to ensure their future success. Soon, it is true, the war between Paul IV. and Philip II., the arrival of the Imperialists beneath the walls of Rome, and the famine, threatened the existence of the establishment, but its founder stood firm, and invented numberless expedients for maintaining his students, and finally weathered the storm successfully. On the 24th of January 1555, he conceived the idea of extending the good work of his college, and wrote in these terms to Cardinal Pole, who had just succeeded in reconciling England for a short time to the Catholic Church:

" I have to announce to your Eminence that everything is prosperous in the house of the professed fathers in the Roman College and in the German College. There are in the Roman College more than seventy people, besides the sixty who live in the house for the professed. Putting aside law and medicine, all sciences are taught, to the great advantage of our men and of the foreigners, who now number more than five hundred. Those who inhabit the German College make very great progress in virtue and learning." He ended by begging the Cardinal to send him young Englishmen on the same conditions and with the same object.

. . . . . .

These chief foundations did not prevent Ignatius from multiplying in different countries of Europe colleges, properly so called, and even universities, the former serving as a preparation for the latter, and supplying them with pupils capable of rising, step by step, by means of the possession of the " lower learning," to the rational acquirement of the " higher learning." Duke Albert of Bavaria, and, to a still greater degree, Ferdinand I., King of the Romans, whose zeal for the Society we have seen, helped him materially, so that a short time before his death he was gladdened by the inauguration of new colleges at Ingolstadt and at Prague. He had secured for many ages to come the triumph of Catholicism in Southern Germany and on the banks of the Rhine.

Was the need less pressing, or was the difficulty more subtle in the two countries of his youth, Spain and France? Both hypotheses may be maintained. Ribanedeira, being sent to Flanders with Philip II., laid stress on the first fact, and advised his master to direct his efforts elsewhere. It is quite certain that the clergy of the King of France and of Philip II. intended, as a rule, to do without these auxiliaries, who put out their arrangements a little. They were especially reproached, says Crévier,[1] (and the Bishop of Paris, Eustache du Bellay, constituted himself the mouthpiece of common complaint), with the name which they had assumed, by which they claimed, it was said, to monopolise the patronage of Christ ; also with the injury which they must necessarily inflict on communities and hospitals by taking part of their alms ; with their privileges, contrary to the rights of parish priests, bishops, and even of the Pope, contrary also to the rights acquired by the universities ; with their abstention from office said in choir, and the small amount of their austerities. Lastly, it was charitably observed that, as they had offered themselves for fighting the infidel, their first duty was to go among the Turks at Constantinople. Thence arose one of those universal storms, at first low and muttering, then violent, such as periodically burst in France; with the exception of a very small number of prelates, everyone, lawyers, ecclesiastics, and men of the people, wished to take part in it at any cost.

This outburst did not affect him against whom it

[1] Crévier, *History of the University of Paris*, *VI.*, 6.

was directed. It was suggested to him that he should answer by a written protest. He asserted, smiling, that he should do nothing of the kind, because the only result of a reply would be the perpetuation of polemics. Moreover, he thought that in this case, as in many others, the reasons publicly alleged were probably not the real ones. He did what he had already done more than once; he busied himself in collecting as many and as important testimonies as possible in favour of the Society, in the countries where their work had been most extensive. When all those documents were in his hands he had no need to use them, tranquillity had been restored.

Portugal was still under the dominion of John III., the most religious prince in Europe and the most zealous for the Society, which naturally made visible progress in his dominions. Indeed, a certain excess of piety not "according to knowledge" almost became a danger there. The mystical Simon Rodriguez, with the simple and good Oviedo, were for a short time on the point of altering the spirit of the Institute by making the love of contemplation and prayer predominate over practical work. Ignatius from a distance saw what was happening. He alternately employed indulgence and authority, allowing for what might be required by the temperament of Rodriguez, to whose aid he had already been obliged to come under similar circumstances. He provided him for some time with a pleasant place of retreat, "which will give you," he wrote, "for your external delight, the sea and all the

beauties that can be desired, and where you will
have as much time as you like for your spiritual
consolation." He refused to enter with him into a
discussion about the difficulties caused by the insufficiency of his direction. "Learn," he said, "that
everyone everywhere loves you, let that suffice for
you." At last, when the time had come, he recalled
him to Rome by virtue of obedience, but in such
terms that the only sentiment of Rodriguez was
that of almost delirious joy at again seeing the
companion of his youth, his friend and master.

The King of Portugal was reserving for the end
of the life of Ignatius an expedition which bore
promise of glory. When the hostile faction of Paris
recalled the fact that the Society had promised to
evangelise the heathen they were giving themselves
unnecessary trouble. The master had not forgotten
this obligation. I put aside a project of a crusade
which he set forth, says Genelli, in a document
destined for the Emperor. We do not possess many
authentic details about this magnificent scheme.
But it is certain that he designed the foundation of
colleges at Jerusalem, Constantinople, and in Cyprus.
As to more distant countries, is it necessary for me
to mention the martyrs of India, China, and Japan?
The Congo and Brazil were also visited by missionaries. Lastly, in the year preceding his
death, the General was organising his mission to
Ethiopia.

It is said that after having been converted by
the apostle St Matthew, and by that eunuch of their
queen Candace, who had himself been baptised

by St Philip, the Ethiopians had become half Jews
and half Christians. Later they had joined the
Greek schism, then, finally won over by the presents
and good offices of the King of Portugal, their king
David had sent a respectful address to the Pope. It
was in order to strengthen this reconciliation that
the Society of Jesus was requested to send to
Ethiopia twelve Fathers, among whom (as an exceptional thing) were to be a patriarch and two
bishops.

This mission was inaugurated with the greatest
solemnity, and set sail in an imposing fleet. It
carried to the king Claudius, the ancestor of
Menelek, a letter from Ignatius. With a certain
amount of Spanish impressiveness, mingled with
Italian grace and skill, he sought to make him
accept the unity of the Church, by arguments
borrowed from the Bible, the temple of Jerusalem,
and the glory of Solomon. Then he presented his
missionaries, and this he did in two sentences which
are noteworthy, for they are distinguished by that
condescension towards kings which the captious
critics of the Society have reproached them with
combining with their unquestionable courage. "They
come disposed," he said, "to help souls by their advice,
their work, and even, if need be, by their death."
Then he ended by saying: "The patriarch and his
companions intend to render to your Highness all
the honour and all the submission due to you, and
even to show you all the indulgence which religion
will allow them."

This enterprise was one of the last over which

our Saint was able to preside. In 1556, he underwent a trial which would have seriously disturbed anyone else; he saw elected to the Papacy, under the name of Paul IV., that Cardinal Caraffa, whose presence he dreaded on the occasion of his first visit to Rome. Paul IV. was to the end, shall we say, an enemy to the Society? At any rate an overseer and a censor, who gave an equivalent for some of his benefits in suspicions and threats; the latter were the more to be dreaded because he hated the Spaniards, accused the Society of entering into a compact with Philip II., and lastly, if we are to believe a recent historian, " he was a man whose intemperate spirit could only form extreme resolutions " (George Duruy).

Ignatius was for a short time very much disturbed at the news, and his secretary observes that it was the only occasion on which he was betrayed into a visible change of countenance. But he recollected himself quickly, knelt down before the altar, and, after a short prayer, said with his usual tranquillity: " We shall have a friendly Pontiff, though the Society must expect trials, which will practise it in patience." The storm was in fact destined to be threatening, but of short duration.

Scarcely was Paul IV. enthroned than he manifested, in a mood that was the reverse of encouraging, a desire to examine thoroughly, not merely the rules and constitutions of the Society, but all the bulls and letters patent that it had obtained from the preceding Popes. Moreover, he plainly expressed the intention of requiring two very serious modifica-

tions; the first called in question the powers of the
General, whom he desired to see appointed for three
years and not for life; the second referred to the
obligation of regularly assisting at office in choir.
The Society did not display any scheme of resistance, but before long the Sovereign Pontiff appeared
to lose his interest in these first ideas, and left the
matter to be settled by the Society, which deliberated and expressed a desire to preserve the constitutions of its founder intact. The silence of Paul IV.
was considered in the Institute, in the Sacred College,
and lastly in the Church, as decided confirmation.

Even had the trial been in the lifetime of Ignatius
still more heavy the resignation of the Saint and his
absolute trust in Divine Providence would not have
been taken unawares. One day, when he happened
to be ill, the doctors had advised him to dismiss from
his mind everything which might sadden him. He
profited by this counsel to try and discover by what
his soul could be troubled to any extent, and he
naturally began to think of the possible destruction
of his Society. But he did not stop there; he examined himself more deeply, and asked himself how
long his emotion would last. "If this misfortune,"
he then said to himself, "were to fall upon me, provided it had not happened by my fault, even if the
Society were to melt like salt in water, I believe that
a quarter of an hour's recollection in God would be
sufficient to console me and to re-establish peace
within me." Does it not seem as though he were
answering beforehand those who have so often suspected him of putting his Society before the Church,

and of seeing in it an end rather than one among many other means, employed in the service of God?

In any case, the brief struggle of Paul IV. and of the Institute was not even known in its entirety by St Ignatius.

In the beginning of the year 1556, his health grew very weak, and he resigned the government to the three Fathers, Polanco, Madrid and Natal. He died on the 31st of July 1556.

I have spoken more than once of the imperceptible continuity which links together without dramatic effects, without unexpected resolutions, all the parts of St Ignatius' life after his conversion. This characteristic lasted to the end. Certain of his approaching death, foretelling it to Polanco and begging him to go and announce it to the Holy Father, he seemed merely to consider it as an accident which could not in any way affect the destiny of his Society. He simply told Polanco to go and ask the Pope for a blessing and the plenary indulgence for himself and Lainez, who were in equal danger. He charged him to add that if he "climbed the holy mountain," he would pray for the Sovereign Pontiff as he had done in his mortal life. His secretary, who had not gathered from the doctors that there was such great cause for alarm, asked if he might wait a little, so as to have time to send off the courier for Genoa. "I should prefer to-day to to-morrow," answered the Saint, "the sooner the better; still, do as seems good to you, I put myself in your hands." They were almost his last words. He had no one summoned, he left neither will nor instructions, and what is more incomprehensible at first sight, he did not ask for Extreme Unction.   One of his sons has explained this by saying that the doctors (whom according to the precept of Solomon he had always honoured) disputed the seriousness of the disease, and that, therefore, if he had asked for the Last Sacraments, he would either have cast open doubt on the knowledge of those who were attending him, or admitted that he obtained his certainty from a supernatural revelation.   His humility would not contradict them in any way this time, and he let things go.   When it was seen that he had been right, those with him asked for the holy oils; it was too late.   After some hours, during which he had spoken alone and aloud, he had just died peacefully.

In consequence of urgent entreaties, supported in turn by Henry IV. and Louis XIII., the Holy See did not delay long in placing him in the ranks of the "Blessed."   When canonising him later, March 16th, 1628, Gregory XV. mentioned, according to custom, the claims which the new saint had on the gratitude of the Catholic world. |He left to posterity the task of bringing into prominence the genius for organisation and government of the illustrious founder.   But, and this is what makes his words specially valuable, he showed, with simplicity and eloquence, what is the main source whence the Church requires that her greatest servants should draw the sanctity which she expects from them.

Ignatius constantly helped the poor and the sick in the hospitals, distributing to them the alms which he received from charitable persons.   From the beginning of his conversion he occupied himself in a special manner in instructing children and the ignorant, in Christian doctrine.

It was he who by his example introduced the custom of visiting and relieving the prisoners. It was he who founded missions in all the countries of the world, built churches and colleges, particularly in this city of Rome, where, not to mention the Roman College, in which instruction is given free, he established the German College. It was he who originated orphan asylums and the institutions for catechumens, the convents of St Martha and St Catherine, and a number of other pious institutions. It was he who settled disputes, gave wise advice, drew up the book of the *Spiritual Exercises*, encouraged the frequentation of the Sacraments, reconciled enemies and made them pray for each other. All these works prove to what an extent he loved his neighbour for the love of God.

CHAPTER TENTH

CONCLUSION

IN these latter days, the psychology of societies and the psychology of those who manage them, have been the subject of much study. In the observations, as yet somewhat confused, which have been collected on the latter head, we often find the words "seer," "leader," "apostle," used as though they were synonyms which might be put indifferently one for the other. There is no manner of doubt that the man whose life we have been sketching was an apostle. He was not a "leader," if the word is taken to mean one who draws the multitude on without revealing to it all that is required of it, and who, simply by means of his contagious enthusiasm, causes it to credit delusions which are later scattered by time and by visible ill success. The author of the *Exercises* did not address himself directly to the crowd. He sought out the best among those who appeared capable of understanding him, he invited them to make in retirement a thorough examination of conscience, to study spiritual things deeply, to practise the *Exercises* with due reflection, and, although this may seem strange at first sight, it was chiefly when he had imbued them deeply with his spirit that he required obedience from them.

Neither was he a " seer," if by that is designated, I will not say a man suffering from hallucinations, but one who, by dint of having desired and imagined things, finally creates the outward semblance of them, and allows himself to be led away by this seduction before alluring others with it. I know very well that, in the eyes of some people, every mystic is a seer, every believer a fanatic, and that the life of a saint like Ignatius is, as has been written, a " systematising of all the visions of the Middle Ages." Those who have just followed, step by step, the efforts of this man so wonderful in his self-knowledge, in his self-conquest, in his power of adapting himself to circumstances, of profiting by his own experience and making others profit by it, of repressing within himself everything that might distract him from study and hinder him from acquiring knowledge, as definite, wide, and exact as was possible at that period, those I say, are sufficiently well-informed concerning the frivolity of these absurd accusations.

Let us then take our Saint—assuredly not as an ordinary man, but at any rate as a man—and try to follow, if only from afar, the development of his destiny. As one of his best historians, Father Genelli, has said: " Grace, like nature, does nothing by violence or by leaps and bounds, neither does it create fresh elements, but uses those it finds to hand, develops them and grows with them."

In order to explain this growth, is it a good thing

to seek out, as has been done in the case of so many writers and men of action, the dominant faculty? Yes, provided that we are careful not to overlook the complexity of those rich organisations in which nature first multiplies contrasts, and grace then establishes harmony. There is no room for doubt in this case; it is evident that the dominant faculty of Ignatius was will, will at the same time humble and bold; humble in everything that only concerned his self-love, bold in everything touching the honour and the triumph of the cause that he served; a will which in the beginning recognised neither difficulties nor limits, but which soon became in the highest degree prudent, pliable, and consequently persevering, since it found no difficulty in sacrificing shadow to substance, the contingent to the necessary, the transitory to the eternal; lastly, a will that was efficacious, because it incessantly strove to eliminate from the least fragment of its work everything that might be a cause of division, weakness, or decay.

Therefore, this will did not belong to the category of wills which set up themselves as their own end and rule, and reject everything which does not correspond to their egotistical requirements. In St Ignatius, intelligence and sensibility are united to the will and subjected to it, just as in his opinion learning ought to be subjected to action. He wished, we have seen, that the teaching of his Society should be, as far as possible, one, because in everything unity is a token of strength and success. With regard to his sensibility, he cultivated everything

R

which might inflame the ardour of action, and set himself to moderate everything that threatened to chill it.   He held that when one had done everything enjoined by duty to save a soul, all that remained, in case of non-success, was to recover one's tranquillity, and not be more disturbed than the guardian angel of the obstinate sinner must needs be.

Subordination is very different from sacrifice.   It cannot be said without the grossest inaccuracy that St Ignatius did not obtain, though a little late, from his unusually high order of intelligence, everything that it was capable of giving; nor can it be denied that he showed to his sons an affection, the feeling of which, as he wrote to St Francis Borgia, overwhelmed him with joy and gladness.

It will be recollected how he loved to contemplate, not only the representations of sacred mysteries formed in his own mind, but also the splendour of the starry skies.   He took delight in this last in the early days of his conversion; he did so yet more in his old age, for this sight, whence he drew philosophical comparisons to explain the rules of order in every social system, touched him to the point of drawing tears from his eyes.

"Music carried him out of himself to such a degree as to relieve his bodily sufferings.   Hymns sung at his side by his brethren were sufficient to mitigate the severe pain he endured in his stomach. Another of his favourite pleasures was to behold flower - besprinkled meadows and fields.   Those tastes often led him into a little garden belonging to the house, where he became so rapt in God that the Fathers hurried to their windows to watch him and to enjoy this spectacle" (Bartoli, iv. 7).

Nevertheless, it must be acknowledged that in his effusions as in his thoughts, the greater part came from the will and tended to fortify it increasingly. He had gained such self-mastery, that it has been said that his original constitution was metamorphosed. According to the disposition of the persons whom he was reproving or consoling, he would assume an angry tone and countenance, then would suddenly calm down and exchange the signs of irritation for a kindly smile. He had, says Ribanedeira, an extraordinary facility for "finding God," and he had, shall we say it once more? the power of suspending within himself, if it was necessary, and for as long as it was necessary, the transports in which his piety took the greatest delight. In his *Exercises*, in his Constitutions, in his letters, he is prodigal of the most minute advice, he despises no useful form either of prayer or of obedience; but at the same time, in order to obtain from his devoted sons wills which shall be as active and as efficient as his own, he desires that they too shall be able to set themselves free from anything superfluous which there may be, at a given moment, in formalities, in devout scruples, in the seeking after spiritual consolation, usually allowed or even recommended. He waits a year to say his first Mass. Through obedience, most certainly not through sensuality, he consents to eat meat on Good Friday; and lastly, in order not to contradict his doctors, he allows himself to be deprived of the supreme help of the sacrament of the dying. It is true that God was always in him, since he "found" Him with such facility, and that love like his, made everything easy to him.

Did his different surroundings count for anything in these transformations, or rather in this continual and harmonious evolution? It will be recollected that he himself sketched out for St Francis Borgia as it were a programme of their mutual life and vocation, telling him that they must produce "thoughts, words and works, ardent, clear and correct." His Spanish temperament made ardour easy to him, intercourse with France could not fail to help him to clearness, and correctness was attained by the judicious, sound, practical, and in the full force of the word sincere, study of exact traditions. It only remains to add that his residence in Italy bestowed on him an increase of grace, delicacy, diplomatic skill, and lastly of condescension for the weakness of men.

His work remains with us to testify what vigour and fertility these gifts have conferred upon his efforts. It has excited much opposition, and those upon whom has devolved the task of carrying it on through centuries and nations have been subjected to attacks of peculiar violence. When we come to look into things impartially, we realise all the fairness and the delicacy of these words of Lacordaire, which absolutely contradict, or at least are very far removed from, the prejudices of a Melchior Cano. "By intercourse with the Jesuits I have learnt to know them better and have especially admired their faith, their

zeal, their good education, their facility for understanding everything, and for putting themselves on
a level with everything, which has always been one
of their characteristics, lastly their sincere detachment from political passions, ready to recognise
order wherever it may be, and religion before every
other interest."

Such is without any doubt, despite prejudices,
the general and enduring spirit of the Society. Is
it the case that some of its members have run the
risk of compromising or belittling it by misusing the
prudent instructions of their founder?   A Catholic,
pre-eminent for his generosity, whose premature loss
we deplore, namely Abbé Leprune, said that some of
them had abused subtlety to the degree of liking
"subtleties" in pedagogy, in casuistry, in their relations with governments and laws.   We will not enter
here into this dispute; possibly the parties interested
would reply that these ingenuities, which have been
considerably embellished by their enemies, must
frequently have saved the existence of the Society.
Let us rather, in conclusion, call to mind how many
of the sons of St Ignatius have, on the other hand,
enhanced the reputation of their Order, and have
even drawn very near to the glory of their Father,
by giving to Christendom apostles and martyrs like
the successors of St Francis Xavier and of St Peter
Claver; by training theologians like Suarez and
Bellarmin, preachers like Bourdaloue and Perè de
Ravignan, scholars like the Bollandists; by establish-
ing the study of those classics whence ancient
literature drew its life; by delivering the soul of the

French nation from the hard yoke of Jansenism; lastly, in our day, by exposing themselves to the fire of the Commune, and by serving, at the risk of their lives, the cause of learning and of the French dominion on the plains of Madagascar.